A PASSION DENIED

Herne touched the pressure sensitive strip at the neck of her treksuit.

"Don't. Please stop." Merin pulled back.

"I thought you wanted this."

"I do. You'll never know how much I do. But I can't. Whatever you were planning to do to me, it is forbidden."

"Of course." In his voice was all the scorn he felt for the Oressian strictures that kept her from accepting him as her lover. "I should have known. You did warn me, didn't you?"

"I'm sorry. It's my fault, Herne. I allowed you to touch me."

She looked so forlorn that his heart melted. The ever-present anger, which had been rising in him, was dissipated, and the passion that had roared in his ears and his mind was muted into a controllable level of desire. He tried to reassure her.

"We are both at fault. I instigated it. I pursued it. You only allowed it."

NO OTHER LOVE

FLORA SPEER

LOVE SPELL ✦ NEW YORK CITY

*For my brother David,
who asked for a story about
the lost city of the telepaths.*

LOVE SPELL®

December 1993

Published by

Dorchester Publishing Co., Inc.
276 Fifth Avenue
New York, NY 10001

The name "Love Spell" and its logo are trademarks of Dorchester
Publishing Co., Inc.

Printed in the United States of America.

Part I
The Explorers

Chapter One

Only Herne saw the woman.

He stood up so suddenly that his companions turned to look at him, four surprised faces illuminated by the campfire. Even Merin lifted her head at his abrupt movement, her white coif shining in the firelight.

She sat a little apart from the others, her self-imposed isolation arousing Herne's curiosity. He had been idly imagining what color her hair was beneath the neat folds of the coif—from her eyebrows and lashes he would guess it was a light brown—and wondering if her body was as delicately made as her facial bones suggested. It was hard to tell about her figure when she wore an oversized orange treksuit every day and never changed into lounging clothes as the other colonists did. Withdrawn, self-sufficient, interested only in the performance of her duties—that was how he would describe Merin if anyone were to ask his opinion of her.

Sensing that she was aware of his attention, he looked away from where his fellow explorers sat, glancing instead toward the ruins of the old city of Tathan. The wind sweeping down from the high plateau and across the wooded plain caught at the leaping flames of the campfire, sending patterns of light and shadow along the sleek body of their shuttlecraft and onto the broken buildings just beyond it. Herne was a physician, not an archaeologist or an historian, but after seeing the maps made by the first group of explorers he had felt an unexplainable compulsion to join this second expedition. The need had been so strong and so unusual that he had volunteered to come along . . . and the city had proved to be nothing but a pile of half-buried rubble. He wasn't sure exactly what he had expected of Tathan, but he was disappointed.

It was while he stared at the remains of the city and asked himself what he was doing there that he saw the woman.

She stood between a stone pillar and a tree, where the two soaring shapes formed an enclosed niche. She was deep in the shadowed area of the niche, and for an instant he thought he could see right through her. Wondering if what he was seeing was some trick of the fire-light, he blinked twice. She was still there, and solid now. Real. Substantial. But she could not possibly be there.

She was slender, her willowy grace barely concealed by a flowing white gown. A short cloak was draped across her shoulders to float behind her, its edges lifted by the wind. Light golden brown hair tumbled in lustrous curls reaching to below her waist. Her eyes were shadowed, their color indiscernible at such a distance, but he could see curving light brown brows and darker lashes. She was an apparition designed to capture the full attention of any man, and Herne could not take his eyes away from her. She lifted one hand, beckoning to him. He thought he heard the sound of laughter. Herne rose with a swift motion, took one step toward the woman, then stopped as good sense overcame impulsiveness.

"Did you see something?" Tarik asked. "You look odd, Herne. What's wrong?"

"The woman. Right there." But in the second or two it took for Herne's eyes to flick to Tarik's face and back to the niche, the woman had disappeared. "She was standing there."

"What woman?" Osiyar said. "I saw no one."

"Really, Herne," said Alla, "I wish you would try to stay awake while we are planning our work for tomorrow. You were dreaming. All of our scanning instruments show no life in this area except for vegetation and a few small animals."

"Merin," said Tarik, "did you see anything unusual?"

"No." Merin's voice was as soft and quiet as always. "I'm sorry, Tarik. I was watching the fire and listening to your discussion. I saw nothing."

"She was there," Herne insisted.

"Describe exactly what you saw," Osiyar commanded.

Herne did, including his first impression that the woman was nearly transparent. Even in the flush of firelight he could see Osiyar's face grow pale. Tarik saw it too.

"Who is she?" he demanded of Osiyar.

"By her white gown and gold cloak she must be the one my ancestors called Ananka," said Osiyar after some hesitation. "She is one of the Others, the spirits of this world. They were here before my ancestors settled on this planet. There was such an entity in the sacred grove near my old home. I can tell you no more than that because as a mere High Priest I was never admitted into the most arcane mysteries, which were reserved for women."

"Ananka," Tarik mused. "The name is familiar. Something to do with Old Earth, but I can't recall just what."

"Ancient Rome," Merin said in her quiet voice. "She was one of the Fates, who formed the destinies of men."

"Of course." Tarik smiled at his colony's historian, who showed no sign of response, but sat with downcast eyes, looking at the fire. "I remember now. Thank you, Merin."

"What could a period in Old Earth's distant past have to do with Dulan's Planet?" Alla asked. "And did Herne actually see this creature, or was he dreaming?"

"Perhaps we'll find the answers to those questions tomorrow, when we begin serious explorations," Tarik said before Herne could protest again that he had not been imagining anything. "Since we can see nothing there now, and it is too dark to search for evidence, I think we should douse the fire, retire to the shuttlecraft for the night, and set the scanning instruments to sound an alarm if anything, living or mechanical, approaches us before morning."

Merin told herself that she had not lied to Tarik. She really had seen nothing in the dark area beyond the fire. But she had not been staring into the flames as she had claimed. She had been watching Herne.

From the first day she had met him Herne had piqued her interest, in part because she sensed that he was as secretive about himself as she was forced to be on the subject of her own past life. She was skilled in the technique of observing people without revealing that she was watching them, and she often watched Herne.

He was a fascinating subject for study. His thick, ash brown hair, cropped short to suit Jurisdiction Service regulations, had a tendency to curl when the weather was damp or when he ran his hands through it in frustration, a frequent gesture with him. His rugged face and fine gray eyes might have led others to call him handsome had it not been for the tense quality of his posture, which combined with the peculiar alertness of his expression to give him the appearance of a tightly leashed animal who, once attacked, would fight to the death without asking for or granting quarter. He would carry that watchful, wary attitude with him forever, Merin felt certain, because he was from Sibirna. One of the most terrifying of all the Races of the Jurisdiction, the Sibirnans were almost as fierce and warlike as the Cetans. But from her observations she knew there was more to Herne than the stereotype of his people.

"Are you sure you saw nothing?" he demanded of her.

"I have already said not," she responded, fixing her eyes on his feet. "I was watching the fire and listening to the conversation, just as I told Tarik."

Silence fell between them. Merin knew he was looking hard at her, trying to discover if she was telling the truth. He made a sound of disbelief before he left her to help Tarik douse the fire. Merin remained with her eyes still on the place where Herne had stood, the half lie heavy on her conscience. She wondered if the shiver up her spine was the result of not telling the entire truth or if it had been caused by the entity Herne had seen, or whether, just possibly, it was because she knew he had been watching her while she watched him.

Chapter Two

Herne . . . Herne . . .

He wakened in the folded-down navigator's seat that was serving him as a bed. Lifting his head, he looked around. By the pale green light of the scanning instruments he could see that everyone else was asleep. Alla lay next to Osiyar with one arm flung over him in a possessive way. Tarik was across the aisle from Herne, in the pilot's chair, now converted to a bed like Herne's. Farther back, in the seat next to the cargo bay door, hands folded upon her chest, Merin was distinguishable by the white coif she never removed. The only sound was the faint humming of the scanners. Yet someone had called his name.

Herne . . . it is time. . . .

He rose from his bed and stepped outside the shuttlecraft. The night had grown colder. He shivered as he turned toward the place where earlier he had seen the mysterious woman.

She stood there again, in the same spot, but the ruined pillar and the tree, and the dark niche, were gone. Instead, a low building faced with smooth white stone confronted him. Where the niche had been there was now an arched opening, shining with the golden light from within. As she had done before, the woman beckoned to him, and Herne followed her.

They entered a long, columned hall of shining white. The center half of the roof had been left open to the sky, and in the exact center of this area was a pedestal of white stone. On it, twice as tall as a man, stood the golden statue of a bird with its beak open and its wings outstretched.

"That's a Chon," Herne said, pausing to look at it. Though larger than any Chon he had ever seen, the statue was perfectly lifelike, the detail on every feather exactly modeled. The long-ago sculptor had successfully conveyed all the grace and nobility of the great, intelligent creatures who, while now much reduced in numbers, still inhabited Dulan's Planet. It occurred to Herne that he ought to be surprised to understand that what he was seeing was part of Tathan during the days six hundred years before his own time, when the telepaths who built the city still lived there, but everything that was happening seemed completely natural to him. "Why did the telepaths make a statue of a Chon and put it in a place of honor?"

The woman did not answer him. She had barely slowed her steps when he stopped to look at the statue. Now he hurried to catch up with her. She led him out of the hall, then down a few steps and across a garden that lay green and silver and quiet beneath twin crescent moons.

"Where are we now?" Herne asked.

Come.

The woman did not speak. The bidding was inside Herne's mind, and it was irresistible. He went with her to where more steps led downward. Soon they were underground. They needed no lights; a white luminescence surrounded them, moving with them. Herne looked backward once, and saw how dark it was behind them.

On their right hand as they descended was a stream flowing downward into an underground lake that extended so far that Herne could not see the end of it. The water was dark blue, as if it lay beneath the purple-blue sky of Dulan's Planet and reflected its color. The water was also lit from within. It shone like a priceless jewel held before a brilliant light.

The steps ended when they reached a white stone grotto, and there the woman stopped. On the right rippled the blue lake; on the left was a room hung with shimmering white fabric, its long side open to the lake. The woman pulled aside a sheer curtain and entered, then stood waiting for Herne.

She offered him food, tiny cakes on a silvery-white dish, and a drink poured into a crystal cup. The liquid was pale blue and clear, the cup cool when Herne took it in both hands. He lifted it to his lips but did not drink, for he recalled something Tarik had once said in one of his many speeches about old history and the need to remember it. Tarik had spoken of an ancient legend about a man who ventured into the world beneath the world, who had been warned not to eat one crumb or drink one drop in that underworld, or he could never again return aboveground. Herne set the crystal cup down upon an intricately carved white stone table, then faced his mysterious hostess.

"Who are you?" he asked. "What do you want of me?"

"You know my name." Her low-pitched, quiet voice reminded Herne of someone, but he could not think who.

"How do you know that? And, come to think of it, how do you know *my* name? You have called me Herne from the beginning."

"From the beginning," she repeated. "Herne the hunter, Herne of the forest. You know what I want. What you want." She moved toward a wide couch half hidden by netlike draperies that billowed and swayed with the movement of air.

"Ananka." He used the name Osiyar had called her and she stood still, smiling at him. Again he felt that odd tug of recognition.

"Ananka," she said, putting out one hand to him. "I am your Fate, for this night at least. Come. Accept it, for there is no breaking the threads spun before time began."

He saw that the golden cloak she had worn when first she had appeared to him was gone. She shrugged her shoulders and her gown fell open down the front, revealing porcelain skin. He noted the rich curves of her breasts and the curling luster of her golden-brown hair. And then he realized that he wore no clothing at all. It did not surprise him. In this place, nothing could surprise him.

Ananka took his hand, drawing him with her to the couch. When she lay down upon it he stood above her, enjoying the elegant display of gleaming limbs, the tempting possibilities revealed, concealed, then opened to him again as she shifted position, making room for him.

"Come. Join me," she murmured. "You do not remember, but I do. As I once promised you, this night is our time." Her beautiful lips parted and her eyes smiled into his. He still could not tell what color those eyes were, whether brown or purple or some other shade.

Herne was a healthy male in the prime of life, and he had not lain with a woman for half of a Jurisdiction year. Suddenly he did not care about the color of her eyes, or if she was real or a mirage of some kind, or whether she would poison him with food or drink or the touch of her luscious body. He wondered briefly if he would ever see the sky or his fellow colonists again, before Ananka drove everything else out of his thoughts. He lowered himself to the couch and she put her hands on him.

She was vibrant with experience, ripe with lush womanliness. She was alluring beyond any man's dreams. Again and again she roused Herne to wild desire, then granted him intense, prolonged pleasure. But she took from him, took and took until he felt drained of his very life force. At last, when her eager mouth and searching fingers could stimulate him no longer, he drifted toward exhausted sleep with Ananka propped above him on one elbow, watching the failure of her most recent efforts.

"Poor, weak man," she said with a ripple of mocking laughter, "not like my kind at all. But, still, an interesting experiment, to know human sensations. . . ."

"Herne. Herne, wake up." Tarik shook him hard. When that effort failed, Tarik pushed the button that converted the bed back into a chair and swung it into navigator's position.

Jolted into sitting upright by the movement of the chair, Herne opened his mouth to utter an oath most improper to use with one's commanding officer. He stopped when a small hand entered his line of vision. In the hand was a mug. The fragrant steam curling upward from the mug began to clear his groggy brain.

"Here," Merin said. "Qahf will help."

Something about her quiet voice touched a memory in him. He made his bleary eyes focus on her face, but it was the same Merin he had seen nearly every day since he had joined Tarik's colonists. Beneath the stiff white coif her face was thin and rather sharp-featured. Her skin was pale, her lips a milky coral shade. As always, she kept her eyes demurely lowered. Just the same old Merin, cool, distant from everyone, never showing a trace of emotion. But she could be kind. The qahf was just what he needed. Herne gulped it.

"If we are all awake at last," Tarik said, "we ought to get started."

"I'll work with Osiyar," Alla informed him.

"We'll make two groups," Tarik ordered. "I want a historian with each, so Merin, you work with Herne, and I'll join Alla and Osiyar."

"We won't need you," Alla began.

"Oh, yes, you will," said Tarik, in a voice intended to remind Alla just who was leading this expedition. He touched a few buttons at the shuttlecraft controls. "The computer will monitor our movements. Each of us is to check in every hour, on the hour. If anyone doesn't call in, the computer is programmed to send an alarm signal to all of the others."

Osiyar and Alla left the shuttlecraft. Tarik prepared to follow them.

"Tarik, wait." Herne got to his feet. "I need to speak to you, in private."

"I'll be outside." Merin slipped through the hatch and closed it behind her.

"Well?" Tarik looked impatient.

"That woman I saw last night came back," Herne began. "She took me with her to an underground room."

"Before you awakened," Tarik said, "I checked the scanning instruments. Nothing living approached the shuttlecraft during the night. No one left it, either."

"I tell you, she was here! And I did leave!" Angry now, and feeling more than a little guilty over what he had done with the woman, Herne recounted his adventure of the previous night, ending with, "I have no idea how I got back to the shuttlecraft, nor any recollection of dressing myself. I don't even know where my treksuit was after we reached the grotto. Except—except just a moment ago when I stood up I thought I saw myself standing beside my sleeping self, and the standing Herne was naked until I merged with the body wearing the treksuit.

"By all the stars." Herne drew a shaky breath. "I've been spending too much time with Osiyar. His telepathic abilities are rubbing off on me."

"I know you well enough by now to be certain that you are not a telepath," said Tarik with a chuckle.

"It's not funny," Herne declared, insulted by Tarik's humor. "This was not just an erotic dream. I *was* with a woman last night, or with something that looked and acted like a woman."

"I believe you. We sometimes forget," Tarik said, laying a friendly hand on Herne's rigid shoulder, "that this planet is in the Empty Sector. The reason space travel is forbidden through this part of the galaxy is because the laws of physics don't always apply here, because legends tell of dreams more real than waking life, and of strange life forms flourishing."

"Like telepaths," Herne frowned, trying to make sense of his experience.

"Like telepaths," Tarik agreed. "This planet's isolation and the laws against travel in the Empty Sector made this a safe place for the telepaths to found their colony of Tathan, so long ago. For the same reasons we came here, to build a listening post to monitor the Cetans, to make certain they keep their recently signed treaty with the Jurisdiction.

"You were right to inform me of this incident, Herne. Be sure to tell me if anything else happens to you that seems strange. Do you feel well enough to work today?"

"Absolutely." Herne nodded. "Thanks to Merin's hot qahf, my brain is starting to function again. Look, Tarik, I know you said we would start our excavations with the building you found yesterday, but if you don't mind, I'd like to study the area where I first saw that woman. Perhaps I can find some evidence of what really happened."

"That's a good idea. Just be careful," Tarik advised. "How much will you tell Merin?"

"She will need to know what I saw," Herne decided, "but I don't intend to reveal every intimate detail."

"Merin is an intelligent woman." Tarik surveyed the physician, taking in his bedraggled appearance, and Herne knew his leader was trying not to show any further sign of amusement. Still, Tarik could not resist a last teasing comment. "I wouldn't be at all surprised if she is able to guess what you've been doing all night."

Chapter Three

Merin could tell that Herne was not feeling well. When she reentered the shuttlecraft she found him drinking a second cup of qahf, swallowing the hot liquid as though it was an unpleasant but necessary medicine—which, from his appearance, it probably was. His face was a pasty-white color, there were dark circles under his eyes, and his step was none too steady. This she learned by quick glances while he was occupied in gathering together his kit and strapping it on his back. She did not allow their eyes to meet. It would not be right. But then, nothing would ever be right again, not till she died.

It had not taken her long to understand that she should not have come to Dulan's Planet.

But she hadn't belonged in the archivists' carrels at Capital, either. There was no place in the Jurisdiction where she could possibly fit in and feel comfortable now that her home planet was forever closed to her. All she had left in her exile was her need to make herself useful in order to justify her continued existence.

When she had heard two other Capital archivists discussing in sneering terms the rumors about a group of misfits whom Commander Tarik was gathering to take on some mysterious expedition into the unknown, she had realized that he would need someone to keep his records. She had once helped Tarik's older brother, Admiral Halvo, with some difficult and confidential research that he had wanted done immediately. He had been so pleased with her work that he had offered to use his influence in her behalf if she ever needed it. Merin went to Halvo, to ask him to recommend her to Tarik. Within a day she had been signed on as a member of the colony. Seven days later she was on her way to Dulan's Planet, where, she hoped, no one would ever learn what she really was.

She found Tarik's colonists a disparate lot. There was even a Cetan among them, although Gaidar seemed a mild enough character and had mated with a Jurisdiction woman, Suria. Both had tried to be kind to Merin. So had Tarik and his wife, Narisa. Still, Merin felt ill at ease with them, because she could not tell them the truth about herself.

On Oressia it was accepted, a necessary thing, but it was an aspect of Oressian life that could never be revealed to outsiders. The few who left Oressia to live elsewhere were sworn to eternal secrecy by the most solemn oaths. At the time of her own leaving, it had not seemed a great thing to ask of her because it was clear that those who lived on other Jurisdiction worlds would be incapable of understanding the very good reasons for the Oressian way of life.

"I'm ready. Let's go." Herne had gotten himself and his gear together at last. For the second time that morning Merin left the shuttlecraft, but when she started walking toward the area of the ruins where Tarik and the others were working, Herne stopped her. "Not there. This way."

She saw where he was going. With a lifting of interest, she followed him.

"Are we going to search for evidence of the woman you thought you saw?" she asked.

"The woman I *did* see," he corrected her. He pointed toward a pile of stones. "As a historian, what is your opinion of that pillar?"

"By Jurisdiction time, it is six to seven hundred years old," Merin replied, glad to forget her personal troubles in work. Quickly, she pushed the buttons on the hand-held recorder that communicated with the shuttlecraft computer, entering information on the dimensions, composition, and exact location of the pillar.

"Six to seven hundred years would be about right," Herne mused, looking at the ground near the pillar. "Isn't that when the telepaths settled here? They must have built this."

"It seems likely." Merin watched him scrape at the ground with one foot. "For what are you searching?"

"For the other side of the arch."

"I see only a broken pillar, with no evidence of an arch," she told him.

"It was here. It was part of a one-story white building that had a garden behind it."

"You think this was the arch?" Merin stood where Ananka had stood the night before. She waved the hand holding the recorder. "And on this side was the interior of the building?"

"Yes. The garden was that way," Herne insisted, noting that, measured against the masonry of the pillar, Merin was almost exactly as tall as Ananka had been.

"Show me." Still Merin's eyes were on the recorder. Her fingers flew over the buttons, adding more data. "Count the steps, or if you can't remember how many steps you took, then just approximate the distance."

"You believe me?" He sounded surprised.

"What is important is that you believe in whatever you think you saw," said Merin. "Describe it to me as we go along. I will record it all. Even if we can make no sense of it, perhaps the larger computer at Home can. Or perhaps your information will fit with any discoveries made by Tarik and the others."

"Here," Herne said, stopping by a slight elevation in the overgrown debris. "At this spot was a huge golden statue of a Chon."

"If it was valuable metal, the Cetans probably hacked it to pieces and carried it off when they destroyed the city," Merin told him. She made notes on the recorder while Herne attempted to clear the dirt away from the mound. Stooping, he picked up an oblong chunk of solid material that had fallen away as he worked.

"Look at this. It was down here, near the bottom, as if it had fallen off the pedestal. Perhaps it's a piece of the stone the statue sat on." He scraped at what he held in one hand, using his fingernails until a spot of dark metal was revealed. "What the—? This isn't stone."

"If it is an artifact and not just a piece of dirt, you ought to use the proper tools," Merin said, handing over a brush and a small pick from her own supply of instruments. When Herne took them she went back to her recorder. "I need to note exactly where and how you found it."

Surprised and pleased that she had not claimed a historian's right by insisting on taking over his discovery to clean and examine it herself, Herne worked at the chunk of dirt and metal for a while. Because he was so intent on what he was doing, it took a few minutes before he realized that she had finished recording the data on his finding and was watching every motion of his hands.

"Do you want to do it?" he asked, irrationally irritated by her quiet patience.

"Why, when you are doing an excellent job? It appears that the hands of a physician are every bit as gentle and precise as those of a trained archaeologist. Which," she reminded him, "I am not. I am only a historian, not a discoverer. Please, continue. I will make the notes." She bowed her head so he could not see her face, but only the crisp white coif with its neat chinstrap.

"Thank you for your confidence in me." Had she been anyone else, he would have touched her arm or her shoulder in grateful acknowledgment of the compliment she had just paid him, but he knew that Merin did not like to be touched. He had seen her shy away when someone came too close and, in the manner of all observant physicians, he had stored that fact in his memory, for future use. He went back to work on the object in his hands. He had only uncovered a portion of it before he knew what it was. Merin knew it too. He could tell by the sound of her indrawn breath.

"It's impossible," she said. "It cannot be. Not buried by six centuries of dirt."

"Luckily, this special metal doesn't corrode." Herne chipped away a piece of solidified earth, revealing part of the upper surface. "You can read the serial number right here. This is a Service recorder, current issue, just like the ones we are using."

"Herne." Merin's hands were shaking. "That is the number on my recorder. There cannot be two recorders with the same serial number. The final five digits are always different, and they are checked often enough at the factory to avoid duplication." She held her own instrument out for him to see.

"The same object cannot be in two places at the same time," Herne insisted, looking at the one in his hand.

"Tarik has often enough warned us about distortions of time and space in the Empty Sector," Merin said. "Perhaps here, under certain conditions, the impossible is possible. Tarik should see this at once."

"Not yet. I want to look around a bit more before we go to him. Come on, we're going to do some exploring."

"By the Jurisdiction's rule of archaeology," Merin said, "you are required to leave that recorder exactly where you found it until your commanding officer verifies the finding. Under these peculiar circumstances, I suggest you take it with you instead. It might not be here when we return."

"It's good to know you do have an imagination." She missed Herne's brief smile because her eyes were on the clean recorder in her hand. He wrapped the dirt-encrusted one in an artifact bag and put it into his kit.

"Shall we go on?" Merin asked in her soft, unemotional voice.

"Be careful," Herne warned. "There are steps here, or there should be. We are entering the garden now. Just over there is the stairway to the grotto."

"You haven't mentioned a grotto before. How do you know it is here? I see nothing to indicate steps."

"Perhaps you would be able to see something if you would occasionally take your eyes off the ground or that recorder," Herne snapped, suddenly irritated by the way she had put aside her distress over the duplicate recorder to resume her usual calm demeanor. He glared at her, but of course she could not see his expression. That annoyed him even more. Believing she would soon begin asking questions about the previous night that he would rather not answer, he attacked with a question of his own. "Why don't you ever look at anyone when you speak? I detest people who don't look me straight in the eye."

"On my homeworld it is considered rude to so challenge another person," Merin responded with quiet gravity. "In order to avoid provoking conflict, we do not look directly at each other."

"You aren't on Oressia now. Look at me." Herne almost told her to take off that stupid white headdress, too, but stopped himself just in time. It wasn't Merin's fault if he was disoriented and in a miserable mood this morning, or if he was blaming himself for what had happened during the night. He had finally realized how he might have put all of his companions in jeopardy by going off with that accursed woman. If he *had* gone off with her. If there actually had been a woman. If he had not dreamed it all. He shook his head, trying to sort out his memories, trying to think rationally.

At least he could be grateful that in spite of the lack of any solid evidence, Tarik had not reprimanded him or scoffed at his story. Nor had Merin laughed at the insane things he had been saying. She had only asked for more information. He was about to apologize to her, to tell her she need not break her native customs in order to accommodate his irascible demand that she look directly at him when, apparently having wrestled through the problem on her own, she lifted her eyes to his.

Herne was rocked back on his heels. Her eyes were light brown with purple flecks in them, wide and clear and innocent, and lashed in darker brown. Her entire face was changed when she looked upward, her sharp features, untouched by any trace of cosmetics, softened into delicate prettiness. Her lips trembled a little at this breach of Oressian custom, and a faint blush turned her cheeks pink.

But the thing that shook Herne to his bones was the way her features resembled those of Ananka. It could not be, unless it was some trick played on his mind by forces he did not understand. He longed to pull the covering off

Merin's head, to see if her hair was the same light golden brown as Ananka's had been. What in the name of all the stars was going on here?

She looked right at him with those wonderful eyes and said in all innocence, "I have recorded everything I can from this position. Will you show me the grotto stair, please?"

There was nothing for it but to stop gazing into her eyes like a star-struck boy and begin searching for the steps. Knowing where they ought to be, he found them soon enough, buried beneath six centuries of dirt and leaves and overgrowth. He and Merin started down the slope, all that was left of the ancient masonry.

"Take my hand," he advised. "You don't want to fall."

"I need both hands for the recorder." That wasn't true. She could have put the recorder away until she reached the bottom of the slope, but she did not want to touch him. Until just a few moments ago she had never looked directly at a man who was looking back at her. When she had met Herne's eyes she had felt stripped, ravished, lost forever, and she had understood why she had been trained to keep her gaze always lowered in the presence of others. Appalled at her own response though she was, and horrified to find herself speaking an untruth for the second time in less than a day, still she wanted to raise her eyes to his again. But she dared not; in such uninhibited behavior lay the seeds of disease and disaster, complete social disorder, war and all its terrors. . . .

She kept her eyes fixed on her recorder. Because she wasn't watching her footing, she tripped over a root. The slope was too steep for her to regain her balance. She bounced against Herne, who was a little ahead of her. He grabbed at her to pull her upright, but he missed and they both went down, rolling and sliding, trying to catch branches and bushes and rocks along the way until they stopped in a heap of bodies and shoulderkits. Dazed and breathless, Merin felt the heavy strength of a masculine body pressed firmly on top of her. She was so shaken that she scarcely noticed the way her head was hanging over the edge of a large dark hole.

"That," said Herne, his mouth pressed close to her ear, "is the entrance to the grotto."

"Last night there was a stream running along here," Herne told her.

They were using the lamp he carried in his shoulderkit to light their way down the slippery, earth-clogged steps. Merin looked where he indicated, but saw only a rock channel worn smooth by the passage of water at some time in the past.

"There was a lake here," he added when they reached the bottom of the steps, "a beautiful blue lake. And draperies blowing in the wind. And a couch, right there."

What they saw now was a small black pool.

The walls and roof of the underground chamber dripped viscous moisture. There was no sign of billowing draperies, nor of any luxurious couch. Instead, there was a ledge of bare rock, and on it the skeleton of a small, batlike creature. The breeze was gone too. The air was heavy, and as still as the water in the stagnant pool. All of this Herne and Merin saw in bits and pieces as he moved the lamp about, and where the light did not reach weird shadows loomed. Merin moved closer to him.

"How did you know this chamber was here?" She did not look at him. She concentrated on the recorder. Tarik would expect detailed notes on this discovery. "You cannot have seen everything you are speaking of in the second or two during which the woman appeared to you by the campfire, and what I have seen since we began to explore this site does not match the descriptions you have been providing to me."

"It was later," Herne said, speaking slowly and, Merin thought, reluctantly. "In the middle of the night she brought me here. Unless I dreamed it."

Glancing upward just then, Merin saw his face by the light of the lamp in his hand, saw his mouth compressed and his expression hard as he looked around the grotto.

"I assume from your manner that it was not a pleasant experience," she said, fingers poised to record his answer.

"No. Yes. I'm not sure."

"Ah, I see." She quickly repressed the pain he had unwittingly inflicted upon her with his disjointed response. She was not well informed on intimate subjects, but even she could guess what Herne believed had happened in that chamber. She reminded herself that jealousy was a destructive emotion. No true Oressian would allow herself to feel it. Besides, Herne wasn't even sure whether the entire episode had happened or whether it had been a dream. She tried to keep her voice neutral, telling herself that questioning him on the matter was her duty, to ascertain the truth for her report. "I have noticed that when men speak in such a confused way, it is usually the result of an experience about which they feel guilty."

"You see nothing!" he responded with barely contained fury. "You with your eyes always on the ground and your body entirely covered except for your face and your hands. What do you know about men?"

"Nothing at all," she replied quietly. "I regret that you find my costume disturbing. The exact opposite was my intent. As for my questions or comments, they are required to elicit as much detail as possible about an incident that Tarik will doubtless find most interesting, and possibly threatening to the expedition."

"Tarik already knows. I told him." He held the lamp closer to her, trying to read her expression.

"What's this?" He caught her face, turning it

so he could better see her right cheek. "You've hurt yourself."

"It does not matter." She stood with her eyes still downcast, fighting his grip on her chin.

"It certainly does matter," he told her. "We don't know what organisms live here, what infection you might develop. Sit down on the ledge there, and let me look at that cut more closely."

Obediently, Merin selected a spot on the ledge as far as possible from the tiny skeleton. After pulling off his shoulderkit Herne sat beside her, shining the light full on her wounded cheek.

"Why didn't you tell me about this at once?" he asked, reaching one hand into his medical supplies. "You know the rules about reporting all injuries."

"It is insignificant." She tried to stop the trembling that seized her when he thrust the lamp into her hands before moving her face about to examine the damage.

"Merin, it is your duty to take proper care of yourself. Tarik needs a healthy company." Herne broke open a vial of sterilizing antimicrobial salve and began to apply it.

"I will remember in the future." The salve stung, but she would not flinch. Herne pressed a piece of flesh-colored plastiskin over the wound.

"I don't think you will develop a scar," he said, "but if you do, I can perform a cosmetic repair after we return to headquarters. It would be a shame to leave a scar on your skin when it's so perfect. You don't have a single blemish that I can see."

"Thank you for your help." Setting down the lamp, she rose, putting distance between them, and her trembling eased a little.

"Do all Oressian women have such beautiful complexions?" he asked, repacking his kit while he spoke.

"I do not know."

"Covering up so completely probably helps, though of course your face and hands are exposed to the elements. Why do you always wear that outfit, and the headgear?"

"I don't know! Don't ask me!"

"Don't know, or won't say?"

"It is rude to question the customs of others!" Blazing anger roared through her, filling every nerve and vein, heating the very marrow of her bones. This was why Oressian discipline was so strict, to prevent just this kind of violent emotional reaction to another person. She struggled to control herself.

Merin's rage was not the result only of Herne's words, nor of her growing frustration at her inability to fit into Tarik's colony. She was frightened by the way she had felt when Herne had touched her while treating her cut face. She was so careful never to touch anyone. She had been warned since childhood of the danger. But his hands had been gentle on her face. She could still feel his fingers on her chin and her cheek. She wanted to put her own hands on the spots. She resisted the impulse, but she could not stop the urge to strike out at him, to say the same kind of cruel things to him that he had said to her, for though he did not know it, his curiosity was cruelty.

"Shall I be equally rude and challenge you about the customs of Sibirna?" she asked, her voice as cold as the winter wind on his home world. "Where you were born and raised the vile natures of children are quelled with harshness, with constant painful punishment, until those children grow up into sour-tempered, irritable men and women, quick to take offense, eager to quarrel. Say what you will about the Oressians, my people have never started an interplanetary war."

"Who knows whether they have or not, when they are so secretive that they will allow no outsiders on their planet?" he retorted. Then, suddenly, he gave her a lopsided smile. "I don't even know enough about your people to insult them properly, unless it's by accident. That's a fine situation for a violent Sibirnan, isn't it, when you are saying those terrible things about my folk?"

"Every word I spoke is true. I have studied your world's history, and I have observed many racial types while at Capital. But Herne"—her anger dispelled by her brief verbal attack, she took a step toward him, looking directly at him now, as he had earlier told her to do—"there is in you a streak of kindness and gentleness that is at variance with your own traditions and upbringing."

"On my world," he said, "the sick and injured are left to themselves, to die or recover as the local gods ordain."

"Did it hurt you to see that?" Something in his voice told her it had hurt him deeply.

"Once, when my mother's sister was ill, I took bread and drink to her. She died anyway, and I was beaten for trying to help her." He was still sitting on the ledge, staring down at his hands. "It was then I knew I could not live all my life on Sibirna."

"So you left and became a doctor?" she asked, fascinated by these revelations. How different Herne was from the harsh man she had first imagined him to be, and how hard he tried to hide the gentle part of himself. Yet the attempt was not completely successful. She had seen through it. "Was the practice of medicine your way of channeling your kindly impulses into useful work?"

"Something like that," he admitted. "But I'm still a product of my upbringing. Is that why you left Oressia? Because you didn't fit in either?"

"Oh, no," she said. "I fit in perfectly. There and nowhere else."

"Then why leave?"

"You would not understand." Because he was looking at her with a sweet half smile that tugged at her heart, she added, "It was done because my age group was too large."

"You mean excess population is sent away? That's been done often enough on many worlds. Younger sons or daughters, people with no economic opportunity where they grew up, political or religious dissenters, all have migrated and colonized elsewhere since history began. You know that. It's the same old story. You go somewhere else and build a new life."

"As you did?"

"I haven't done too badly, considering my past," he said, thinking that this was the first time he had ever spoken so freely to another person about his early life. Odd that it should be Merin who had generated his openness. Emboldened by the apparent friendliness of their conversation, he added, "Why don't you ever take off that headdress?"

"I cannot. It is forbidden." Her voice was so calm and quiet that he persisted.

"Not on any world except Oressia. And this is a new world, freer than any other place I've ever been. Take off that stupid contraption and let your hair blow free. I assume that Oressians do have hair."

She stared at him in such disgust and horror that Herne imagined she was afraid he would try to rip off her coif. When he rose from the ledge and stepped toward her she backed away, terror in her eyes, and he felt a stab of remorse tempered by something darker.

Having just opened his heart to her, he had

expected in return some revelation of her own private feelings. He was disappointed by her continued reticence, and angered by it too. He knew he ought not to expect intimacy from her. Oressians were reputed to be incapable of emotional closeness, though they were so secretive that no one could be certain of what they might feel. Herne forced himself to swallow the frustrated anger that was so much a part of his own cruel upbringing. He tried to understand her reaction to what he had just suggested so he could soothe her obvious fear of him.

"Here, now," he said, catching her shoulders with hands that shook a little from his effort to be gentle with her. "Don't look at me like that. I'm not a complete beast. I won't hurt you, Merin, I promise."

Merin stood trembling, knowing she ought to pull away from him, especially when he bent his head, put his lips against hers, and pressed. She had seen other men and women do this, and had been shocked by such a gesture. Thankfully, it had never been done to her before now. It was an obscenity. She should not permit it. And yet . . . .

"Merin?" He drew back a little, looking puzzled. His hand caressed her chin, then her wounded cheek, and the sensation was sweeter than it had been the first time he had touched her face. She lifted her head, following the motion of his hand, keeping the contact as long as possible. He steadied her face with his fingertips and put his mouth on hers again. There was a sweetness in his lips, and a warmth toward him building inside her. . . . When she whimpered in fear of her own emotions he let her go at once.

"I never really noticed you before we came to Tathan," he said. "Not as a woman."

"Do not notice me now." She made her voice cool and crisp. "Never touch me again. I am not like other women you know; I cannot respond as you want."

"You just did."

"You are mistaken." She turned from his bewildered look, trying to think of something that would prevent him from ever kissing her again. Picking up the recorder from the ledge where she had left it, she paused, fingers·ready for work. "Is this where your encounter with Ananka took place? On this ledge? Please recite a detailed account for the colony archives."

"Damnation!"

"I would hardly call that a precise explanation," she said, "though there may be some grain of truth in it."

"What in the name of all the stars are you, that you can ask a question like that after we just kissed?" he demanded.

"I see no connection whatsoever between the two events," she told him. "As for what you did to me, it was wasted effort on your part. I felt nothing."

"You're lying." He sounded angry, as well as bewildered.

"Oressians never lie. It is against our law."

"But you aren't an Oressian anymore, are you? That's one thing I do know about your people. Once you have left the planet, you cannot return. You are no longer an Oressian citizen."

She favored him with a look from those wondrous purple-flecked eyes, a look that would have stopped an attacking Jugarian crab dead in its own slime.

"If you have completed your survey of this chamber," she said, turning off the recorder and tucking it into her belt, "we had best return to the surface. We are overdue with our hourly report to the computer. Tarik will be worrying about us. And he should see that artifact you found as soon as possible."

"You did feel something," he muttered, watching her begin the climb up the dirt-covered steps. If she heard him, she gave no sign. "And I am going to find out why you repressed every normal response to me. No woman who can become as angry as you were could possibly be as frigid as you pretend to be."

Chapter Four

As anyone who knew him might have predicted, Tarik was fascinated by Herne's discovery of a recorder with a serial number matching that of the recorder Merin was using.

"There is simply no reasonable explanation," Tarik said, holding the partially cleaned instrument. "This model has been manufactured only during the last five years, yet here we have the same recorder found in ruins six centuries old."

"Some quirk of time?" murmured Osiyar, his telepathic training leading him to consider possibilities others might find frightening or unnatural.

"Here in the Empty Sector," Herne began, for once apparently ready to back one of Osiyar's peculiar theories.

"This is nonsense." Alla cut into their talk. "I am certain there is some scientific reason for what Herne has found. Given enough time and thought, we will discover it."

"My dear," Osiyar told her, smiling, "after our intimate association you should have learned that not everything in the universe has a rational cause or effect."

"I must admit," said Tarik, "that all the theories occurring to me are unreasonable, and so unscientific I'd rather not consider any of them till we have more information."

That seemed to close the discussion. The recorder was packed away in the cargo hold to await further cleaning and examination upon their return to headquarters at Home. Merin continued to use her own, matching recorder every day.

Feeling oddly disturbed by the duplicate recorder and frightened by her emotional and physical reactions to Herne, Merin tried to avoid him as much as possible. It was not terribly hard to do. For a place built by only a few telepaths, Tathan covered a large expanse of land. The telepaths had surrounded their houses with spacious gardens and had maintained many parks and open areas. All of this, as Tarik observed, would have made it a green and pleasant place in which to live. The visible ruins stretched over many acres, with still more buildings buried under earth, trees, and bushes. Their aerial surveys had shown evidence of outlying farms and villas, but those areas had yet to be thoroughly mapped.

In all this space it was easy for Merin to stay away from Herne. By saying she wanted to record every detail of Osiyar's impressions as he explored the city his ancestors had built, she was able to convince Tarik to switch places with her, so that he worked with Herne. Osiyar said nothing about the change, accepting Tarik's decision with his usual serenity, but Alla was another matter.

"So you can't stand working with Herne any longer," Alla said. "Why don't you just fight back when he's being difficult, instead of withdrawing into yourself as you always do?"

Refusing to say anything about what had happened between Herne and herself, Merin kept her eyes and her fingers on the recorder. Alla would not be discouraged.

"He was in one of those black moods of his after he saw that invisible woman. That was the day you worked with him. Did he say or do something to offend you?" Alla asked, adding, "I suspect Herne only became a doctor so he could have a legal excuse to torture people. I will never understand why Tarik chose a Sibirnan for our colony doctor."

"Tarik probably chose Herne for the same reason he chose the rest of us," Merin replied mildly. "Because we are all misfits in one way or another."

51

Flora Speer

She had been watching with interest while Osiyar eased a piece of stone out of a mound of dirt and weeds. When he looked up, laughing at her words, their glances met for an instant.

"Indeed," said Osiyar, his sea-blue eyes twinkling. "Even those added to Tarik's colony after he reached this world are oddities."

"I, at least, am not a misfit, or an oddity," Alla declared, looking at Merin in a way that made her wonder if Alla planned a lecture on the subject of Oressian aloofness.

Osiyar stopped whatever Alla might have said. "We are here to work, not quarrel. Now come, my dear, help me to clean the dirt off this carving."

"This entire trip is a waste of time," Alla told him. "We need more workers and heavier equipment if we are ever going to do any real excavating or make any important discoveries."

"That's not entirely true," said Osiyar. "Tarik and I have been working with Merin to map the location of specific buildings and some of the streets."

Merin stopped listening to them. She respected Osiyar but found it impossible to understand how he could be so patient with Alla. Perhaps his telepathic powers gave him special insight into Alla's true feelings, buried beneath her constant barrage of sarcasm and criticism toward others. It might be that the strength of their bond to each other lay in the mysterious physical relationship between male and female. Merin dared not speculate on that fearful subject, but when she tried to clear her mind Herne's voice intruded on her thoughts.

He stood a short distance away, discussing something with Tarik. Since their visit to the grotto he had occasionally tried to talk with her. When she did not respond to him except on archaeological matters, and then as briefly as possible, he gave up and began to ignore her. It was better so. The thought that he might want more from her than the kisses he had already stolen made Merin feel ill.

While she was able to endure the busy days by avoiding Herne completely—and when she could not avoid him, by not looking at him and declining to enter into extended conversation with him—the nights were another matter. With all five of them crowded into the shuttlecraft, it was harder to pretend that Herne was just one of the others, no more to her than Tarik or Osiyar. His kisses had changed that safe relationship forever. Merin found it increasingly difficult to sleep in the same shuttlecraft with him.

One night she lay wakeful in the darkest hours, refusing to allow herself to turn over one more time, or to sigh, or even to stretch out her cramped legs. But she could not control the twinges in her limbs or make herself fall asleep. Nor could she keep herself from thinking forbidden thoughts. She knew the discipline imposed upon her for her entire life was weakening. The fault was mostly her own, though Herne did bear some of the blame. If only he hadn't kissed her; if only she had been able to stop her response to him before he noticed it. For the tenth time that night she tried the regular breathing exercises that had always before brought rest.

With her eyes half closed and her mind at last beginning to slip toward repose, she thought she saw a movement at the front of the shuttlecraft cabin. The only light came from the green glow at the control panel, where Tarik had set the scanning instruments for security. Something moved between Merin and that green light, then drifted toward the main hatch.

Herne! It must be Herne, because from where she lay, Merin could see Tarik's head, and in the two flattened seats behind him the dark shapes of Alla and Osiyar. She was certain there could be only one place where Herne could be going in the middle of the night. He was going to search for Ananka. It was foolish of him, possibly even dangerous—to him and to the rest of them.

So far had the strictures of discipline slipped from her that Merin, with no forethought at all, did something equally foolish and dangerous. She was still wearing her treksuit, with her boots and shoulderkit laid neatly by the seat on which she lay. Swinging her feet to the

54

floor, she reached down to sling the kit over one shoulder and pick up the boots. Then she crept to the hatch, opened it as quietly as she could, and stepped into the night.

It took only a moment to pull on and fasten her boots, a moment more to find the handlight she kept in her kit. Then, guided by twin moons that were each half full, she set off toward the ruined building and the grotto.

Inside the shuttlecraft, the green security signal began to blink steadily and emit a beeping noise. Tarik came instantly awake, sitting up to check the scanning instruments. He had barely touched the control panel when Osiyar was there, kneeling in the aisle beside him.

"Is it an intruder?" Osiyar asked.

"No." Tarik switched off the beeping alarm and the light stopped blinking. "Someone has left the ship."

"Not Herne. He's right here." Osiyar indicated the motionless shape across the aisle from Tarik. "How could he sleep through that noise?"

"He's not asleep." Alla had awakened, too, and was using a diagnostic rod on Herne. "He's unconscious. It seems to be some kind of altered state of existence. There is no indication of drugs or injury. It's just that his mind is elsewhere."

"It has happened before." Quickly, leaving out the few erotic details Herne had confided to him, Tarik told them about the physician's previous experience. "Herne spoke of returning to this ship and standing beside his own body for a second or two before he became one with it again."

"What you are describing is not unknown to telepaths," Osiyar said. "It is possible that at the instant of separation between body and consciousness an electrical discharge could be created, but would it be sufficient to produce a signal on our instruments? That did not occur during Herne's previous separation."

"Merin is gone," said Alla, glancing around the cockpit.

"When she opened the door that set off the alarm," Osiyar remarked, "but where would she go?"

"Where Herne went," Tarik told him. "Alla, is it safe to leave Herne alone in that condition?"

"I don't see why not," Alla said. "There is nothing any of us can do for him until he reintegrates himself."

"Then we will secure the shuttlecraft and begin a search for Merin."

The faint silver glow coming from the chamber at the bottom of the grotto stairs made her handlight unnecessary. Merin went down carefully, picking her way through rubble and avoiding broken steps. The light grew brighter. By the time she reached the barren chamber at the heart of the grotto, it had become a shimmering globe centered on the ledge at one side of the chamber. Silhouetted against the light was a figure.

"Herne!" Laughter followed her cry to him— not Herne's laughter, but that of a woman. Disregarding the sound, Merin called again. "Herne!"

He gave no indication of hearing her. As he slowly merged with the globe she could see him clearly. He was unclothed. The sight should have revolted her, made her ill with disgust at the obscenity he represented, but he was beautiful . . . beautiful. He was a tall man, large boned and muscular, with his proud head held high as he walked into the light. What a marvelous creature he was . . . how easily he moved, how graceful was the shape of his hands and feet and legs. . . .

"Herne!"

There were sounds behind her, voices, clattering feet, and flashing lights.

"Merin, why did you come here in the middle of the night?" Alla demanded. "You know you have broken security."

"I followed Herne." Merin had not taken her eyes off the ledge, but all was now dark except for the light cast by the lamps the others had brought with them. "Herne was here just a moment ago, but he's gone, and the light too."

"You saw him?" Tarik was staring at her.

"Of course I saw him. How else could I have followed him?"

"Extraordinary," murmured Osiyar. Merin ignored him. Her concern was all for Herne.

"Tarik, he may be in danger. We have to find him."

"Herne is back at the shuttlecraft," said Tarik.

"No, he's here," Merin insisted. "Or he was."

"Only you saw him leave the ship." Osiyar's eyes bored into her. Merin had her own eyes properly lowered, but she could feel his on her, searching, seeking information about her.

"I think," said Osiyar, "that it is time for my thoughts to touch yours."

"No." Merin wanted to flee from him, as though mere physical distance could protect her from his telepathic power. "I cannot allow it."

"Merin, it is necessary." Tarik's voice was kind, but he could not ease her fear. "We don't know what this entity is that can separate Herne's body from his mind, why this grotto is important, or whether there is any serious danger to us, or even to the others back at Home. We have to learn all we can about what has happened here."

"Since you were capable of seeing what the others did not, your mind offers the best pathway to the knowledge we need," Osiyar added.

"Herne's mind would be a better pathway," Merin suggested in desperation.

"At the moment there is nothing in Herne for me to contact," Osiyar told her.

"I regret that I must order you to do this," Tarik said. "It is for the safety of all those under my command."

"No!" Merin was close to panic.

It was then that Alla came forward; sharp-tongued, unfriendly Alla, who never said a kind word to anyone when she could scold or criticize instead. She took Merin's hand and led the protesting young woman to the ledge, where she made Merin sit.

"I was afraid too," Alla said, sitting beside Merin. "The first time I was terrified. But it doesn't hurt. There is only a faint prickling in your mind. It can be a beautiful thing, to join your thoughts to those of another. Osiyar will not harm you, will not take anything away from you. You will still be yourself when he has finished."

"You don't understand. It is impossible. I cannot do what you want."

"Is it the Jurisdiction prohibition against telepathy that frightens you?" Alla asked with a surprising amount of sympathy. "This is a new world, a different place. No such stricture applies here."

"No, I will not do it."

"You must." Alla was growing impatient, her voice taking on its usual sharp edge. "It could mean our lives, including Herne's. At the very least, you could save Herne's sanity."

"She's right," Osiyar said. "Herne has no training in telepathy. His lack of training combined with his deep resistance to the very idea of telepathy makes me fear that he cannot endure repeated separations of body and consciousness. The being we know as Herne will simply disintegrate, will cease to exist, if he is not permanently restored to what he *is*."

"He will die?" For a fraction of a second Merin allowed herself to look directly at Osiyar, to try to read his face, to discover if he was telling her the truth. He was so serious that she was forced to believed every word he had said. Tarik looked equally solemn, while Alla regarded her with increasing impatience. "I do not want Herne to die," Merin said.

"Then help him," Alla pressed her. "Help us all. You owe it to us, Merin. Let Osiyar enter your thoughts."

"There is no need. I will tell you everything I know," Merin offered, still trying to avoid what would happen if she allowed Osiyar to do as he wanted.

"That's not good enough," Tarik said.

"Accept me," Osiyar urged. "I can learn facts and details you yourself do not understand."

That was exactly Merin's concern. Osiyar ranging through her mind would learn the truth about her. He would tell everyone. They would cast her out forever, and she had nowhere else to go. She could not bear the pain of it, nor the fear.

But she could not bear the thought of Herne dying, either, not when she might help him. Behind her lowered lids she saw his image again, naked and proud, walking into the mysterious light. She lifted her hand to her lips, feeling his kisses once more. With a deep, shuddering sigh she abandoned her past for his sake, sacrificing any chance she might have had for an ordinary life.

"Yes," she said, and lifted her eyes to Osiyar's.

He gave her no chance to change her mind. His sea-blue gaze burned into her, his hard, determined will brushing past her paltry last-minute defenses as if all her training in control of her thoughts had succeeded in erecting only cobwebs against him. She fought him in panic for a second or two before she gave up and allowed him to take the information he needed.

She became aware of the prickling Alla had described, followed by a sensation as if the edges of her mind had grown vague and were being stretched. It was exquisitely painful. She felt Osiyar's surprise; it should not have hurt either of them. Then she experienced his deep shock, and knew that he had reached her secret, that he now understood what she was. She felt his revulsion, and his pity. And then, as the prickling ended and his mind withdrew from hers, he directed a surge of admiration and respect toward her. It did much to alleviate her terror over what

61

would happen next, when he told Tarik and Alla about her.

To Merin's surprise, Osiyar said nothing to the others of what he had discovered in her mind. He discussed only Herne and Ananka.

"I have seen in my own mind what Merin saw when she looked at the light," Osiyar said. "I believe the light is the creature the telepaths once called Ananka. Or, to be more precise, the womanly form and the name Ananka are aspects of the light."

"I don't understand what you are saying," Alla objected.

"There is no way you could understand," Osiyar told her. "You have only five senses, plus a rudimentary version of what humans call a sixth sense. Even I, with my well-trained telepathic abilities, cannot begin to comprehend all the senses and possibilities contained within the light that Merin saw."

"Is it friend or enemy?" Alla wondered.

"So far as I could tell, it will not harm us," Osiyar answered.

"Unless we step on its toes," said Merin, and they all stared at her in surprise. She could look straight at Osiyar now. There was no need to hide anything from him, so she kept her eyes on him. "What you describe is a life form far superior to humans, even human telepaths. How can we tell what acts of ours will make it angry, make it strike back at us? Its values, if it has any, will not be the same as ours."

"True." Osiyar gave her an approving look. "But we have not angered it so far, just by being here and poking around the old city."

"Perhaps it doesn't care about the city," Merin said. "What about Herne? He was the reason for your invasion of my mind. What did you learn about the creature's intentions or feelings toward him?"

"I regret to say, very little, except for a gust of mocking laughter and an impression of fondness. But I felt no hostility."

"Fondness?" Alla interrupted whatever Osiyar was going to say next. "Was that Ananka's emotion, or Merin's?"

It was a remark so typical of her that Osiyar did not even bother to frown or tell her to be silent. But Merin began to blush, the heat rushing upward to her throat and face. It had happened to her only once before, with Herne. Her self-discipline had always prevented any outward sign of her inner feelings. Fortunately, in the fragmented illumination provided by the handlights, the others did not notice. Except for Osiyar.

"If the creature is gone from this grotto, then it seems to me there is nothing more we can accomplish here," Tarik said briskly. "We ought to return to the shuttlecraft to see if Herne is completely himself again." He motioned Alla up the steps, then followed her. Osiyar was still watching Merin.

"When my thoughts touched yours," he said, "I understood your deep concern lest I reveal all of the contents of your mind to Tarik and Alla. You used the word 'invasion.' I think you do not understand the laws that have bound all telepaths on Dulan's Planet. I would never enter your thoughts without your permission unless it were an emergency or to save a life. Nor can I reveal anything I have learned from you that does not relate to the problem at hand. Your past and what you are have nothing to do with what has happened here. Your secret is safe with me."

"I felt your shock."

"Say, rather, my surprise. There is little that can shock an experienced telepath. I have no right to condemn the decrees of the Elders of Oressia. But, Merin"—here Osiyar touched her, took her arm so that Alla or Tarik, looking backward, would think he was guiding her toward the stairs—"in spite of your terror at the thought of being found out, in spite of your fear of me personally, you did what was right for Herne and for the safety of this colony. I admire and respect you for the sacrifice you were willing to make, at a possibly terrible cost to yourself."

"I was not so willing," she said.

"For Herne, you were willing." He smiled. "On that subject, also, I will be silent."

Now he did lead her toward the stairs, his hand still on her arm, and Merin, though trained since earliest childhood to abhor and avoid the touch of another anywhere on her body, was comforted by Osiyar's warm fingers. She found comfort, too, in his promise of silence. A part of him lingered still in her mind, assuring her he could be trusted, could be depended upon if she should need a friend.

Friend. She had never had a friend before. Oressians were so separate from each other, so steeped in stern discipline, that friendship was impossible for them. There could be no thought that Osiyar imagined anything else in regard to her, for his heart and mind were deeply bound to Alla. He would be Merin's friend, no more. But his friendship was a priceless gift. Merin emerged from the grotto with something very close to a smile on her usually expressionless face.

They found Herne apparently sleeping normally. When, after much effort, they succeeded in waking him, and after Merin had given him two large cups of qahf, he recounted his version of the night's events.

"It was the same as before," Herne said, "except that when I reached the grotto suddenly Ananka and everything else vanished, and I was lost inside a black, whirling tunnel, until you woke me and I found myself back here."

"You told me that the first time you went into the grotto the large chamber was furnished," Tarik said. "Was it the same this time, the draperies, the tables, the illuminated lake?"

"Exactly the same," Herne said.

"But it was a barren, damp chamber, unchanged since the day when you and I explored it together!" Merin exclaimed. "I was there, Herne. I saw you, and the light. There was no woman, and there were no furnishings."

"And," Tarik added, "your body remained here, inside the shuttlecraft."

"Are you saying it was all an illusion?" Herne looked so relieved that Tarik laughed out loud. When Alla began to explain what had happened while Herne was unconscious Merin tried to fade into the shadows near the cargo bay door. But, as Alla finished her detailed account, Herne's qahf-sharpened eyes found hers.

"Thank you," he said, "for your willingness to help me."

His eyes held hers for much longer than was necessary, until Merin wisely dropped her own.

Chapter Five

It rained during the night, briefly but violently, leaving the shuttlecraft surrounded by mud. Dawn brought a dull gray sky, heavy with the threat of more rain. Only Herne ventured out to wander about the ruins. The rest of the explorers lingered inside the shuttlecraft, drinking qahf until an urgent call from Home brought their desultory plans for further exploration of the city to an end.

"There is a rainstorm with severe winds headed in your direction," Narisa told Tarik. "We haven't monitored the weather on this planet long enough to be absolutely certain, but the computer projects repetition of such storms, some of them with monsoonlike rains. It seems to be the standard weather pattern for both hemispheres at this time of year. We are expecting heavy snow here at Home in three to four days. I recommend that you return at once, while you can still travel safely. Besides, I miss you."

"We will leave Tathan by noon," Tarik replied, smiling at the personal message. "I'll see you soon, my love."

"About time too," Herne grumbled when he was told of the change in plans. "We should have left this place the day after that creature first showed itself to me."

"If you wanted to leave," Alla told him, "you should have said something before this. Do be careful; you are just tossing the medical supplies around instead of putting them where they belong. If we hit turbulent weather, we'll have a terrible mess to clean up after we land."

"I don't care." Herne threw his favorite diagnostic rod into the locker on top of a delicate calibrator. With a squawk of outrage, Alla snatched up the rod so she could rearrange the calibrator.

"What is the matter with you?" she shouted at Herne.

Standing behind them, Merin tried to hand the last of the medical equipment to Alla while at the same time attempting to shrink into invisibility. Relieved when Alla snatched the packages from her hands and began to stow them, she turned to leave the shuttlecraft. Herne's answer to Alla's question stopped Merin with one hand on the hatch.

"I think this part of the planet should be permanently quarantined, and I'm going to tell Tarik so," Herne said. "Osiyar believes this Ananka creature only exists here, at Tathan, and can't move elsewhere. If we stay out of this area, it shouldn't bother us again."

"You are the one it bothered, Herne." Alla shot him an amused look. "Did you have a good time with her?"

"You know, Alla," said Herne, red-faced and flashing a quick glance in Merin's direction, "you have a remarkable talent for saying exactly the wrong thing at the wrong moment."

"If you had a woman of your own," Alla told him, "you wouldn't have to resort to mysterious spirits."

"Tarik believes it was all an illusion and so do I," Herne grated, not hiding his anger.

"Illusion is even worse," said Alla sweetly. "Merin, where did you put—now where did she go?"

Too upset by this conversation to listen to any more, Merin had left the shuttlecraft to stand beside the ruined pillar, where she stared toward the grotto while struggling with bitter jealousy, an emotion she had never dreamed she was capable of feeling until a few days earlier. Osiyar found her there.

"I have wanted to speak with you in private," he said. "Merin, I know you are frightened and lonely. It need not be so. If Tarik were to learn the truth about you, I think his reaction would be far milder than you imagine. Tarik is a tolerant man."

"Others are not," Merin snapped at him with unusual spirit. "Alla, for instance. Or Herne. But it doesn't matter what others might think. I took an oath and I can't break it."

"Circumstances change," he said. "I was once bound with the twin bracelets of a High Priest and sworn never to touch a woman. Yet today my wrists are bare and I regularly make love with Alla. I am only suggesting that you consider your present situation and do what seems best to you."

"I can't change, Osiyar. You know that."

"So stubborn." His smile softened the effect of the hard word. After a moment he seemed to move on to another subject. "Have you pondered the mystery of the recorder you found here? The only possible explanation that occurs to me seems incredible. Yet I, of all men, know how easily the impossible can become reasonable and simple."

It was only later that Merin realized he was still talking about her, and it would take terrifying alterations in her life before she could comprehend that Osiyar had understood the mystery of the recorder all along.

The return trip northward was smooth and uneventful, though from the high altitude at which they flew the travelers could see heavy clouds gathering along the northwestern horizon, forerunners of the expected snowstorm. When the shuttlecraft had landed at Home, near the round white building set on an island in a lake, Merin watched Tarik greet his wife with a long kiss and a close embrace. To her surprise, for the first time in her experience among these overly demonstrative non-Oressians, she was not disgusted by the sight of openly expressed emotion. Pondering the meaning of this change in her sensitivity, she took the path toward the center of the island, to the headquarters building. Herne fell into step beside her.

"Come to surgery later," he said, "and I'll do the final repair on your cheek."

"Thank you, no." To get away from him, Merin hurried into the building, to the room she shared with Carlis, one of the communications officers. Carlis wasn't there. Grateful for the privacy, Merin began to unpack. She had not quite finished when there was a tap on the door. Without waiting for her permission, Herne entered.

"I know it's only a small scar," he said, "but I would like to remove it."

"I said no."

"How have I offended you?" When she did not answer Herne said, "You know Tarik wants all of us to get along together. There are too few of us to allow the luxury of quarrels."

71

"You are the one who quarrels most," she said. "With Alla on subjects best not discussed at all, with Tarik now and then, and frequently with Osiyar."

"You don't seem to understand the distinction between an honest difference of opinion among friends and a real fight."

"I do not quarrel," she said.

"No, you just drift around the edges of any gathering, saying nothing, contributing no opinions. You display no emotion, except for that one time when you were angry with me. It's not healthy to repress your emotions so rigidly."

"I am what I am," she said. "I cannot change."

"You are an intelligent human being," he told her. "Of course you can change. Merin, I would like to be your friend."

Even with her complete lack of experience with men, Merin understood that what Herne was offering would be something very different from Osiyar's friendship. He proved the truth of her assumption at once. She should have been watching him more carefully. If she had, she might have prevented him from tilting her chin upward and planting his mouth over hers. If she had been prepared, she could have kept her lips pressed tightly together and endured the pressure of his mouth until he realized there was nothing in her to give him any pleasure. But she was not prepared. Her lips were half open on an intake of breath and his tongue slid past them to touch the tip of her own.

"*No!*" He had not been holding her, so it was easy enough to pull her chin from his fingers and spring backward. "I warned you not to touch me. Go away!"

"Why are you so afraid?"

"If you want a woman," she said coldly, recalling his verbal skirmish with Alla while they were still at Tathan, "go to your chamber and dream of Ananka."

She managed to control her trembling, keeping her eyes on the floor and standing perfectly still while he stared at her for a long, silent moment. Then, when the tension between them had stretched out until she thought she would begin to scream, he left her, closing the door after himself with deliberate care. She sprang at the door, to seal it shut so he could not return and so no one else could disturb her. By then she was so weakened by the unwelcome emotions raging through her that she could no longer stand. She started toward her bed, but did not reach it. She sank onto her knees, her head resting on the corner of the mattress. And then, for the first time in her twenty-five years of totally disciplined life, Merin gave way to tears.

Herne stalked out of Merin's chamber, across the central room of headquarters, and through the main door with a face so set and grim that even Gaidar the Cetan warrior did not dare to speak to him. He knew Alla expected him in surgery, to help her unpack their equipment and afterward to take inventory of the medical supplies left on the shuttlecraft. He had reports to feed into the computer, the medical records made during his absence to read, the duty roster to check, his personal unpacking to do. All of that would have to wait until he had calmed himself enough to think and speak rationally.

He avoided the path that led to the beach where the shuttlecraft sat, knowing he would find people there cleaning and refueling the ship. He did not want to talk to anyone. He wanted privacy. He headed for the other side of the island, moving with long, angry strides until he had reached the shore. Drawing a deep breath, he rested one foot on a rock, crossed his arms on his knee, and let his mind go blank for a while.

The scene before him almost always brought peace to his chronically troubled spirit. The cold western wind was whipping up waves on the lake, sending spray and foam far up the beach. In the far distance rose the single snowcapped peak that Tarik had named Mount Narisa. Nearer was the forest that grew right down to the edge of the lake. When he had left for Tathan the trees had flamed with brilliant shades of autumn reds and golds, but now they were bare. Gray or black branches lifted toward the cloudy sky, their wind-driven rustles and creakings sounding like prayers for protection against the bitter winter soon to come. Herne wished he could raise his own arms and shout out his anguish.

He had never in his life been happy for more than a few moments. His native Sibirna had demanded toughness and too-frequent violence from anyone who wanted to survive there. Herne had been forced to hide the gentler part of his nature, having learned early that no one would understand his feelings. His attempts at disguise had not always been successful, most notably in the incident with his dying aunt and, a year before that, with a girl he had cared for who had called him weak and cowardly when he did not beat her as she had passionately hoped.

He had left Sibirna with his parents' approval and their fervent wish that he never return. They had another son who would carry on their bloodline, and they thought Herne was a disgrace to his family. The time of his medical studies had been a difficult period, but eventually he had learned to direct his Sibirnan hardness toward the disease or the injury he was battling, which left him free to treat his patients with the kindness they deserved until they were well again. Herne knew he had become a good physician.

As for women, there had been a few, and might have been more, since women seemed to like his brown-haired, rugged looks. Certainly, there were times when he would have welcomed a companion who would love him and no other. But Herne had stayed free of serious emotional entanglements because of his growing disillusionment with the rigid Jurisdiction laws and with anyone who could accept them. He had sensed that a day would arrive when he would want to leave the Jurisdiction, and then a woman would only be an encumbrance.

In his disenchantment he was no different from anyone else now on Dulan's Planet. Like the other colonists, he had seen it as a place where he could begin a new life. But he had brought his past with him, and the inner battle continued between his harsh and brutal upbringing and the gentler nature he ached to set free.

To Herne's left, not far from the island shore, rose the cliffs where the Chon lived. He watched the birds soaring on the wind, diving to snare fish from the lake, then winging back to their caves in the rock. Here, with the mountain in the distance, the lake at his feet, and the Chon going about their business, he could usually relax. But not today, not while Merin crowded his thoughts no matter how hard he tried to banish her. He could still feel the way her soft lips had moved against his mouth, the heat of her tongue when he touched it with his own. And then, before she could begin to respond completely, had come her implacable withdrawal from him and her scornful words. Never before had he continued to want a woman who had shown so positively that she wanted nothing to do with him. He could not understand his own reactions.

After a while he decided there was no point in wasting any more time staring at the landscape. He wasn't going to feel better no matter how long he stood there. He ought to go back to the building and get to work.

With a rustle of emerald wings, a Chon settled on the pebbly beach near him. It was so tall that Herne and the bird were of a height, and when he turned toward it, the Chon regarded him with its head cocked to one side, as if it were studying him.

"All right," said Herne, kicking a stone into the lake, "since you are supposed to be so star-blasted intelligent, why don't you give a friend some advice? Why don't you tell me the reason Merin is so withdrawn from all emotion and what I can do about it? Why can't I reach her? And while you're answering questions, tell me what really happened at Tathan and why that creature in the grotto looked almost like Merin. Would you know if I were going mad? Would you tell me?"

The bird stood quietly, watching him from shining black eyes.

"Shall I touch you, the way Osiyar does?" Herne wondered, taking a step forward. The bird did not move. If it wanted to, it could peck out his eyes with its long, toothed beak. A swipe of its wing would dash him to the ground. Herne lifted one hand, but something in him, some deep Sibirnan inhibition, kept him from touching the bird.

"There is—was—a golden statue in Tathan," he said, and stopped speaking, because the bird's head had moved closer to his.

For an instant, for just a flash of time, as soft green feathers brushed against his cheek, Herne's mind was filled with the image of that white hall in Tathan, of the statue of a Chon, and of people, men and women and a few nonhumans, all in brightly colored robes, crowding the hall, mingling with the Chon. Even in that brilliant assembly, the birds of green or blue shone like fabulous gems. Herne imagined he saw himself standing beside a woman in a gorgeously jeweled gown. Then the picture was gone, and he felt as if his brain had been forcibly torn out of his skull. Drenched in pain, he stumbled toward the rock where he had been standing, reaching out with both hands to hold on to it and thus support himself.

"What does it mean?" he gasped.

"What does what mean?" Osiyar had appeared from among the trees and now walked down the beach toward Herne.

"That bird—my head is splitting." Herne rubbed at his forehead.

"I shouldn't wonder." Osiyar regarded him calmly. "I saw what you were doing, and I would advise you not to try to communicate with the Chon again. Sibirnans don't have the right kind of minds for telepathy."

"Believe me, if I survive this headache, I won't ever forget that," Herne promised.

"What were you trying to learn?" asked Osiyar.

"Just what you'd expect," Herne replied in a sour voice.

"The Chon, and I, are telepaths, not magicians," Osiyar chided him. "If you want your fortune told, you must look inside yourself. If you want to know another person's thoughts, ask that person."

"And what do you suggest I do," Herne demanded, still rubbing his aching head, "if I ask and I'm given no answer?"

"Then you have a choice to make," said Osiyar, smiling at the bird. "Give up the question. Or ask it again, in a different way."

The Chon bobbed its head up and down, then ruffled its feathers. Herne laughed in genuine amusement.

"Does it understand us?" he asked.

"Every thought," said Osiyar, his hand reaching toward the bird.

"Perhaps I'll take your advice." Herne suddenly felt much better. "Yours and his. I'll wait a while and ask the question again."

The predicted snowstorm arrived on schedule and lasted for a day and a night. By the second morning more than a foot of dry, crunchy flakes had accumulated on the island, and the heavy clouds suggested more would fall before long.

Merin was given the job of clearing a path from the headquarters building to the shuttlecraft on the beach. With the snow so light in texture, the work was easy. Soon she was well beyond the central clearing, working her way through the swath of leafless trees and bushes that ringed the island. When she heard the sound of boots on snow behind her she straightened.

"Medical supplies for the shuttlecraft," Herne said, indicating the boxes in his arms.

He brushed past her and continued on his errand while she stood gazing after him. She did not lift her shovel again until he had disappeared through the shuttlecraft hatch. By the time he had reemerged she had shoveled all the way to the beach and it had begun to snow again. Herne stopped beside her. Glancing at him, she saw a flash of humor in his eyes.

"Did you ever have a snowball fight?" he asked, pulling off his gloves. "Or have you ever washed with snow?"

"No." She did not add that either sounded

like a foolish activity to her.

"Does it snow on Oressia?" He bent to scoop snow into his hands.

"Sometimes." She remembered large, wet flakes falling into the gray Southern Sea, and the sharp edge of a seawall softened by a blanket of white, until Herne's actions snapped her back to the present. "What are you doing?"

"Asking the question in a different way," he said, his words only mystifying her further. "This stuff is too dry to make good snowballs, but not too dry for a nice wash. Hold still. It won't hurt." His hands were full of snow. He raised them to her face. With a gentle, almost tender motion, he began to rub the snow against her skin. Mcrin was so surprised by this unexpected gesture that she could not move.

She was blushing again. She could feel the blood rushing into her cheeks, and the snow was wonderfully cool and moist as it began to melt. When he rubbed a little of it on her forehead flakes fell on her brows and lashes. The wet drops trickled into her eyes, blurring her vision. The outline of Herne's face became unclear. . . .

An instant later she saw him more precisely. Behind his head the sky was a deep purple-blue, and a golden late summer sun shone upon them. Herne's face was tanned; he was grinning at her, white teeth flashing, his eyes crinkling with laughter. She knew him so well, knew the feel of his warm skin beneath her fingers, knew what it was to be held in his arms. The way she felt inside was familiar to her, too, the warmth, the lightness, as though her heart and brain would burst with the intensity of it. Sunlight and warmth. Peace and comfort. And something else, an emotion she had never experienced, yet an emotion so familiar to her that it was an instrinsic part of her being.

"Merin." Herne's hand brushed her cheek. . . .

"Merin?" The sky was gray and cold. Delicate snowflakes fell between them. Herne wiped half-frozen moisture off her face. "Well, how did you like your first snowwash?"

"I—I'm not sure." Snow had gotten into the neck of her jacket and melted there. She shivered. "Did you—did I—have we been here all the time?"

"Right here on the path." He looked at her with that intense, wary gaze of his. "You're almost as white as the snow. I didn't think a little bit of cold would send you into a state of shock."

"It wasn't the snow," she began, wondering how she could possibly describe to him what had just happened—or, perhaps, what she had just imagined. She was spared the need for explanation when Alla came down the path carrying more boxes of medical supplies.

"I thought you were working in the shuttle-craft," Alla said to Herne in an accusing tone. "I came to help you. What have you been doing to Merin? Her jacket and coif are soaked and she's shaking with cold."

"It's nothing," Merin responded, pulling herself together and trying to sound normal. "Herne was only demonstrating an ancient Sibirnan custom."

"It looks like an unhealthy custom to me, if it involves standing in the cold in wet clothing. Don't either of you have any common sense?"

"Alla, let me help you with those boxes," Herne said after another hard look at Merin.

"Put on some dry clothes, Merin," Alla advised, heading toward the shuttlecraft.

Herne followed her through the hatch, but Merin stayed in the same spot for a time, staring after him and trying to decide what it was that had just happened to her.

"Osiyar," Merin said when the evening meal was done and they were the only two left at the table, "are there residual effects after your thoughts have touched another's?"

"Rarely, but they can occur." Osiyar sat back in his chair, folded his arms, and waited serenely for Merin to continue.

"I saw sunshine and felt warmth on a cold and snowy day," she said.

"Perhaps it was only a memory of your own," Osiyar suggested.

"I had never seen what I saw then," Merin declared, "nor felt that emotion, either."

"Was it unpleasant?"

"No, only unfamiliar. But it was unacceptable to me. I should not have felt what I did."

She knew Osiyar would understand what she was trying to say, even if she could not describe the emotion exactly. "I was somewhere else for a moment. The sun was at a higher angle in the sky. The light was different."

"How do you feel now?" Osiyar's sharp blue eyes probed into hers.

"Perfectly well," she said. "It's as though the episode never happened. It only lasted for an instant. I thought I should report it to you."

"I wouldn't worry about it," Osiyar advised, smiling at her.

After Merin had left the table Tarik sat down in her vacant seat.

"I heard," he said. "Has it anything to do with Herne? She has been rather pointedly avoiding him this evening."

"She is changing," Osiyar said. "They both are. It was inevitable after Tathan. They need time now. Just a little more time . . ."

Part II
The Kalina

Part II
The Kethno

Chapter Six

The spaceship *Kalina* was a captured Cetan vessel, refitted at Capital in order to carry the colonists to Dulan's Planet, and rechristened in honor of Tarik's mother. Now in permanent orbit above the planet, the *Kalina* was never left unattended. Each colonist was periodically expected to serve a four-day stint aboard the ship. As he did with other routine duties, Tarik allowed the computer to make random selections of personnel for this purpose. Gaidar and Suria had just completed their turn on the *Kalina*, and Merin was assigned to the next four-day period. Herne was to be her partner.

She wished she had the courage to ask for a reassignment. Always before she had gone aboard the *Kalina* with another woman. The thought of spending four days alone with Herne was terrifying. How could she possibly maintain the necessary tight discipline over herself if he was there, trying to touch her, to put his mouth on hers? The memory of his mouth and his tongue left her weak-kneed and breathless; the images of him standing in the sun and touching her cheek, of him beneath gray skies gently washing her face with snow came to her unbidden and far too often.

"You needn't worry," he told her, as if he had read her mind. "I won't attack you. The last thing I want to do is hurt you."

"I'll get my luggage. I won't be long."

He watched her bow her head and walk away to her room. If she was upset about this assignment, he was even more disgruntled at the prospect of spending days alone with her. He foresaw only continuing frustration for himself.

He could not begin to comprehend what motivated Merin. Each time he thought they might be approaching a more friendly relationship she withdrew into that invisible emotional fortress of hers. And the more she withdrew, the more Herne wanted to know what she was really like beneath her unemotional surface. He could not look at her without aching to put his arms around her and kiss her sweet, unresponsive mouth. He knew if he tried she would only rebuff him once more. Damnation! How could a usually sensible, well-educated man be such a fool? Dreading the time he would have to spend alone with her, he tossed his softbag aboard the shuttlecraft and strapped himself into his seat.

The voyage skyward was accomplished in silence except for the necessary comments pertaining to navigation of their vessel. When they brought the shuttlecraft into the docking deck of the larger ship, Gaidar and Suria were waiting for them, ready to help unload supplies before they boarded the second shuttlecraft to return to the planet.

"There is something unusual to report this time," Suria told them. "A slight fluctuation in the planet's magnetic field, the result of electromagnetic storms caused by violent solar flares. There has also been occasional disruption of our communications with Home. It's nothing dangerous yet; just something to be aware of and to watch carefully. We on the surface will probably have interesting aurora to observe over the next few nights. Other than that, the ship is functioning normally."

"Let me help you stow this cargo before we leave," Gaidar offered, lifting a large water tank to his shoulder. "Bring the other one, Herne."

Suria saw the men out of hearing distance before she spoke again to Merin.

"You don't look well."

"It's the shuttlecraft." Deeply distressed by the need to tell yet another untruth, Merin gave the first excuse that came into her mind. "Riding in it always makes me feel ill." She wished it were not necessary to dissemble so much, but she could not tell Suria that the real source of her queasiness was the pat followed by a gentle caress that she had seen Gaidar administer to Suria's buttocks before he went off with Herne to stow the water tanks. But Suria had good eyes and a well-trained memory. She was a midwife as well as a navigator, and was therefore accustomed to asking intimate questions without seeming to pry.

"You don't like to see men touch women in a familiar way," she said. "I've noticed your reactions before. Why is that?"

"I cannot speak of it."

"Did a man hurt you some time in the past?"

"What you suggest would never happen on Oressia. There, no one harms another."

"It must be an unusual planet." Merin could not see Suria's expression because her eyes were on Suria's feet, but she heard the sarcasm in Suria's voice.

"The men have returned," Merin said, hoping to change the unpleasant subject.

"If you really don't feel well," Suria said, putting out one hand but not quite touching Merin, "speak to Herne about it. That's an order. We can't afford to have our people falling ill."

After Suria and Gaidar had gone, and Herne and Merin were in the shiny black passageway that led to the bridge, Herne stopped walking.

"I heard what Suria said. If you are ill, you should have mentioned it before we left Home. Someone else could have taken your place here."

"I am not ill." She would have continued on her way, but Herne stopped her, catching her by the shoulders and holding her still beneath one of the recessed ceiling lights so he could examine her features more closely.

"Look at me, woman. I've told you before how much I dislike it when you won't look at me while we talk."

"And I have told you before not to touch me. What made me ill was the way Gaidar touched Suria. Sickening. Disgusting."

Her voice was quiet, but so compelling that he lifted his hands from her shoulders and stood there, looking into her eyes, his hands still raised, until she feared he would catch her face instead of her shoulders and kiss her. He did not. His hands fell to his sides, but his eyes remained locked on hers.

"Yes," he said slowly, "you flinch every time you see anyone touch another person. It isn't just men touching women, as Suria thinks; it's anyone at all showing affection or emotional concern. Why? What's in your past? What kind of conditioning did you undergo on Oressia?"

"You know I cannot answer any questions about my home planet," she said. "I ask only that you respect the customs I am compelled to observe."

"How can I respect them when I don't know what they are?" he asked.

"I have told you," she replied with forced patience. "Do not look directly into my eyes. Do not touch me. And do not, ever again, put your lips on mine."

"But I want to," he said, a barely suppressed smile quirking one corner of his mouth. "I want to do all of those things, along with other things that would doubtless shock you to the depths of your Oressian soul. The human psyche is so constituted that if you forbid a person to do something, you only make him want to do it more."

"Herne," she said sternly, "we have a large amount of work to accomplish before we return to headquarters. I must insist that we concentrate on it, and that you behave in a professional manner toward me. If you do not, I will complain about you to Tarik."

"Merin—" But her eyelids were down again, the glory of her brown and purple eyes hidden from him. Her face was carefully blank, every feature sharp and tight, revealing nothing of her feelings.

Herne's own strongest feeling at the moment was despair. He had seen hints of another woman behind her controlled facade, a woman of strength and spirit. A woman he wanted to know. He had to find a way to convince her to reveal her true self to him and to talk freely about her mysterious past.

"As you wish," he said, searching for some sign of relaxation in her. There was nothing. The real Merin was gone again, hidden behind the mask, and he could think of no way to make her return. He gave up the attempt to reach her—for the moment. "Let's get to work."

The rule for those serving aboard the *Kalina* was an eight-hour watch, the last hour overlapping with that of one's partner. During this overlap meals were eaten together and reports were made. Merin had chosen the first watch, so it was Herne who prepared their meal and brought it into the conference room just off the bridge.

"There is another large storm moving across the northern hemisphere. There will be heavy snow at Home," Merin reported. "There have been two more major solar flares, and a series of large sunspots has appeared. A message has been received from Capital. I relayed it to Tarik at once."

"From Capital?" Herne looked up from his soup. "Anything serious?"

"Commander Tarik's mother wishes him a happy birthday. The lady Kalina's timing is accurate, if not her wisdom or sense of propriety."

"I assume from your tone of voice that you don't think Kalina should be using official communication bands for personal messages," Herne noted.

"Tarik may well be embarrassed by the contents. In any case, only the most urgent messages should be sent to us," Merin said. "Each transmission makes Cetan detection of our settlement more likely and thus jeopardizes our mission here. Were the Cetans to discover that we are monitoring their activities, they might decide to abrogate their treaty with the Jurisdiction."

"Oh, come on, Merin, that's taking one short message too seriously. Hasn't your mother ever done something affectionate that embarrassed you? Even my mother, much as she disapproved of me, embraced me in public once or twice and smoothed down my hair in front of my friends. When I was still very young, of course. Never after I reached the age of six." Herne's amusement ceased as he watched Merin freeze. He decided he was not going to let her get away with that old routine. Not this time. He was going to push at her reticence until he had learned something more about her. "Tell the truth, now. What did your mother do that embarrassed you?"

The uncomfortable silence stretched on and on, until Herne thought she would never answer. But, eventually she did, in a small, strangled voice.

"I have no mother."

Damnation! Every time he opened his mouth with her he made another mistake. Almost at once he realized that it hadn't been a mistake at all. He had hurt her by bringing back sad memories, but he had also succeeded in opening the door to her past by just a crack. He knew from his work with patients that if he wanted more information, he had better continue asking questions right now, while she was still upset.

"I'm sorry," he said. "Were you very young when she died?"

"I have never had a mother." Still that same pinched voice. She pushed back her tray and rose from the table. "Thank you for the food, but I find I am not at all hungry."

She was gone, leaving Herne cursing himself for his clumsiness and his stupidity. Merin wasn't a patient, compelled to answer his questions in order to procure the best medical treatment he could give; she was someone he wanted for a friend, and for more than a friend. He thought he understood what his prying had done to her. It had reopened an old wound.

Death in childbirth was rare, but it did occur now and then, and when it did it was a terrible tragedy that left its scars on the entire family. The one most hurt was always the child whose birth had caused the loss. The death of her mother when Merin was born could explain a great deal about her character, especially if Oressian fathers were distant and unloving, like Sibirnan fathers.

Believing this was what had happened to her, Herne thought it was no wonder that Merin found it difficult to give or accept affection. She had probably never received it as a small child. Yet he had seen her begin to unbend toward others, particularly toward Osiyar. It was possible that she could eventually learn to trust Herne, too, and even to care for him. That sweet reward would be worth any amount of patience on his part.

Merin sealed the entrance to her cabin and turned off every light, even the red emergency bulb that was supposed to be lit at all times. She stood in the middle of the blackened room, taking deep breaths, willing herself into a peaceful state, the condition she had known in First Cubicles and had seldom achieved again since. Advancement to Second Cubicles had brought light, stimulation, order, and rules. From then on it had been one rule or law after another, all of them to be memorized and obeyed. Failure had meant instant extermination. She had seen others moved out of Cubicles, never to return. But she had a mind well suited to detail. Memorization was easy for her. She had advanced faultlessly through the milestones of her tenth year, her fifteenth, her twentieth. At twenty she had learned her fate, had taken her oath of silence, and then had left Oressia. And now, every day, she broke another rule, violated another Oressian law.

She should never have spoken those words to Herne. They had been the truth, and yet they would mislead him, would make him believe something other than the truth. Nor would he stop asking questions. Just as his touches and his kisses would continue and increase with the passing of time, so would his questions besiege her mind and her heart. The advice she had been given just before leaving Oressia was correct. The slightest offered opening, the least breach of secrecy, would lead others to pry more and more deeply, would make those others eager for the truth. So it would be with Herne. He would not stop until he knew everything. And when he knew he would never again look at her with tenderness, or take her face in his hands, or put his mouth on hers. To him, she would be an abomination.

Merin stood in the dark, fighting the tears that ran down her cheeks in salty betrayal of all she ought to be, searching for the peace she had known as a Young One, a peace that could never more be hers.

During the next day the solar flares increased in size and frequency. As the electrified particles emitted by the flares streamed toward Dulan's Planet, the upper atmosphere began to glow. The resulting auroral displays were visible from the *Kalina*. When her duties permitted Merin left as many bridge lights off as she could and sat watching the curtains of light sway and change color from green or blue to white and back to green again. So entranced was she by the show that she was only momentarily distracted when Herne slid into the seat next to hers.

"Magnificent," he breathed, his face glowing with reflected light. "Look there. And there."

"It is tempting to forget one's duties," Merin agreed. "You are early, Herne. You aren't required to be on the bridge for another half hour."

"I couldn't sleep. Perhaps I sensed what is going on out there." He waved a hand toward the rippling curtains of light.

"There have been some minor instrument malfunctions, which are to be expected under the circumstances," she told him. "Tarik is growing a bit concerned about the increased solar activity."

"The atmosphere will protect the planet," Herne said, "and the *Kalina* is well shielded. We should be safe enough."

"But not in the shuttlecraft, which has less shielding. We may have to remain aboard for more than the usual four days." Merin's distaste for that possibility sounded in her voice. "Tarik has also suggested that if there is a chance of the more sensitive instruments here being damaged, we ought to take the *Kalina* out of orbit and travel elsewhere for a while till the sun calms down."

"Lost in a solar storm," Herne murmured. "Adrift on a sea of ions."

"Your humor is misplaced," she said. "Since neither of us is an experienced pilot, a forced departure from Dulan's Planet is not a pleasant prospect."

"I have piloted this ship before, several times," he replied, grinning. "So, if Tarik decides he does want us to leave orbit, you will just have to trust me, won't you? And I promise to trust you, whether you have ever acted as pilot on a large ship or not."

Refusing to respond to what she considered a deliberate provocation on his part, designed to trick her into revealing something more about herself, Merin did not answer. She flipped a couple of switches, reset a dial, then stood and made ready to leave the bridge.

"It's your watch, Herne." With that, she officially turned the ship over to him for the next eight hours.

"See that you eat something," he called after her. "You have been starving yourself."

Again, she did not answer. She knew he had been monitoring her food consumption, but she did not care.

She moved easily through the ship, comfortable in the confinement of its black and gray walls, secure in the knowledge that so long as Herne was on the bridge she would meet no other person. In the galley she poured a cup of hot qahf. Herne had left a tray of pastries on the counter. He had a tendency to eat sweets when something else would have been a better nutritional choice, and he assumed that others would want sweets too. Merin thought it was an odd attitude for a physician. She would have preferred a piece of fresh fruit. Reminding herself that personal preferences were irrelevant, she picked up a piece of the pastry and took it with the qahf to her cabin. It was almost time for sleep.

She was back at the grotto at Tathan, watching the globe of white light grow larger and more brilliant, until she could clearly see every inch of Herne's naked body. He was a glorious creature, beautiful to her eyes, totally, excitingly male.

A wave of emotion swept through her, shaking her to the foundation of her being. Everything in her—heart, spirit, mind—yearned for him. Her body ached for his touch. Herne took a step toward her, and Merin felt the air stir against her bare skin. She was without clothing. Even her coif was gone, so that her hair tumbled freely down her back.

She waited for him, her heart pounding, knowing that in another moment he would take her into his arms. His skin would touch hers. Her breasts would be scratched by the rough brown hair on his chest. His mouth would be on hers, his tongue inside her. She would be held . . . touched . . . kissed . . . caressed.

"No! No!" She awoke, sitting up on the bunk in her cabin aboard the *Kalina,* clutching a blanket to her chin. She still wore her treksuit; her coif remained firmly fastened to her head. On the shelf beside the bunk was half of the pastry and the empty qahf cup, her recorder next to the food.

She had been dreaming. It had been a terrible, a terrifying dream, but nothing more. Only a dream, and it was over. All was well. Nothing had happened. Herne had never seen her unclothed. No one had, not since the day when she had first put on garments. She understood the need to stay completely covered at all times except for the very brief moments required for hygenic purposes. She had never failed to obey that rule. Until recently, she had always obeyed the rules.

It was her mind that had betrayed her into that forbidden dream, her thoughts and the emotions she ought not to have—could not possibly have—would not allow herself to have. Not after so many years. She had passed all the tests. She would have made a perfect Oressian had it been possible for her to remain on Oressia. Even during her years at Capital she had never faltered for an instant. Not wanting to know about forbidden subjects, she had deliberately kept herself apart from the activities of humans while she lived in a city where access to any vice was possible so long as one had enough money and free time. Merin had never been tempted. Not once.

Only since coming to Dulan's Planet had she begun to weaken. She was not certain whether the fault lay with the planet itself, or with the other colonists. Perhaps it had begun when Osiyar's mind had touched hers. Or with Herne's kisses. Herne's kisses . . .

Merin lay down, pulling the blanket up to her nose and tucking it tightly around herself, to make herself feel safe. In the dream she had felt air on her skin because, once a day, she removed all her clothing to bathe. She had felt her hair loose and falling down her back because, twice a day, she took it down and brushed it. But she had not felt the touch of Herne's naked flesh on hers because a dreamer could only recall physical sensations that had been experienced in waking life. The trouble was, she should not have had the dream at all. That she had was a sign of how dangerously far she had fallen from Oressian discipline. Were she on Oressia, she would have been honor-bound to turn herself over to the Elders, to be exterminated for the good of society.

But here, outside Jurisdiction boundaries, on a lost planet in the Empty Sector, there was nothing to stop her from dreaming again—and again.

"There's food ready for you." Herne indicated the tray next to the science panel. "I fixed it for myself, but I couldn't eat. No point in wasting it."

"Thank you. Relieving you of duty." Neatly avoiding any opportunity to touch him, Merin mounted the two steps to take the science officer's seat. Herne did not leave the bridge promptly, as she had hoped he would. Instead, he stood on the deck directly behind her. She could almost feel him there. If she moved her head backward just an inch, it would rest upon his chest. Then he would surely put his arms around her. She could relax against him.

Vile, disgusting thought! Never touch again . . . never allow anyone to touch . . . She stiffened her back, sitting rigid before the panel of blinking lights. He had to leave the bridge before she lost control of her emotions. He had to . . .

Herne leaned forward, his left shoulder brushing against her coif, his right hand pushing a button.

"Pay attention to what you're doing, Merin. You might have missed that solar flare. You know we are supposed to watch and record each one."

"The computer will do it," she said absently.

"Not if the flares interfere with the computer's power, which is a distinct possibility." He spun her chair around so quickly that she gasped in surprise. "What's wrong with you? I can see you aren't concentrating. The records in ship's stores indicate that you have scarcely eaten since we came aboard. Does my presence offend you so much that you lose your appetite?"

"I seldom eat much," she said. "You didn't eat the latest meal yourself." She glanced toward his untouched tray.

"Look at me." She had heard him use that voice before, when he was performing surgery and meant his orders to be instantly obeyed. She could not deny him now. Intense, worried gray eyes bored into hers. He pulled from his pocket the diagnostic rod he always carried, and used it to scan her body quickly, from head to toe. "You are a bit undernourished and dehydrated, but otherwise healthy. See that you eat properly, and increase your fluid intake. That's an order."

"Please," she whispered, "keep your eyes lowered."

"You said once that to an Oressian, a direct glance constitutes a challenge," he recalled, setting one hand on each arm of her chair so that she could not escape him. "A challenge to what? Physical combat? Lovemaking?"

"No." It took every ounce of willpower she possessed to keep herself from giving way to total panic, and so the truth slipped out before she could stop the words she ought not to say. "Never lovemaking. Leave me alone, Herne."

"Why do you find me so repulsive while I find you incredibly attractive?" he wondered, half to himself. When she did not answer, but sat wringing her hands in distress at how much she had revealed to him in the last few days, he added, "Can't we at least be friends?"

"Friendship is forbidden." That much she was permitted to say to anyone who might approach her.

"No love, no friendship. Yours is a cold world, Merin. An inhuman world. Yet you are human. I have just proved it with this diagnostic rod." He straightened, releasing her from the prison of his closeness. He paused before leaving the bridge. "Someday even you will know how human you are. I hope that day is soon, before you break from all the emotions you are repressing."

Chapter Seven

The overlapping hour between their watches
had become a torment to Merin. When she had
first come aboard the *Kalina* with Herne it had
been the one time when she could not ignore
or avoid him, but at least it was only an hour.
If it was the end of her own watch, she cut the
time short by leaving as soon as she had made
her report to him. At the end of his watch,
when she came on duty, she pretended to be
absorbed by her work until he left the bridge
to seek his own cabin or to wander around
the ship, checking on the various systems that
kept it in orbit. Now, however, a disruption had
occurred in one of those systems, and Merin
and Herne were going to have to work together to repair it. Thus, the most unpleasant and

difficult hour of her day would be extended to an indefinite length.

In the engineering chamber, where the controls for the *Kalina*'s propulsion system were housed, Herne pulled the grate off a shaft in the lowest section of bulkhead and shone a handlight inside it. At his command Merin squatted beside him, craning her neck to look where he indicated.

"There," he said, moving the handlight to give her a better view. "Can you see the dial? And that loose cable? The cable will have to be reconnected and the dial reset."

"This should not have happened." After looking into the shaft, Merin scrambled to her feet to call the ship's plans onto a nearby computer screen. "According to this information, when the ship was refitted at Capital new cables were installed in this section and then double-checked to be sure they were properly connected. I'm no engineer, but this diagram looks simple enough to me."

"I'm glad to hear it," Herne interrupted her disparaging comments about whoever had originally made the cable connection, "because you are the one who is going to fix it. That shaft is too small for me to fit into."

"Herne, I'm a historian, not a mechanic," she protested, now regretting her hasty remarks.

"We are all supposed to be able to perform every necessary chore on this ship or on the planet. You have accomplished every other task

Tarik has set for you. I'm sure you can do this one too. Are you afraid of small spaces?" The look he gave her was kind but determined. "If you are, I'll give you a relaxant so you won't feel frightened, but that cable has to be repaired, and you are the only one to do the job."

"Small places are home to me," she told him, with a murmur of silent laughter at how true that statement was. "I will not need drugs to enable me to enter the shaft. I was only concerned about the work itself. I have never reconnected a cable before."

"I'll show you how to do it." From the computer Herne called up another screen to demonstrate the repair process. "Think you can do that?"

"I'll try my best." Merin looked at the hole through which she was expected to crawl. "Isn't it bad planning to build a shaft too small for the average man or woman to crawl into?"

"No one has ever accused the Cetans of careful advance planning," Herne said. "Gaidar certainly wouldn't fit in there. At Capital they have a narrow trolley, a flat gadget on wheels that rolls right into tight spots and does the work automatically. I've seen it in action. It only takes a few seconds to make a repair like this."

"We should have one on the *Kalina*," Merin said.

"Complain to Tarik when we get home." Herne strapped a flexlight to her left wrist and set it for full brightness, then handed her the tools she would need, explaining the use of each. "There isn't much room for you to move around in there. You won't be able to get your arms over your shoulders in that space, so you will have to lie down on your back with your arms over your head out here. Then I'll push you inside. When you're done I'll pull you out again."

Startled by this proposition, she looked directly at him. He gazed back at her with a reassuring smile. She thought he was trying to convey to her, without putting it into embarrassing words, that he would not touch her in an improper way or take advantage of her inability to defend herself while the upper half of her body was inside the shaft. She sank to her knees, then stretched out as he had ordered, holding the tools and putting her hands into the opening of the shaft.

By bending her knees and pushing with her heels she was able to help at the beginning, but the shaft was deeper than she had anticipated. Before she reached the disconnected cable, Herne's hands—on her thighs, then on her calves, and finally around her ankles—were all that moved her forward. She knew, with a sickening jolt of her heart, that when she dreamed again she would feel his hands on her. Deliberately, she used her will to blank out all physical sensation so she could concentrate on her work.

It was not complicated, but the position was

awkward and she was unfamiliar with the techniques required. Minutes ticked by as she tried to fasten the end of the cable to the terminals, failed, and tried again. Herne's worried voice came to her like a tinny echo through the layers of metal. He seemed to think she must be suffering from claustrophobia. She called back that she was perfectly fine. And she was. She felt safe and comfortable in that narrow shaft. It felt like home. She was almost sorry when the cable was fixed, the dial reset, and she could tell Herne to pull her out.

She was free as far as her knees when a loud popping sound behind her head reverberated through the metal bulkhead. Immediately, the shaft was filled with gray smoke. She felt the urgent pressure of Herne's hands on her thighs, pulling hard at her, sliding her through the shaft as fast as he could. Then he had her by the hips. An instant later she was out of the narrow shaft and Herne, who had been kneeling across her legs as he worked her body forward, was holding her in his arms, crushing her against him while smoke billowed out of the hole where she had been. When she put up one hand to adjust her coif he gave a shaky laugh.

"That cursed thing never comes off, does it? Blessed stars, I was frightened for you! Are you hurt? Merin, can you say something?"

"I'm not hurt." He didn't seem to realize that he was still straddling her thighs and that she

111

could not move. He did release her from the tight embrace of his arms, but only to take her face between his hands while he kissed her. And she, thoroughly shaken by the explosion in the shaft, lowered her defenses enough to put her arms around him and kiss him back. Then they were down on the cool metal of the deck, Herne sprawling on top of her, his weight pressing hard on her, holding her there, while his hands at either side of her head kept her immobilized through a wild, deep kiss. Still she clung to him, trying to pull him closer, reveling in the unfamiliar pleasure of masculine hardness and taut muscles.

"Merin, Merin, I thought I had lost you." He held her gently now, pulling her partly off the deck so they were side by side as he rocked her.

It was sweet, so very sweet, to be held like that, to know he cared enough to fear for her. No one had ever cared for her before. No one. Merin buried her face against his shoulder.

His hands touched her coif, trying to unfasten the strap beneath her chin, trying to push away the fabric. That brought her back to reality. Breaking apart from him, she sat up.

"We need to attend to the ship," she said.

"For a while there, I forgot about it," he told her. "I forgot everything but you, and whether or not you were hurt."

"You must never forget your duty for my sake."

"When we have the ship repaired," he began, "when we are back safe on the planet, at Home again—"

"Then all will be as it was before." She had regained her usual self-control. "Nothing has changed."

"Nothing?" He stared at her, then reached out to pull her close again, but she stood up and moved away from him. He followed her, a hard-muscled hunter stalking his prey. His next words sounded almost like a threat. "I want you, Merin. I dream about you at night."

So he dreamed too. Did he imagine her unclothed, walking toward him, as she had dreamed of him coming to her? He had never seen her without her treksuit and coif, but he was a doctor; he would know how a woman was made. Did he dream of putting his hands on her bare skin, of pulling her against his naked body? Merin ran her tongue across dry lips.

Herne. Oh, Herne. They were looking into each other's eyes and, like the mesmerized prey she imagined herself to be, she could not tear her own eyes away from the hunter who would destroy her. But she must. She must.

"Stop this," she said, fighting for calmness through her fear and through that other emotion she refused to acknowledge. "We have a faulty cable that needs correction. Since I have failed in my amateur attempt to fix the malfunction, I suggest we contact Tarik and ask what he recommends. We should do it at

113

once, before the problem is compounded by any more errors on our part."

"How can you do that?" he asked. "You change so easily from deep passion to complete coldness and control."

"It was not passion. As usual, you have misunderstood me, Herne. I was only a little startled by the explosion."

"I know when a woman is responding to me."

"Will you call Tarik, or shall I?"

He could tell she had closed him out of her mind for the present, so he started back to the bridge, to contact Tarik. He was not at all downhearted. After the embrace they had just shared he felt certain that Merin's withdrawal—her prim claims to feel nothing, her insistence on rigid standards—were merely a disguise for her emotional nature. Sooner or later there would come another moment of surprise or of danger when she would forget her strict rules of behavior and open herself to him again. He would be better prepared when it happened the next time, and the time after that. Eventually, with patience on his part, he would learn what she was really like beneath all the conditioning and the rules. Then he would understand how to make her his. For he knew now that she would be his, when the time was right.

Merin got to the bridge first and opened communications with headquarters, explaining their problem with the cable and what had happened when she had tried to reconnect it.

"Hold on, let me confer with Gaidar," said Tarik. "He knows the ship as well as I do, perhaps better."

The receiver went silent except for occasional static. Herne looked down at Merin. A wave of tenderness swept over him. Her usually crisp white coif was wrinkled and soiled. There was a streak of dust across the shoulders of her treksuit. Her back was held stiffly, her shoulders squared. When she turned her head to watch one of the lights on the control panel he put out his hand, then drew it back, certain that if he were to touch her now she would be deeply offended and would withdraw even more from him. He contented himself with a mildly teasing comment.

"There is a smudge on your cheek. And another on your nose."

"Time enough to worry about cleanliness after that cable is repaired." Her voice was cool, unemotional, a little abrupt. "Ah, here is Tarik again."

"Gaidar and I agree that you will have to go back and try again to repair that connection," Tarik said. "I'm going to let him give you the instructions."

"Listen carefully, Merin." The Cetan's deep voice rumbled out of the receiver. "Go in by the shaft on the opposite side of the propulsion system from the one you used before. That way, you will have more room to move your arms.

115

It will be easier to make a firm connection."

"She will be crawling at an angle that will put her almost upside down by the time she reaches the cable and the terminals," Herne objected. He had called up the diagram of that section of the ship and was studying the screen where it appeared.

"Let her wear one of the harnesses from the cargo bay of your shuttlecraft," Tarik ordered. "The ones we use to lower people through the cargo bay doors when we can't land the shuttlecraft."

"There is a length of metoflex rope stored in a locker on docking deck. Attach it to the harness." Gaidar gave them instructions on where to find the rope, adding, "Herne, you will have to keep Merin from sliding down into the main propulsion duct, and when she has finished her work you will have to pull her out again. It would be all but impossible for her to crawl backward out of that shaft."

"I'm sorry about this, Merin," Tarik said. "There is so much solar activity right now that it would be dangerous for us to send anyone else by shuttlecraft beyond the protection of the atmosphere to help the two of you."

"I understand. I'm not worried about my personal safety," Merin replied, "only about my ability to make a successful repair."

"I will rehearse you again," Gaidar offered. In fact, he went through the entire procedure three times, making Merin repeat his instructions back to him twice before he announced, "What you have just learned will have to do. Good luck, Merin."

After adding his own good wishes, Tarik signed off. When Merin turned from the communications console Herne was watching her with a worried expression.

"I wish you didn't have to go in there. I would gladly do this job myself," he said, "if only I could fit into that confounded shaft."

"While you find the rope Gaidar told you to use," she said, ignoring the sentiment implicit in his words, "and bring the harness from the shuttlecraft, I will locate this second shaft and remove the grate so we need waste no time. The repairs grow more urgent with every hour that passes."

"You are absolutely fearless, aren't you? You don't mind going into those cramped shafts at all. I admire your courage, Merin."

"If I am not afraid," she responded, "there can be no courage in what I do. As I understand it, to achieve courage, one must first overcome fear."

"I wish I knew what you really are," he whispered. "Sometimes I suspect you aren't human at all."

After he had left her Merin slumped a little, shaking her head at the irony of her present situation. She had gone into the first shaft indifferent to her own safety. Indeed, at one level of her mind she would have been pleased to die in there, so that the torture of her recent existence might end in a place similar to the Cubicle where her early life had been spent.

But in the shock of the explosion in the shaft she had made a frightening discovery. As Herne had pulled her out, as he had held her and she had clung to him, she had suddenly wanted to go on living, not because her life was valuable or even because she hoped for anything pleasant in the future, but because she did not want to leave Herne. He had become so important to her that the thought of never seeing him again, or hearing his voice, or perhaps occasionally being touched by him, was intolerable. If she died, she would leave him for all eternity. Thus, she would enter this second shaft in fear for her life, an emotion entirely new to her.

Perversely, she savored the fear while she made her way back to the propulsion controls chamber to locate the shaft Gaidar had told her to use. There she called up a diagram screen and double-checked the shaft location, then began to remove the grate covering its outlet. This shaft ended high in the bulkhead instead of at deck level, like the first one. By the time she had the grate off and was lowering it to the deck, her hands were shaking so hard she dropped it.

"Watch that!" Herne had reappeared, carrying the harness and the rope. "Keep your mind on what you're doing or you'll botch this attempt too!"

Through the fear that threatened to stifle her breath, Merin was able to see that he was seriously concerned about the repairs, and rightly so. Both their lives might depend on the work she did. Summoning all her Oressian training, she asserted control over her fear as she would over any other emotion, banishing it to a small, dark corner of her mind, commanding it to stay there until she had finished what she had to do.

With no outward show of feeling, she let Herne fit the harness around her chest and shoulders and fasten it at the back. Next he attached the narrow metoflex rope, a combination of plastic and strands of metal.

"Centuries ago," he told her, his fingers busy on the rope, "surgeons used to cut their patients open with knives and then sew them up after the surgery was completed. I once saw diagrams of the knots they used, in an old book. I used to practice tying the knots, just in case I should ever need to know how to make them. Now, here I am, remembering that book and tying knots in a rope. There, that should hold."

"It won't come undone until I'm out again?" Merin twisted her head around but could not see what he had done. It was hard to reach behind her back to feel the knot with both hands. She tried once more. The knot felt firm and tight. "You are sure it will hold?"

"If that particular knot hadn't held," Herne told her, smiling a little, "then over the course of almost a century, a lot of patients would have bled to death. Of course, surgeons didn't use sutures for very long. Better closures were invented. But until they were, the knots held. So will this one."

His smile faded. He looked hard at her. She kept her eyes on the flexlight he had once more strapped to her wrist. She adjusted the brightness with fingers that trembled a bit in spite of her efforts to control her feelings.

"Merin, are you frightened? You needn't be ashamed if you are."

"Certainly not." She made her voice as crisp and calm as she possibly could. "Oressians are never afraid."

"Is that also one of your laws?" In contrast to her voice, his was gentle, and as tender as the large hand that stroked across her cheek. Merin fought the urge to catch his hand, to kiss it and hold it against her face. Instead, she bent to pick up her tools. Still not looking at him, she fastened the tools to her shoulder harness so she would have both hands free.

"I will need the steps to reach the entrance," she said, nodding toward a nearby rolling ladder.

"They'll just get in the way. I'll boost you up. Remember, I'll be right here, with the other end of the rope wrapped around my waist. It may go slack at times, but even if you slip, you won't go far. I know how long that shaft is, and I can always pull you back."

"I am ready," she said.

Herne made a step of his hands and Merin put her foot into it. He lifted her with easy strength until her face was level with the shaft opening. She put her arms and head inside. Herne pushed her a little higher, and now her waist was in too. She felt him lifting her legs so that her entire body was at a slant, head down, face toward the floor of the shaft. There was more room in this shaft than there had been in the first, so she could maneuver her arms more easily. She began a squirming, slithering crawl at a downward angle, stopping when she felt the tug of the rope at her back, then inching forward when Herne played out more rope.

Approaching from this direction, she was farther away from the disconnected cable than she had been in the other shaft. She estimated that she had moved about three times her body's length before she saw first the cable, swaying gently with the motion of the ship, and then the dial. To reach both, she had to push herself out across the width of the main duct that led directly downward into the ship's propulsion system. Why anyone would place these essential elements in such an impossible-to-reach spot, Merin could not understand. She wondered briefly if their position was some weird Cetan joke. She must remember to ask Gaidar about it.

She had by now progressed far enough along the slanting shaft to poke her head out over the main duct. Grasping the metal edge of her own shaft, she pulled herself forward into emptiness until her arms and half of her chest were free. She wiped her sweaty palms on the sleeves of her treksuit before she detached a tool from her harness. If she dropped it, it would be lost to her and, falling into the main propulsion system, it might cause irreparable damage. For a moment she looked straight downward into the glowing, churning heat of the ship's engines. Then, taking a deep breath and willing herself not to look again, she reached across the empty space and began to work.

Gaidar had been right; with more room to maneuver, it was much easier to reattach the cable to its terminals, even though her head had begun to ache from the downward angle at which she was lying.

With the cable repaired and the connection tested several times to be sure it would hold, Merin replaced her first tool and took the second one, then reached toward the dial to reset it. To her horror, as she stretched toward the dial she felt herself slip forward, until all of her body from the waist up was out of the shaft and hanging over the main duct. Surprised, not having expected to lose the support of the shaft floor, she naturally bent forward at the waist, the motion pulling her out of the shaft by another few inches. She nearly dropped the tool she was holding. Awkwardly, pressing with her free hand against the side of the main duct, she straightened herself and once more reached to the dial. It was quickly reset. Within a few moments she could see that the connection was working properly and the dial was registering normal numbers. From where he was, Herne would be able to see on the lighted panel near him that the repairs had been made. Merin reattached the tool she had been holding and prepared to be pulled back up the shaft.

Only now did she realized that the knot holding the rope to her shoulder harness had slipped out of the shaft with her. As Herne drew on the rope, pulling her backward into the shaft, the knot caught where shaft and main propulsion duct joined. Merin pressed herself downward, trying to make more room between her back and the top of the shaft, so the knot could fit into the narrow space. Her arms, hanging loosely into the main duct, were useless, and the tools fastened to her chest further impeded her reentry into the shaft. She dared not remove them and toss them away for fear of damaging the ship's propulsion system. She felt the rope tighten, jamming the knot more firmly against the entrance to the shaft. The rope tugged at her again as Herne tried to pull her out.

"Herne!" She shouted as loudly as she could, but she wasn't certain he could hear her. "Herne, I'm stuck!"

Frantically she searched with her fingers along the side of the main duct, trying to find a projection or rough section of metal that might give her leverage to push herself back into the shaft. The walls were perfectly smooth except where shaft and duct joined. There, she suddenly noticed, the walls of the shaft projected outward about two inches, ending in jagged edges. Against the upper edge the knot was rubbing each time Herne pulled on the rope. By twisting her arm at a painful angle she could feel where the metal had already cut into the thin rope. It would not be long before the knot was severed, and she would fall to her death in the propulsion system. She knew there was no way she could possibly be rescued. Not without taking the ship apart.

"Merin! Merin!" She heard Herne's voice from a great distance. When she took a deep breath to answer him as loudly as she could she slipped forward a little more.

"Merin, try to help me. I can't get you moving!" Herne pulled harder on the rope, trying to help her but only making matters worse; each time he pulled the jagged edge of the shaft cut deeper into the knot that was the only thing keeping her from certain death.

An hour or two earlier it wouldn't have mattered to her. Merin began to laugh at the injustice of fate, and then to cry. The hysteria lasted only a few moments before she grew sober again and began to consider her situation.

If Herne could not help her, if everything he tried to do to move her out of the shaft only made her predicament more serious, then she would have to help herself. She could no longer depend on the rope, but her arms and her chest were free, and she did have one advantage— the same protruding edge that appeared to be dooming her.

She swung herself upward as high as she could, lifting her torso off the floor of the shaft. At the same time she reached down and grabbed the metal edge of the shaft with both hands. Then, using all her strength, she pushed backward as hard as she could. The upper edge of the shaft bit deeper into the knot on her back. She felt the knot give way and heard the rope slither back up the shaft as Herne pulled it. She heard him shout at the sudden loss of her weight.

She had no time to think of Herne or of what he might do. She was too busy to think of anything but her fight against the ship's gravity in the deadly downward slope of the shaft. She had succeeded in pushing herself backward into the shaft by a few inches, but the sharp edge of metal had cut into her hands. Still holding on to the edge, she pushed again, but her hands slipped on her own blood. She wiped both palms on her sleeves, lifted her chest once more, caught at the edge, and pushed backward, gaining another inch or two. She wiped the blood off her palms and tried again. And again. She had to stop to adjust the tools she could not jettison, losing an inch or two to gravity in the process, though she tried to brace herself against the sides of the shaft with her legs. On the next try she got all of her chest into the shaft.

Now her work was harder; her arms were beginning to be restricted by the sides of the shaft, but inside it she felt safer. She kept pushing herself, an inch at a time, until her head and her arms up to her elbows were inside too. She rested a moment, then began again. When even her extended fingertips were inside the shaft she began pushing on the floor, using her legs as much as she could, working her way slowly backward, uphill, fighting the downward slope all the way.

It occurred to her that she hadn't heard Herne for a while. She wondered what he was doing. Perhaps he had called Tarik or Gaidar for advice. She couldn't think of anything any of them could do for her, and so she kept trying to help herself.

She became unbearably tired, her overworked arms and hands aching from the strain. She wanted to stop and rest but feared if she did, she would fall asleep and begin to slide downward again. To counteract her weakness she placed both hands on the floor of the shaft and pushed as hard as she could.

"Merin!" From behind her, far up the shaft, she heard the sounds of banging and the ripping of metal. It continued, growing louder, then stopping while Herne called her name again and again. The banging, tearing sounds started once more. Her headache, which had begun earlier, became worse from the noise.

Periodically, Herne stopped whatever he was doing to call her name. Occasionally, she responded, but she thought he couldn't hear her answers, and there was no point in wasting her breath. She needed all her strength just to keep moving. By the flexlight still strapped to her left wrist she could see the trail of blood she had left in the dust along the shaft floor. When she got out of the shaft, Herne would want to fill her with medication to prevent infection. If she got out. No, she *would* get out. *She would.*

"Just keep pushing," she told herself. "You are making progress. An inch at a time adds up, and soon—soon—" But it took a long, long time.

Then, suddenly, all the noise on metal stopped. There were no sounds but her panting breath and the rubbing of her exhausted body moving up the shaft. A moment later her feet were no longer touching the floor of the shaft. They felt as if they were in open air.

"Merin!" Herne sounded as though he were standing at her shoulder. She felt him grab her feet. Now she hardly had to push herself along at all because he was pulling her. He had her knees, her thighs, her waist. He was lifting her over twisted metal and open panels, past a tangle of wires where the last two sections of the shaft ought to be. She had a quick impression of the control panel dangling by one cord. Then she fell downward out of the shaft onto the ladder, her tools clanking against her chest. Finally, her feet touched the deck of the propulsion control room, and Herne was holding her upright, staring at her. He was wearing heavy work gloves and his face was white and hard. Oddly, she was not the least bit shaky or upset.

"I cut my hands at the end of the shaft," she reported very calmly.

"Cut the rope, too, you idiot." Despite the rude word, she could tell he was not angry, only relieved.

"I slid a little too far into the main duct," she told him, watching him remove the gloves, knowing his eyes were on her face. "At least your knot didn't come untied. It had to be sliced apart, little by little, as you pulled on the rope."

She saw his hands tighten into fists over the gloves when she said that, and she shut her ears to the curse he uttered. Afraid to look directly at him, she glanced around the chamber instead. Surprised and a little dazed at the sight, she noted the neat pile of all the ship's medical supplies at one side, and the almost total destruction of the bulkhead into which the shaft opened.

"Did you tear all of this away to try to reach me?"

"It was the only thing I could think of to do."

She wished she could burst into tears and throw herself into his arms. She wanted to beg him never to let her go. But even at such an emotional moment she found she could not disgrace herself in that way. Instead, to cover her feelings, she took refuge in a cool, professional manner.

"It's really too bad you did so much damage. Now you will have to put it all back together again or Tarik will be angry."

"Are you all right?" He was frowning, as if he expected some wild, emotional reaction from her.

"Perfectly," she answered.

"I envisioned you falling into the main propulsion duct," he said, in a tone that suggested he was trying to frighten her into an emotional response. "How did you get out?"

"I crawled." She paused to take a breath while he repeated the words, staring at her again. "You may report to Tarik that the cable is reconnected and the dial reset. I am certain the repair will hold."

"Are you sure you're all right?" She wasn't, and she knew he knew it, but she wasn't going to admit it to him.

"Of course. Why wouldn't I be?" She was finding it increasingly hard to speak clearly.

"Let me see those hands." He took them in his. "Merin, these are serious cuts."

"Then repair them, please. I notice you have your supplies handy." She found she had to choose each word with great care. Her tongue was unexpectedly thick and slow. "I would like to clean up and put on a fresh treksuit and coif."

"*Merin.*" He was holding tightly to her wrists.

"I am off-duty now, am I not?" He seemed so far away to her. There was a ringing in her ears. Merin fought to keep her voice steady. "Would you please repair my hands so I can go to my cabin? I am a bit tired."

"So you should be. Sit here." He led her to the ladder, where he made her sit on one of the steps. She could not relax. If she did, she might not be able to stand up again. She sat at rigid attention while he cleaned the torn flesh on her hands, used the sonic regenerator to repair a ligament or two, closed the wounds, and covered each palm with plastiskin. As she had expected, he gave her two injections against infection, then scanned her with the diagnostic rod to be sure she had no other injuries.

"You need rest," he said, his hand on her elbow to help her rise.

"As soon as I am clean again, I shall endeavor to sleep," she replied, moving toward the hatch with care so he would not see her stagger.

"I don't think it's going to be much of an endeavor." He was smiling at her, but his eyes were serious. "You are suspiciously calm and controlled."

"Why should I not be? Isn't your usual complaint against me that I am always well controlled and disciplined?" It was taking more and more effort for her to speak coherently.

"If you want anything, if you feel unwell—" he began, his smile fading.

"I know where to find you. Thank you, Herne. My hands feel better already." With that, she left him.

She had not gone two steps into the passage leading away from the propulsion controls chamber before she had to hold on to the railings along the bulkhead to keep herself from falling. There were brilliant whirling spots before her eyes, and the ringing in her ears was now accompanied by an insistent buzzing in her mind. Wavering and stumbling, she slowly made her way along the passages to her cabin.

She still had sense enough to seal the hatch behind her so Herne could not enter to disturb her without using special security clearance. Calling up all her Oressian discipline to keep herself erect, she pulled off her soiled coif and ripped away the torn and dirty treksuit. She battled rapidly weakening knees and a growing nausea to stand for the necessary minute in the cleansing chamber. That made her feel a little better, since it was narrow and close, like the Cubicles she had known as a Young One. But when she emerged into her cabin again the ringing in her ears had blotted out the vibration of the ship. She could no longer focus her eyes, nor would her knees hold her upright. But she did make it to her bunk before her Oressian training finally gave way, allowing her to do one more thing that she had never before done in her life.

Merin fainted.

Chapter Eight

Herne watched Merin come onto the bridge. She was pale, a little strained about the eyes, but otherwise she looked normal. He wanted to put his arms around her, to hold her close and protect her from all harm.

It had taken him hours to repair the bulkhead he had torn to pieces in his desperate attempt to rescue her. He could only imagine what her thoughts must have been when she had known she was almost certainly doomed to a terrible death. But she had not given up. With incredible determination, she had worked her way back to safety. He was still fighting his own rage and frustration at his inability to help her through that ordeal. Before replacing the grate in the restored bulkhead he had climbed

133

up on the ladder, to shine his handlight into the shaft. He had seen the scrapes she had made in the metal during her slow, backward, uphill progress, and he had seen the bloodstains. Shaking his head in admiration of her courage and anger for what she had endured in that shaft, he had slammed the grate across the opening with a savage gesture.

Now he saw her looking cool and distant in a fresh orange treksuit, her clean white coif neatly in place and strapped beneath her chin, and he wanted to shake her. She was so determined to hide her feelings, yet when he had kissed her after pulling her from the shaft she had reacted with spontaneous passion, a response all the sweeter for its unexpectedness.

"I trust you slept well?" he said, watching closely for any sign that she was trying to hide illness or any delayed reaction to her trials in two different shafts.

"I always sleep well."

He doubted that, but he made no comment on her claim. "I'm glad you are safe," he told her.

"Why would I not be?" She sounded surprised.

"You were far from safe in that shaft."

"But I am safe now."

Herne thought he would go mad if she did not soon change that quiet, unemotional voice and those idiotically neutral responses. He held his arms tight at his sides, clenching his fists.

He wanted to kiss her, to beat her, to hold her in his arms and tell her he'd never let anything hurt her again, to shake her and scold her until she cried—and he wanted to do all of those things at the same time. Most of all, he wanted desperately to make love to her, to hear her cry out his name as she dissolved into rapture.

"May I have your report on your watch, please, Herne?"

Now he wanted to strangle her. His fingers itched to feel her slender neck. He had torn half the ship apart trying to reach her when he believed she was in danger, then had put the entire mess back together again, and the only reward he got for all his trouble was her cool little voice asking for a star-blasted report. If she said one more word, he was going to kill her and send her body into deep space through the decompression hatch the Cetans had once used for disposal of their unwanted prisoners.

He'd be damned to everlasting torment if he ever did anything for her again. She could fall through any blasted shaft she wanted and burn to a cinder in the propulsion system and he wouldn't care. If she were wounded, he'd let her bleed to death, physician's oath or no. He wanted nothing more to do with a stubborn, cold-blooded Oressian who wouldn't even say thank you.

"Is something wrong?" She turned the full power of her purple-flecked brown eyes on him. She was almost smiling. There was a definite upward tilt to the corners of her lovely mouth. Herne's frustrated wrath began to drain away.

"I've been worried about you." He took a step toward her, and she did not move backward. Herne's heart began to pound with a heavy, unsteady beat. He was going to kiss her. Before he left the bridge he was going to feel her slender frame in his arms.

"It's kind of you to concern yourself with my welfare," she said, "but as you can see, there was nothing wrong with me that could not be cured by a few hours of rest. Now, the report, if you please."

"Solar flares have increased during the last eight hours. The air circulation system stopped for a few minutes. I'm not sure exactly what was the matter with it, but I turned a few dials for a while and it came back to normal. The heating system also went out, but that's back too." He went on, speaking as if he were a perfectly sane man, when in fact he was drowning in her eyes and slowly going mad with wanting her. "Obviously, the violent storms on the sun's surface are affecting the *Kalina*. I have relayed all the pertinent information to Tarik and have made appropriate entries in the ship's log."

"Thank you, Herne. Relieving you of duty." Merin moved toward her usual seat at the science officer's console.

"Not yet." He caught her arm. "I still have a few minutes left on my watch."

He transferred his grip to her wrist, holding her hand up so he could see it. With a practiced motion of his other hand, he stripped off the plastiskin. The lacerations on her palm were healing nicely, with only a slight pink swelling to indicate how much damage had been done.

"Let me see the other one; then I'll put on fresh dressings." It was as good an excuse as any other he could think of, and it gave him a legitimate reason to touch her. He got out the medkit that was always kept on the bridge and found the plastiskin. After he had finished with her hands she stood rubbing the piece of plastiskin on her right palm. He nodded, understanding. "It will itch for another day or two, until it is completely healed."

"I do appreciate everything you have done for me," she said. "Everything."

He touched her right cheek, where she still bore the tiny scar from her last injury. To his surprise, she turned her head a little, leaning her face into his hand. She caught her lower lip between her teeth, as if to stop it from trembling, but she did not move away from him as he had expected she would. She stayed as she was, with her cheek against his hand. He heard the soft catch of her breath.

"Oh, Merin." The words left his lips like a sigh. Her eyelids fluttered, then lifted, and once again he was lost in the depths of her purple-brown gaze.

She raised her face to him, parting her lips to accept his kiss. He gathered her closer and she did not protest. She was slim yet strong in his arms, and he felt her hands on his back, holding on to him, caressing his shoulders and down along his spine. Herne let one of his hands wander down her back to catch her hips and pull her hard against him, letting her feel his hot need of her. She moaned a bit, but did not pull away. Surprise and delight filled him. While he could still think, he began to consider where the nearest bunk might be. Her lack of protest made him think she wanted him as much as he wanted her. They would give each other such joy. He would see to it that she was completely fulfilled, and as for himself, she was everything he had ever wanted.

He touched the pressure sensitive strip at the neck of her treksuit, pushing it open down to the gentle valley between her breasts. He slid his hand beneath the orange fabric to touch the high, round sweetness, and felt the tip of it spring into instant hardness. His lips found the hollow of her throat.

"Don't. Please stop." Merin pulled back.

"I thought you wanted this."

"I do. You'll never know how much I do. But I can't. Whatever you were planning to do to me, it is forbidden."

"Of course." In his voice was all the scorn he felt for the Oressian strictures that kept her from accepting him as her lover. "I should have known. You did warn me, didn't you?"

"I'm sorry. It's my fault, Herne. I allowed you to touch me, knowing I should not."

She looked so forlorn that his heart melted. The ever-present anger, which had been rising in him, was dissipated, and the passion that had roared in his ears and his mind was muted into a controllable level of desire. He tried to reassure her.

"We are both at fault. I instigated it. I pursued it. You only allowed it."

"Thank you for saying that, even though it is not entirely true."

"I suppose you want me to leave the bridge now." She nodded, her face closed and tight. He had the oddest feeling that if he stayed a little longer she would begin to cry. He thought she would not want him to see her tears. He paused at the hatchway into the passage that led from bridge to cabins. Her eyes were fixed on the deck, her hands twisted together in the way he had seen before, as though she would try to wring out all her problems and her forbidden needs through her fingers. "Merin, you know, don't you, that one day we will finish what we started here?"

"It was finished here, a moment ago," she said.

"You are wrong. It hasn't even begun."

He was gone, and she could catch her breath again. Twisting her hands together, Merin sank into the captain's chair. She was still unsettled from her experience in the shaft eight hours earlier. Upon regaining consciousness after fainting onto her bunk, she had engaged in a fit of emotional tears most unseemly for one who claimed Oressian origins. During her off-watch hours she had slept badly, her rest interrupted by dreams in which she was falling down an almost vertical shaft and out into the wide nothingness of the main propulsion duct. These nightmares had been followed by sensuous dreams in which Herne was touching her legs and her hips. The waking embrace they had just shared had seemed like a continuation of those dreams, until he had opened her treksuit.

Valiantly, Merin faced the debacle in her mind, the ruin of all her childhood conditioning. The recent perils she had undergone and her close brush with death had moved her beyond her previous rule- and law-limited existence to a new mode of thought in which she could accept Herne's desire for her, and even her own growing tenderness toward him.

But there was one barrier between them that could never be destroyed. It was clear to Merin that she could not tell Herne how important he had become to her; if they grew close, he would inevitably learn the truth about her. And when he knew, he would turn from her in revulsion.

She sat rubbing her still-aching arms and shoulders while she planned the performance she must carry out from the present moment into the future, till she died or left Tarik's colony. She could not let Herne see how much she had changed. It was essential that he believe she was still the rigid Oressian-trained woman she had been when they first met. Only in that way could she hope to maintain his respect for her, and perhaps, just perhaps, salvage a modicum of friendly feeling on his part.

The solar flares had risen to levels that repeatedly interferred with instruments on the *Kalina*, and with messages between ship and Home. It seemed likely that Tarik would soon order Herne and Merin to take the *Kalina* out of orbit and away from Dulan's Planet. Because they were expecting the order, they were not surprised to hear Tarik's voice break through the static on the communicator. It was the overlapping hour of the watch, so both of them were on the bridge. Herne had just begun to eat from a plate he had brought in with him.

"You are to leave the *Kalina* and return to headquarters at once," Tarik commanded.

Herne paused with a piece of bread halfway to his mouth.

"Are you saying you want us to leave the ship unattended?" he asked. "That's contrary to your original directive when we first landed on the planet."

He was answered by a crackle of loud static.

". . . return to headquarters at once," Tarik's somewhat broken voice repeated.

Herne pushed his plate aside. Merin caught it just before it would have fallen off the console. She watched him work at the communicator, trying to clear the sound.

"Tarik," Herne shouted into the mouthpiece, "there is a lot of interference. I can't hear you clearly. Repeat again, please. Do you want us to abandon the *Kalina?*"

There was another burst of static before Tarik's voice sounded again.

"Leave the *Kalina* . . . return at once." The communicator fell silent.

"This doesn't make any sense," Herne insisted. "We are safer here than on a shuttlecraft; the *Kalina* hasn't sustained any serious damage; we are not under attack. Why does he want us to leave?"

"Could he have received a communication that we don't know about?" Merin suggested.

"It's unlikely, but then, Reid and Carlis, who are the official communications officers, are at Home with Tarik. I suppose they could have picked up a low-level message that we missed."

"Or perhaps Osiyar is aware of some danger to the ship." Merin set the plate she was still holding down on the captain's chair and went to another panel of lights to check an abnormality she had noticed.

"I guess Osiyar's telepathy is always a possibility." Still Herne sat at his console, pushing buttons. "Now the communications equipment is totally dead."

"Herne, look." Merin pointed to the panel in front of her. "Air circulation has stopped. The heat just went off, and the water reconditioning machinery too. The entire ship is shutting down, one system after another."

"That squares it. Tarik knows something we don't." Herne stood, caught Merin's arm, and pulled her toward the hatchway. "I don't know about you, but I have no intention of staying on a ship with no functioning life systems. If one system went down, we could fix it, but we can't fix everything at once, and we can't stay here with no air or heat and no communications. We are going to obey Tarik's orders, right now, without further discussion."

"What happened just then?" In the central room at Home, Tarik stood over the large computer-communicator, watching Carlis, the communications officer, at work.

"All communications with the *Kalina* are blocked," Carlis announced. "I can't make any contact with the ship. It must be the solar flares."

"Did they get my message to stay aboard beyond their four days, that we aren't going to risk sending anyone up in a shuttlecraft until these storms have ended?" Tarik asked.

"I can't be certain they received that last message," Carlis admitted. "But Herne and Merin are both sensible people. They know better than to leave the safety of a well-shielded ship.

Besides, they know the routine of not leaving the *Kalina* before the next crew arrives."

"It's just possible," said Tarik, recalling what Osiyar had said about them, "that they won't mind a few more days together till things calm down."

In an airy villa some distance beyond Tathan, a dark-haired woman faced a globe of glowing white light.

"Remember, you promised no one would be hurt," the woman said.

"New knowledge is never gained without danger," the light responded. "They have received my false message, and they will be in position shortly. Our preparations are complete. It is too late now to change our plans."

"Then," said the dark-haired woman, "it is time to begin the great experiment."

Part III
Old Tathan

Chapter Nine

"Doesn't it strike you as odd," Merin asked, "that while the entire ship has shut down, everything is working perfectly here on docking deck?"

"I haven't had time to think about it. I've been too busy stowing supplies and cleaning up, and at the moment I'm just glad to be warm again. I never realized how cold space is till the heating system stopped, or how much I appreciate artificial light until we were left with only inadequate red emergency lighting. Not to mention the healthful effects of breathable air." Herne filled his straining lungs with the clean air of the docking deck and felt his body readjust to the improved conditions. He and Merin had rushed through the last-minute checkoff lists, trying to complete them before the environment aboard *Kalina* became unlivable. They were leaving just in time. He had almost reached the shuttlecraft when the full impact of her words struck him. Dropping his softbag on the deck, he walked back to where she stood by the controls console. "What are you implying, Merin?"

"I'm not sure. We are now in the segment of *Kalina*'s orbit that takes us over the southern hemisphere of Dulan's Planet, across the south pole, then northward again. For the next thirty-five minutes, *Kalina* will be south of the equator."

"And?"

She glanced upward, saw his tense expression, and knew he had made the same connection she had.

"When the systems on the ship began to shut down," she informed him, "we were directly over the ruins of Tathan."

"The conditions aboard the *Kalina*," he said, his words slow and careful, as though he was fighting with himself and trying to list his arguments, "are the result of severe solar storms and unusually large sunspots and flares. We are certain of that. To suggest anything else would be unscientific and irresponsible."

"Still, it is an interesting coincidence, isn't it?" She paused before delivering the blow she hoped would make him angry enough to forget his affection for her. "Perhaps Ananka wants to see you again."

"If that is intended as a joke, it's in very bad taste."

An angry silence fell between them. It drew out while Merin waited, her hands still above the buttons. Herne faced her on the other side of the console. She could see his fists clenching and unclenching, in the way he had when he was trying to fight his inner rage. She was surprised at how much it hurt her to remind him of the episode at Tathan. She ought to be immune to that kind of jealous pain, but it seemed she was not. The silence deepened. Herne said nothing more.

"I shall set the outer hatch to open on one-minute delay." Merin spoke at last. "We had better board the shuttlecraft."

"After your remarks about Tathan I'm sorely tempted to leave you behind," he growled.

She hoped that statement meant he was as irritated with her as his frown seemed to indicate, but in case he was not she answered in the meek way she knew would annoy him even more, and she kept her eyes downcast.

"If you wish me to remain aboard the *Kalina*, Herne, I shall do so."

"To die of cold and asphyxiation? What in the name of all the stars do you think I am?"

"A Sibirnan, with a typical Sibirnan temper, which you are not keeping under control very well," she replied as unemotionally as she could. She punched the console buttons with unnecessary vigor. "There. We have exactly one minute till the hatch opens and the docking deck decompresses."

"What are you trying to do?" He was so suspicious that she knew he had seen through her attempts to put emotional distance between them. "Why are you deliberately trying to make me angry with you?"

"I seem to be succeeding." Picking up the softbag containing her few personal articles and toiletries, she started walking toward the shuttlecraft. He moved in front of her, blocking her way.

"A little more than eight hours ago," he said, "I held you in my arms and we almost made love. You admitted that you wanted me. Now you treat me like an enemy and you throw the incident at Tathan in my face. Are you trying to make me hate you?"

"What I am trying to do," she said, "is reach the shuttlecraft before the docking hatch opens and we are sucked out into space."

"I won't hate you, and I won't let you make me angry," he told her. "And no matter what you say or do, I won't stop wanting you."

Knowing that there was, indeed, something she could say that would forever end his interest in her yet sworn not to reveal it, she dared make no answer. She walked around him and got into the shuttlecraft, taking the pilot's seat. Herne sealed the shuttlecraft hatch, then took the navigator's position across the aisle from her. He reached over to take her hand, holding it tightly when she would have pulled it away.

"I think you are afraid of your feelings," he said. "I believe that is what this attempted quarrel is about."

"If you will release my hand," she replied coldly, "I have work to do."

"We will talk about this again when we are safely on the ground," he promised, loosening his grip on her.

She turned her head away, pretending to check a gauge while she fought for self-control. She had assumed that he would take immediate offense at her remark about Ananka. She had not expected him to choose this time to be understanding. And, unfortunately, he was right. She *was* afraid. She was terrified of the way her feelings for him grew every time she looked at him, and she was panic-stricken when she considered the certain result of giving way to those feelings.

"Docking deck hatch is open," Herne reported, his words bringing her back to the job at hand. "Deck atmosphere has decompressed."

Merin gave her full attention to the task of releasing the binding wires that kept the shuttlecraft in place during decompression. The engines started immediately, and the shuttlecraft lifted off the docking deck and through the hatch. Once they were away from the *Kalina* Herne took the downward spiraling course that was the standard maneuver to bring them toward Home, while Merin tried to contact Tarik.

"I get nothing but static," she said.

"I'm not surprised." Herne worked at his own instruments. "There is a major magnetic storm going on. But just a fifteen-minute ride and we can make our reports to Tarik in person."

He broke off as a blinding white light filled the shuttlecraft. The engines shuddered, died, then started again when the light faded.

"What was that?" Merin had lifted both hands to cover her eyes. "I feel nauseated and I'm so dizzy. Herne, was that you laughing?"

He was slumped in the navigator's seat. After a second or two he straightened, shaking his head as if to clear it.

"I didn't laugh," he said. "We must have taken a direct hit from a bolt of lightning, and there is nothing funny about that. Do you know we are off course?"

"How can you tell? The instruments have gone mad. I have no idea where we are." Merin fought back the nausea while trying to keep the shuttlecraft on a steady course. "Let's get closer to the ground and see if that helps. If the instruments don't settle down, I may have to land by sight alone. At least the viewscreen is still working."

Rubbing his forehead as though it ached, Herne squinted at the viewscreen.

"Our present course will take us down on the wrong side of the planet," he informed her. "It's noon at Home, but this is the night side."

"I can see that. There's daylight just ahead." Fighting fluctuating malfunctions in the instruments, Merin guided the shuttlecraft toward the streak of light she could see along the horizon.

"Damnation!" This expletive burst from Herne as they roared just above the treetops of a dense forest, then out across a sparkling blue sea. They were now in full daylight. "Where are we? I don't recognize anything."

"I do." With both hands busy on the controls, Merin could spare only a quick nod of her head toward the viewscreen. "See the plateau and the mountains beyond? That's Tathan, there on the plain. I know the way home now."

"We aren't going anywhere," said Herne, checking the navigational instruments. "We have just lost all power except for the viewscreen."

They both fell silent, Merin wondering if Herne was remembering her comments aboard the *Kalina*, if he was considering, as she was, the possibility that they had been deliberately brought back to the ruined city by the creature who had for a while held Herne under her control.

"If there is no power, then we'll just land on the plain," she told him, trying to sound calm. "Once we are down we can try to get the engines started again. Even if we don't succeed, at least Tarik will be able to find us easily by the emergency beacon."

She was pleased when Herne didn't insist on taking the controls away from her. He let her manage in her own way, let her use the shuttlecraft like a glider, looping round and round until they were low enough for her to land it on the broad, flat plain with some hope that they could avoid a fatal crash. He did help her with the manual brake, which was difficult to use. She welcomed his strong hands next to hers on the lever, pulling back in unison with her efforts until, after a rough landing and a long, bouncing roll across soft turf, they came to a gentle stop.

"Nicely done," he complimented her. She made no response. She was trying to start the engines. She pushed the buttons, but nothing happened. She tried again. Still, there was no throb of smoothly functioning machinery, nor even the sound of a malfunction.

"They won't work," Herne said. "Look at this panel, and this one too. All our instruments are dead. We can't start the engines, and without power we can't call for help. The emergency generator is down, too, which means we have no beacon."

They both knew what that meant. When they did not appear at Home on schedule Tarik would send out crews on the remaining two shuttlecraft to search for them, but without a beacon to mark their location, they would be difficult to find. The search would continue for a predetermined period before it was stopped on the assumption that they were dead. They had all agreed to this arrangement when they had first begun exploring the planet. Now, with no means of communicating with Home, they were on their own.

"Let's look at the engines," Merin suggested. "Lift the deck panels. There must be something we can do to repair them."

They spent almost an hour on the engines.

"There is nothing wrong with either one," said Herne. He finished replacing the movable panels over the engines, then crouched on the deck, watching her reaction to his conclusions. "It's just like the *Kalina*. Everything checks out in perfect condition and fully functional, but nothing works. Every system on this shuttlecraft has shut down."

"Including the viewscreen." Merin was at the controls once more, trying every possibility to bring back the power. "I guess we were lucky we could see through the landing. At least we know where we are."

"Don't be too sure of that. From what I saw as we came in, the sea is too near for this to be Tathan, as you believe. Tathan was miles away from the water."

"I saw the ruins," Merin insisted.

"Perhaps there is more than one set of ruins on this planet." For an instant he thought she might cry. Her eyes grew wide and frightened and her face began to crumple, but within a second she had pulled her usual smooth expression into place, with her gaze on the floor. And he, who at another time would have welcomed any evidence of emotion from her, was relieved to see that she would not give way to it now.

"We cannot remain immobilized inside a useless ship," she said, picking up her ever-present recorder and moving toward the hatch. "If this is not Tathan, then we need to know where we have landed." She stopped, with one hand at her head, to take a gasping breath. Then she straightened with a brave lift of her chin that tugged at his heart. He wanted to touch her but knew she would not appreciate that sign of his concern for her. He confined himself to a question.

"Are you still dizzy?"

"A little," she admitted. "It will pass."

"I'm feeling unsettled, too, ever since that bolt of lightning hit us."

They stepped out of the shuttlecraft into brilliant sunshine, made even brighter by its reflection off a calm blue sea. Herne could understand Merin's insistence that she knew where they were, for to the north rose the cliffs at the edge of the high plateau that formed the center of the continent. From the base of the plateau stretched the lowland plain, its overall configuration familiar after their previous visit. But the forest Herne remembered from that visit was gone, and now a broad river meandered southward across the plain until it finally met the sea at the head of a curving harbor. There, where river and harbor joined, lay the buildings Merin had seen.

"They don't look like ruins to me," Herne said, squinting so he could see more clearly. "They are only about a mile away. Perhaps we can find some answers there." He began to walk eastward, toward the buildings in the distance.

Merin went with him reluctantly, unwilling to be left alone with the disabled shuttlecraft, yet fearing what they might discover among the strange buildings.

"Everything I see is wrong," she objected as they drew nearer. "At Home it is early winter, which means that this far into the southern hemisphere it should be late spring, yet the vegetation is in late summer growth. I see planted farmland where forest should be. Nothing here makes sense.

"Herne." She caught at his arm, then pointed. Two human figures had emerged from a nearby stone cottage, hoes over their shoulders. Taking no notice of Merin and Herne, the figures began walking toward one of the fields that stretched northward. "Herne, where are we? What has happened? Is this real?"

"Good questions all," Herne said. "Those fellows don't look like especially welcoming types, so let's try that settlement up ahead first. If we find nothing there, we can always stop here on our way back to the shuttlecraft." He walked a few paces more before turning to look at her. "Are you coming with me, or are you going to stand there staring?"

"I have to stare," she told him. "As I should have expected, my recorder isn't working. I have to remember every detail, so I can make my report later." With a gesture of complete bewilderment, she hurried to catch up with him. They trudged on, side by side.

As they drew nearer to the harbor area, a salty breeze touched their faces, while above them a pair of seabirds cried. The faint sound of distant surf reached their ears. Merin sniffed the air appreciatively.

"What is it?" Herne asked, watching her.

"It smells familiar." She was so confused that she revealed too much. "I used to live by the sea."

"Oressia has a salty ocean?" Herne asked, fascinated by this spontaneous revelation.

"I should not have said that." Her face grew closed and still.

"Do you imagine we have somehow been transported to Oressia?" he asked. "That is impossible. Though, of course, all of this could be an illusion of some kind."

"It's not Oressia." A terrible suspicion had begun to grow in Merin's mind, an idea so fantastic that she should have rejected it at once. Instead, spurred by Herne's wild suggestion about Oressia, she began to explain to him her theory. It was based on what she had seen as they skimmed over the area before landing, combined with what she was now observing. "I think what we are seeing is Tathan, but not the Tathan we visited. And I hope it *is* an illusion, because if it is not—" Her words trailed off.

"What are you saying?" Herne saw that her face was pinched and stark white, but after a couple of breaths she began again, talking in a quiet, detached voice, explaining the unbelievable as if it were perfectly logical.

"It is possible that over six centuries of neglect a harbor can fill with silt deposited by a river until there is no longer any harbor at all. Or a coastline might be changed by earthquake or volcanic activity. We know both are frequent in the southern half of the continent. That could explain the discrepancy between the geography we discovered on our earlier expeditions and what we are seeing now. Certainly, six hundred years would be time enough to allow a forest to grow on deserted land."

She had his full attention. His eyes were boring into hers, and for once she felt no need to lower her own. There was nothing personal in his gaze, only surprise and a growing interest in what she was saying. She went on, determined to tell him all she suspected before she lost her nerve and became too terrified to speak.

"I believe this is Tathan as it once was, Tathan as we know it from the records we discovered at our headquarters building. This is Dulan's Tathan, but whether it is an illusion or whether it is real and we have been moved in time, I do not know." She saw him considering what she had said, and saw that he would not reject it immediately as she had half feared he might.

"You may be right," he said. He looked at sea and sky, at the farmland nearby and the tall cliffs in the distance. "Tathan."

"Shall we test my theory?" she asked. A surge of pure recklessness urged her forward, an impulse unlike anything she had ever known before. She knew she was still confused and more than a bit unbalanced by what had happened to them, but she did not care. "Shall we set our feet upon that bridge just ahead and attempt to cross the river by it and enter the city?"

"I'll go first," he said. "You wait here until I reach the other side. If there is no real bridge, you can pull me out of the water. That's assuming there really is a river."

She waited only until he had reached the middle of the bridge before, certain the structure was solid, she hurried after him. They entered the city together, and Merin was not surprised to recognize the arrangement of streets and buildings, not after helping Tarik and Osiyar to map Tathan. She was convinced now that she was right. Somehow she and Herne had come to Tathan.

They chose a wide, tree-lined avenue and began to walk along it. The two-story buildings on each side of the street were perfectly simple yet of elegant and pleasing proportions, and all made of a rose-red stone that looked as though it might have been quarried from the face of the cliffs where the plateau ended. Almost every house had a lush garden.

They saw no one, but a murmur of sound drew them onward to where the avenue ended at a large open square. Here at last there was evidence of busy life. The square was filled with people, most of whom appeared to be human, clothed in bright red, blue, or green. Produce was piled in bins beneath the striped awnings of several shops. A few buildings away from the produce market, a weaver worked at his loom, the previous products of his labors draped on frames to display their many-colored patterns. Another shop sold ready-made clothing; still another held racks of leather goods.

"It seems so real," said Herne, turning about slowly in order not to miss a thing in the bustling square. "But who—or what—has done this?"

"Do you really think all of this is an illusion?" Merin asked, looking around, trying to remember everything she saw.

"Let's find out." Herne stepped in front of a red-robed figure. "Excuse me, sir. May I speak with you?" The figure walked past him, apparently unaware of Herne's presence.

Herne caught at the sleeve of a second figure, but again the person simply moved away. A third and a fourth try brought the same results.

"I gather we aren't really here," Herne noted dryly, glancing at Merin.

She had been observing his attempts to make someone notice their presence. Convinced now that he would be unsuccessful, she turned away to scan the crowded square, looking for some clue to their mysterious circumstances. The crowd shifted, giving her a new view of their surroundings. She cried out, pointing to a building strikingly different from all the rose-stone structures they had seen so far. This was a low white edifice, long enough to form one entire side of the square. White stone steps led up to an arched doorway. The dark wood double doors were wide open. She recognized the building from Herne's description. Herne stepped to her side, following her line of sight through the moving patterns of brightly clothed figures.

"That's it," Herne exclaimed. "This square must be where we landed the shuttlecraft when we came to explore, because that is the building I saw then."

"Be careful," Merin warned, but he wasn't listening. He made straight for the entrance. "Herne, wait."

"No," he said. "I intend to find out exactly what is going on here." With that, he mounted the steps and disappeared through the arch. Not wanting to remain alone among figures that bought and sold and otherwise acted as if they were alive while completely ignoring Herne and herself, Merin decided the only sensible thing to do was to follow him inside.

The white stone interior was as Herne had described it to her a month before, while they had explored its ruins. Here was the double row of columns, shaped like the columns of their headquarters building at the lake. In the center of the building, exactly where Herne had once told her, was the statue of a Chon with wings upraised and beak open. There was no roof on this section of the hall. Herne stopped beside the golden statue, and there Merin caught up with him.

"It's beautiful, just as you said," she whispered. She laid one hand on the bird, her fingers tracing the delicately carved feathers. "I have never seen such exquisite workmanship."

"It's not real. It can't be. None of this is real. I'm certain of it now. It's all too much like the dream I had. It's too perfect." As he spoke, Herne was striding down the length of the long chamber, taking wide steps that quickly brought him to double doors at the far end set in an arch that matched the main entrance. With Merin at his heels, Herne burst through these doors into a garden. White flowers in every conceivable shape and size filled the garden, their mingled fragrances almost too sweet and heavy for human nose and throat and lungs to tolerate.

"Where is the grotto?" Herne glared at the high white wall surrounding the garden. He raised his voice. "Whoever you are, since you seem determined to recreate an illusion, show me the entrance to the grotto."

They stood in silence, Herne clenching his fists, both waiting for some response. It came from the far side of the garden.

"How impatient you are," said an oddly scratchy voice. "But then, impatience is one of the attributes of Jurisdiction personnel."

"Who are you?" Herne demanded.

Merin thought he was disappointed, because the short figure now approaching them, hooded and cloaked in pale blue, could not possibly be the Ananka whom Herne had described to her. She could not even see the figure's face beneath the sheltering hood, and she could not tell by the voice whether it was male or female.

"You must relinquish your weapons," the figure told them. The blue robe rippled and two slender but obviously strong hands stretched forward. "Tathan is a peaceful place, but all here remember too well the violence of the Jurisdiction. We cannot allow you to break our peace. The weapons, if you please. *Now*."

It was impossible to resist that voice. Herne placed his small hand weapon into the figure's hands. Merin did the same, making certain to touch those hands as she did so. The flesh was solid, warm, real. Still, she could not see the face, and she sensed a cool reserve more than matching that of any Oressian. She decided to try courtesy.

"I also have a recorder that doesn't work." She touched the strap at her shoulder, from which the useless recorder swung. "Will you want it, also?"

"Since it is not functional, you may keep it."

"Thank you. I am Merin of Oressia," she said politely. "This is Herne of Sibirna."

"Both Jurisdiction planets," said the figure.

"In a way, we are exiles from the Jurisdiction," Merin said. "May we know your name?"

The cloaked figure bowed its head. "I am Dulan of Romesan, also an exile," replied the scratchy voice.

Chapter Ten

"You are Dulan?" Herne's shock was plain to see.

Although surprised herself, and immediately, frighteningly, aware of the many implications of finding themselves in a Tathan in which Dulan still lived, Merin found her voice.

"Is this building your home?" she asked.

"Of course not. Who would wish to live in so large and empty a space?" Dulan gave a short, broken laugh. "This is the Gathering Hall."

"The statue of the Chon is magnificent," Merin said.

"You know of the Chon?" Dulan's short figure exuded tenseness.

"We lived briefly in the northern part of this

continent," Merin said. "We had some contact with them."

"How is it that we did not sense your presence?" Dulan's head bowed, as if the weapons still being held in slim fingers were being examined. "You say you are exiles. Are you telepaths?"

"No, but we know you are." At Herne's words Dulan moved backward a pace or two.

"Have you come here searching for us, to do us harm? If so, you were foolish to hand over your weapons." Dulan turned them over and over, the motions of those pale hands imparting to Merin a distaste and a reluctance to handle them. "They are unusual. I have never seen any like them before."

"That's because—oh, blessed stars." Herne looked helplessly at Merin. "You're the historian, you tell me how we can explain how we got here, or what we think happened, without sounding completely insane."

"There is no reasonable explanation," Merin said to Dulan.

"Your confusion, these strange weapons—now I begin to understand," said Dulan.

"You do?" They both stared at the blue-robed figure.

"If I speak the name Ananka, will it be familiar to you?" asked Dulan.

"It will," said Herne, looking grim.

"As I expected. How many others are with you?"

"There is no one else," Herne said, adding, "We were forced to land here. At the moment, our ship is in need of repair."

"Of course it is. You want to return to your proper place. I shall try to help you. In the meantime, let me offer you my hospitality. Perhaps it will be some small recompense for the inconveniences you have suffered." Dulan indicated with one hand that they should follow, then led them toward the garden wall where they could now see a door that had been partly concealed by shrubbery and white flowers.

"Dulan, how long have your people lived here?" Merin asked.

"For almost exactly one hundred of this planet's years," came the reply.

At this, Merin and Herne exchanged glances. Both had read the records of Tathan that were stored at their headquarters building, so they knew Tathan had been one hundred years old when the Cetans attacked and destroyed it. Behind Dulan's back, Merin touched Herne's arm. Perhaps startled by this unusual gesture on her part, he stopped walking to look at her.

"Say nothing of what we know about the fate of Tathan," Merin whispered urgently.

"Don't worry," Herne whispered to her. "That's a vital piece of information to be kept secret in case we need it later, to bargain for our lives."

"Is something wrong?" Dulan had paused by the garden door, waiting for them.

"Do we appear solid to you?" Herne asked.

"To my eyes you are perfectly normal, substantial human beings," Dulan said. "However, I understand your concern. Indeed, I share it. As soon as we have reached my house, I will do what I can to dispel the mystery that so disturbs you."

Dulan led them through the door into a narrow alley that ran parallel to the garden wall. Along the opposite side of the alley was another stone wall, into which, a short distance away, was set a dark wooden door. Dulan pushed this door open. Inside, they found a pleasant, cozy room with dark wood ceiling beams. Finely woven banners hung on the white walls, wooden chairs were cushioned with more colorful textiles, a fire burned merrily in a raised fireplace. In one wall a series of windows looked out across a salt marsh to the sea. Above the undulating grasses, three Chon were hunting their dinner, diving now and then to snatch at prey.

"My mate is away from home on a brief retreat to Lake Rhyadur," said Dulan, "so it is left to me alone to make you comfortable. I have more than enough food and drink here. Since you are familiar with the Chon, perhaps you will wish to join us tomorrow evening, for our Gathering with them."

"We would be honored," Merin said.

"Actually, we would like to be gone by tomorrow," said Herne. "You offered to help us repair our ship."

"What is wrong with your vessel, or perhaps I should say the conditions I believe resulted in your arrival here, will take more than a single day to repair," Dulan informed them. "Please, seat yourselves near the fire. We chose to build at Tathan because the climate here is uniformly pleasant, but at this time of year, as summer ebbs, the sea breeze can be surprisingly cool and damp. Let me find refreshments to share with you." Dulan left them, passing through an archway to the left of the room.

Once again, Merin touched Herne's arm, then raised a finger to her lips, signaling caution.

"Somehow, we have been moved in time" she began in a whisper.

"No, it's all an illusion," Herne interrupted.

"Whichever it is," Merin told him with a hint of impatience, "we must be careful not to reveal anything we know about the fate of Tathan."

"I have already agreed to that." Herne nodded. "I think it would also be wise not to mention our colony. And, Merin, we are going to let Dulan believe we are mates."

"*What?*" This suggestion so startled her that she forgot to whisper.

"Hush, talk softly. It's a way of making sure we aren't separated through an entire night, until we find out what has really happened to us. We'll have to take turns standing watch. Dulan seems to be friendly enough, but we can't be certain what is planned for us. We don't even know if that is really Dulan in there."

"Your point is well made, Herne. For the time being, I am willing to act as if we are mated while we are with Dulan and the other telepaths whom we will probably meet here."

"Are you sure you know how?" He grinned at her in a manner most unlike the Herne she knew.

Merin wondered if he was experiencing the same occasional giddiness she had been feeling ever since leaving the shuttlecraft, but before she could ask him about it, Dulan returned with the promised refreshments. There was brown bread, a plate of several different kinds of fruits, a pitcher of foaming, golden liquid, and three pottery mugs glazed in a lovely shade of blue. Dulan set the food on a low table, pulled a third chair close to the fire, and sat down to pour out the liquid. It proved to be a tangy, beerlike beverage. Merin drank it with thirsty pleasure, but noted that Herne barely sipped at his.

"I have promised to tell you what I know or can conjecture about your coming here," Dulan said. "To begin, everyone in Tathan or farming on the outskirts of the city is a telepath. Most are human; some are members of the other Races. After the Act of Banishment forced us to leave the Jurisdiction we made a long journey together, ending finally in the Empty Sector, where we found this suitable planet. There were but sixty-four of us left when we founded Tathan a century ago, but on this world all Races live much longer lives than is usual. Sixty of the original founders are still alive. All of us have prospered and multiplied our kin through several new generations until now there are over two thousand of us. We brought with us the technology to build our beautiful city and to make the best use of soil and the sea. For nearly one hundred years we have been safe and content, until recently."

Since this information was familiar to both Merin and Herne, neither said anything, but let Dulan continue the story.

"Among telepaths there are universally understood barriers to the expansion of our skills," Dulan told them. "But in every group of intelligent beings there are those, usually young, ambitious, as yet untried souls, who want to abolish all limits."

"It happens in most societies," Herne put in. "The young rebel for a while, but in time they mature and learn to control themselves. By then, of course, there is a new generation coming along to cause fresh trouble."

"So it was with our previous young ones," said Dulan, nodding agreement. "But in the case of this particular generation two new factors have been added. The first was Saray, a girl born with remarkable powers. She studied with me for several years, until she outpaced her teacher. The second factor is the entity known to us as Ananka."

Here Herne drew in his breath with a sharp sound. Dulan's head turned in his direction, as if the telepath were studying Herne's expression.

"Is there something you wish to add to this story?" asked Dulan.

"Not yet," said Herne. "Perhaps later."

"Very well." The blue hood now faced toward the fire, as if Dulan were gazing into the flames, considering what to say next. After a while the low voice resumed. "We had known of the presence of several similar entities on this world before we settled here. They are creatures of light and energy, without bodies as we know them. Our powers were not great enough to allow us full contact with them, but we received the impression that our settlement was not unwelcome. For almost a century we simply ignored this form of life, and it ignored us.

"Now Saray claims that she has made friends with Ananka, and that Ananka is helping her to enhance her telepathic abilities. I have seen Saray move objects and even herself through space," Dulan continued. "I have also observed a brief though successful attempt at transportation through time. I think that is why you are here. I believe Ananka and Saray were experimenting on you."

Merin and Herne stared at each other, saying nothing.

"You knew the name the entity used," Dulan said, "which makes me believe you have witnessed one of its manifestations."

"I did," Herne admitted. "Twice. She appeared

as a beautiful young woman."

"Where was that?" asked Dulan. Herne and Merin said nothing, as they had earlier agreed, until Dulan spoke again. "I need to know in order to determine how strong the Saray-Ananka alliance has become. If the effects they create can be extended beyond this immediate area, then our problem is more serious than I have believed."

"When the malfunctions in our shuttlecraft began we were directly above Tathan," Herne said, avoiding an answer on the subject of where he had first met Ananka. "We thought the solar storms had affected the instruments."

"The term 'shuttlecraft' implies a larger ship somewhere near," said Dulan. "And to my certain knowledge, the sun is in its quiescent period just now. There are no solar storms."

"We can't tell you," Merin began.

"You must," Dulan interrupted. "If my theories about Ananka and Saray are correct, the lives of everyone in Tathan may depend upon your answer."

"All right." Herne leapt to his feet, almost knocking over the table where the food sat. "Merin, we have to tell Dulan everything. There is no one else who can help us leave here."

"Herne," Merin protested, "we agreed to keep silent."

"Why?" asked Dulan. "Is there something I dare not know?"

Merin bit her lip, thinking about the coming Cetan attack. Herne spoke again to Dulan, expressing an attitude he had voiced before, to Merin.

"Look, could you remove that hood? It covers your face, and I hate talking to someone I can't see."

"I could, but you would wish I had not." Dulan paused for the duration of a sigh. "Long ago, when I lived in the Jurisdiction, I was tortured in an attempt to make me reveal the names of other telepaths. My face was badly scarred, my voice permanently altered. I was fortunate to escape with my life."

"I'm sorry." Herne sat down again, looking hard at the blue fabric covering Dulan. "I'm a physician; perhaps I could help."

"I thank you, but it is too late for that." One of Dulan's hands moved a little. "Please tell me everything you know about Ananka. It is vitally important. I swear not to reveal your secrets to the other telepaths."

Merin sat watching Herne as he produced a carefully edited version of what had happened to him while exploring Tathan. He did not mention Tarik or the other colonists, instead giving the impression that he and Merin had been exploring by themselves. He also made the *Kalina* sound like a much smaller ship than it was. He did not mention the coming Cetan attack.

"So, Tathan will end in ruins," said Dulan when Herne had finished.

"As all cities end, in time," Merin said.

"Time is precisely the dimension we must consider," Dulan told her. "With Ananka's help, Saray was able to change the position in time of a small animal, and later to move you. You will note that the second transference included your ship as well as your persons. We must conclude from this that the power produced by the union of the two is growing stronger."

"Dulan, can you help us?" Merin asked.

"It is possible." Dulan rose. "I want to consult with my friend, Tula."

"You swore you wouldn't tell anyone what we said." Herne was on his feet again, looking angry.

"If you walked to the center of Tathan from the outskirts of the city, then everyone knows you have arrived," Dulan replied. "Thus, there is no breaking of my promise in inviting Tula to join us for the evening meal. You may decide for yourself how much you want to tell him. In the meantime, you will not be disturbed while I am gone. The guest accommodations are in the rooms to your right. Perhaps you would like to bathe, or to sleep for a while. So long as you are my guests, my home and all I possess are at your disposal."

"I'd like to take another look at your Gathering Hall, and at the garden too," Herne said.

"As you wish." With a polite bow, Dulan left them. The moment they were alone, Herne turned to Merin.

Flora Speer

"This isn't real," he said. "It's all a trick of some kind. Did you notice there's no entrance to the grotto from that garden?"

"So you are convinced the appearance of an entire city is Ananka's doing, perhaps with the connivance of this Saray whom Dulan knows?"

"I think there isn't any Saray, just as there isn't any Dulan. I am going to find Ananka and force her to free us from this illusion so we can go home." Herne took a step toward the door to the alley.

"I'm going with you." Merin was right behind him.

"She may not appear to me if you are present," Herne objected. "Stay here, Merin. Investigate this house and look into those guest quarters. If Dulan returns before I do, try to glean whatever information you can that might help to end this illusion. You have done better than I so far. I'm too impatient and I try for direct answers. You are more subtle; you may ultimately be more successful with our mysterious host. And you may find it necessary to disguise my absence."

"From a telepath?" She almost laughed at that idea.

"Osiyar claims all telepaths observe the rule of not entering anyone's mind without permission," Herne reminded her. "But it doesn't matter because this Dulan isn't real. Do as I ask, Merin. I'll be back as soon as I can. I promise." Before she could draw away, his lips brushed her cheek. Then he was gone, pulling the door shut after him, barring her exit.

Merin considered following him, until she realized that he was probably· right about Ananka only appearing if he was alone. She began to examine the sitting room, and after it the kitchen, both inch by inch. She could find nothing unusual about either room, nor any sign of advanced technology. They were just simple, comfortable places in which to eat or sit and talk with friends. If Dulan's house was an illusion, it was a remarkable one. Whatever she saw or touched seemed completely real to her.

Having finished with the main rooms, she decided to investigate the guest quarters as Herne had suggested. There she found another plain white room with a large bed topped by a brightly striped coverlet. There was only one window. Leaning out of it, Merin could see on her right the curving shore of the harbor. The house was set on a slight rise in the land. Directly before her a garden of blue and white flowers sloped down to the wide salt marsh, which had as its farther boundary a row of sand dunes. She watched a herd of long-legged, antelopelike animals browsing among the waving marsh grasses that shone green and gold in the setting sun.

Turning from the peaceful scene, Merin discovered a door that led into a bathing room. A white stone tub was set into the floor, and next to it a bench with a red- and blue-striped cushion. At one side of the bathing room was a tiny enclosed courtyard filled with green plants. There was no sign of any other person, and only the faintest muted sounds penetrated from outside the house.

She looked at the tub with yearning. Oressians were a meticulously clean people, trained to bathe at least once a day, and she had just spent four days aboard the *Kalina*, where water was rationed and the crew had to use automatic cleansing chambers that cleaned by sound waves. Dulan had said to refresh herself. . . .

Nearly overcome by another wave of the curious lightheadedness she had periodically felt since leaving the shuttlecraft, Merin sat down on the bench near the tub and put her head between her knees. When she felt better she lifted her head again, her eyes slowly focusing on the tub. The longer she looked, the more enticing became the prospect of a bath. She knew perfectly well that the strangeness of her situation had affected her judgment. Normally, she would not even consider taking a bath in an unfamiliar place. For an instant she felt giddy again, just as she decided that whether her surroundings were real or an illusion, she was going to have the bath she needed and wanted so badly. She turned the handles that opened the pipes.

While water poured into the tub, she hastened back to the main room. Dulan had not returned and there was no sign of Herne. She made certain the door to the guest chamber was closed before she went into the bathing room once more.

She had been taught to remove her clothing, lather herself with cleansing liquid, then to rinse, dry herself; and replace her clothing as quickly as possible. Shampooing was to be done with equal dispatch. Under no circumstances was this process to be enjoyed. Bathing was a hygenic necessity, no more. But today, whether because of the unusual circumstances in which she found herself and her doubts about the reality of everything she saw, or because she was still unnerved and a bit giddy after piloting a powerless shuttlecraft into a safe landing, Merin found herself sinking into the warm water with a sigh of relief. Her tense muscles relaxed and the headache that had begun to pound at her temples blurred and faded away.

There was no efficient cleansing liquid, just a bar of scented soap that burst into bubbles when the water touched it. The water itself was silky-smooth on her skin. A tiny wisp of steam curled upward into the cool air of the bathing room. Merin dipped her shoulders beneath the water, splashing soapsuds, and then began to wash her hair.

Herne returned to Dulan's house in a state of increasing frustration and with a pounding headache. In the deepening dusk he had been unable to locate the grotto entrance. The garden was surrounded by a smooth white wall, its only openings the door to the alley that led to Dulan's house and the wide double doors into the hall where the Chon statue was. When he had hurried to the main entrance of the hall he had found it locked, so he could not leave the hall to go into the square in front of it. With growing irritation, he had searched the hall from end to end, carefully examining the golden statue and its pedestal before returning to the garden to hunt again for some indication of where the grotto was. Nowhere in garden or building did he see another person or hear any sound but his own footsteps. Convinced that he and Merin were the victims of an elaborate illusion, he retraced his steps, regretting that he had left her alone, hoping he would find her unharmed.

Dulan's sitting room was empty, as was the guest bedroom, but he could hear someone moving in the room beyond. Cautiously, he pushed the door open to look within. A faint mist still hovered above the sunken tub, a mixture of steam and a delicious perfume. The last traces of bathwater bubbled gently down the drain as a woman stepped away from the tub, her every movement flowing with unaffected natural grace.

At first he thought it was Ananka, and he took a purposeful step into the room, intending to

accost her, to demand an explanation for what
had happened to the shuttlecraft as well as for
why she had made an entire city appear where
only ruins should be. Then he saw Merin's
orange treksuit and her coif, both neatly folded on a bench beside the tub. Unaware of his
presence, Merin was drying herself with a thick
white towel.

Herne watched, enchanted by the sight of
slender arms and legs and a perfectly formed
body. Her rounded breasts were tipped with
small, rosy nipples, her neck was a smooth
column of sculptured ivory, her pale, sharp-
boned face, softened by the tender warmth of
the bathwater, was lightly flushed with color.
And her hair . . .

Herne had never seen such hair before. Thick
curls the color of the richest, finest-brewed dark
brown qahf drifted to below her waist. When
she moved the lamps embedded in the bathing
room ceiling struck gleams of gold and deepest
red from that hair. How could any woman bear
to cover such an asset, to keep it hidden from
the eyes of all men?

He wanted her. He had been tormented by
his growing desire for her all during their days
aboard the *Kalina*, and now, with a heavy,
imperative need, Herne knew he had to have
her. She had admitted that she wanted him.
It was possible that it would not take much
persuasion to make her his. He watched her
rub the towel down the outside of one long,

beautifully formed leg, over thigh and knee and calf to ankle, then back up the inward side of her leg, stopping at her thigh. Herne's fingers itched to follow the same path, to stroke that smooth, soft skin, to touch her and then to place his mouth *there*, where she was drying now. At the thought of her moist warmth beneath his lips, his common sense deserted him. With that desertion all his sense of danger from their present strange situation evaporated. He could think of one thing only. *Merin.*

Stepping back into the bedroom, he stripped off his clothing as quickly as he could, knowing he must hurry before she had had time to replace that wretched loose treksuit and her ridiculous coif, to hide her incredible beauty from him or from anyone else who might see her. When he returned to the bathing room she had just finished toweling her hair and was reaching for the treksuit.

Still slightly disoriented and feeling a little dizzy, lulled into drowsy relaxation by the unfamiliar sensuous delights of warm water and perfumed soap, Merin thought it was appropriate that Herne should materialize before her while she was thinking of him. He looked just the way he had when she had dreamed of him that first time.

Of course, he wasn't really there. She was only dreaming again. He would take a step or two toward her, as he had done in her earlier dream, and then he would vanish. And since he wasn't there, and no one but herself could possibly know what she was dreaming, she ought to take advantage of the opportunity to study him. He was the only unclothed person she had seen since she was ten years old. She was unlikely ever to see anyone else undressed, real or imagined, because after this lovely dream was finished she would force herself into the most rigorous forms of Oressian discipline, so that she would never dream again. But for the moment, in this strange and unreal place . . . in this time out of all time . . . .

He came toward her, as she had known he would, and even though it was only a dream, and she knew she could make herself wake up whenever she wanted, she began to tremble. But then he touched her. His hand brushed along her cheek and reached into her hair. She knew the touch of his hand on her face. She had felt it before. She had felt his kiss, too, so it was not surprising that she should dream of it again now. He gathered her into his arms, his flesh against hers, and she shuddered at the contact, half rousing from her dreamlike state, then sinking back into it. She did not want to face reality yet. Not yet, not until after he had kissed her.

"Merin." His mouth was in her hair, at her throat, against her ear. "It's you I want, only you."

Overwhelmed by unfamiliar sensations, her

inhibitions dangerously frayed by the light-headedness that would not go away, Merin half fainted into Herne's arms.

"Let me love you," he whispered. "I've wanted you for so long."

Her hands moved around his neck; her head rested on his shoulder. She knew by then that this was no dream, but she could dredge up no feeling of appalled horror, which would have been the appropriate Oressian reaction to what was happening. All she knew was that she wanted Herne to go on holding her.

"Please," she whispered into his neck. "Please kiss me."

Herne lifted her face, holding her so they were almost mouth to mouth.

"Hold me close." Her voice was a breath, even lower than a whisper. "Let me feel all of you against me for just a moment. When I'm alone again I want to be able to remember you."

She watched the rugged harshness of his face soften into tenderness. He pulled her closer, his arms holding her gently yet firmly. Merin trembled under the touch she had ached to know, yet had for so long refused to admit wanting. His body imprinted itself upon her mind with a vividness possible only to one who for all her life had been denied tactile pleasures.

The heat of his mouth on hers brought with it the memory of the other times when he had kissed her. Under his tutelage she had learned a little of that art. She opened her lips. When he did not respond at once as she wanted she pushed her tongue toward him, across his lips and into his mouth. She tightened her arms around his neck, pulling her body upward and harder against him.

His hands were on her hips, moving them forward. At the same time she felt a stiff, hot part of Herne probing against the place where her thighs joined. She did not understand what he was doing, but she instinctively shifted her position a little, allowing him the access he sought. She stood there for a breathless eternity, pressed so tightly to Herne that she could almost believe they had become one being, with his tongue searing her mouth, her breasts crushed against his chest, their thighs together, and that hard, hot part of him thrust between her legs. Merin tensed, quivering, shaken by previously unknown, yet now absolutely undeniable needs.

"Help me," she moaned when he had freed her mouth enough for her to be able to breathe again. "What do I want? Why do I feel—? Herne, Herne, don't let me go."

She was lifted in his arms, swept off her feet. She was unaware that he was carrying her until he laid her on the bed in the guestroom. Half blinded by uncontrollable sensation, she reached toward him, to pull him back against her. He came willingly, to put his mouth over the tip of one of her breasts while his fingers played with the other. Merin gave a cry that was part scream of alarm, part moan of pleasure. Erotic desire, ruthlessly repressed for all her life, came fully awake under Herne's searching hands and mouth. By the time he carefully separated her thighs she was beyond thought or words. With her eyes closed she felt his touch, and recalled vaguely that no one was ever supposed to touch another person in that spot. But his fingers were gentle. Too gentle. She wanted more, wanted pressure and friction and heat. She opened her eyes just in time to see what he was going to do.

"Yes," she gasped, lifting her hips to offer herself to him. "Please, touch me there."

He moved forward, pushing into her, and she lifted herself again, pushing back as hard as she could, searching for what she so desired. Unexpected joy welled up in her as she felt him begin to stretch her body. Half delirious though she was, she could discern in his face the pleasure her eager response was giving him. It was his openly expressed delight, and the joy that continued to soar and flame in her, that gave her the courage to endure a long, rending pain when Herne continued to push himself into her with a slow and steady determination. She screamed, biting his shoulder in a confused frenzy of longing and discomfort. It was against all her training to accept this kind of pain, but she had no desire to avoid it. Then the pain was gone and Herne was completely inside her, on her, crushing her with his weight, and she was dissolving into him. He was making her part of himself, and she knew in her deepest heart that she would never be separate from him again. She trusted him, so she let him do whatever he wanted to her, while she gave herself to him freely, reacting with feverish intensity to his every hard thrust, crying out with ever-increasing need, over and over again, until at last she found her trust rewarded with pleasure so vibrant and shattering that she thought she would die of it.

The tremors that had shaken her body were stilled at last. Her face was wet with tears, though she could not recall having shed them. Herne lay sprawled over her, one arm across her breasts.

"All my life I've been angry," he murmured, his warm breath against her shoulder, stirring her curling hair. "I've always been ready for a quarrel with words or a physical battle on the slightest provocation. Sometimes I have fought with no provocation at all, just to relieve the rage piled up inside me. But from the moment I took you into my arms my anger was gone. For the first time I'm at peace. It feels wonderful."

"What have we done?" Merin's voice quavered and broke. She tried again. "Herne, what was it that just happened between us?"

"It's called love." He sounded amused. He moved his arm to hug her more closely. When he spoke again his voice held an awed solemnity. "It's true; it was love we were making. That's why I'm not angry any more. It's because of you, and the love you gave me. Merin, my dearest, sweetest love." He lifted himself to bend over her. She knew he intended to kiss her.

"No, I cannot. It's not allowed." When she pushed against his chest he moved aside so she could sit up. She could tell he was puzzled by her behavior, but not frightened as he ought to have been. But then, she should not have expected him to be frightened. He did not understand, he did not know the laws of Oressia. She did. She got off the bed and ran into the bathing room. The place between her legs, where he had pushed so hard and hurt her, ached now when she moved. She looked down and saw a smear of red on her inner thigh. She sank to her knees beside the bench, fingers groping toward her coif.

"Merin, what's wrong?" Herne was there, kneeling beside her, his beautiful naked body now an affront to her eyes. She was so frightened that when he pulled her against his chest she cried out in abject terror. Despite her panic-stricken struggles, he would not let her go. He held her close until she had some control over her emotions.

"My dearest, I know I hurt you," he told her. "But I know you enjoyed it, too, and I promise it won't hurt the next time, nor ever again.

From now on it will just get better."

"What am I to do?" she cried, seeming not to hear his attempt to comfort her. "There is no Tribunal of Elders here, so how can I be punished? And you, Herne, how can I save you?"

"If it's impossible for you to be punished for what we've done, I don't think I have much to worry about." Herne did not know whether to be amused or concerned by her fears. Never having made love to a virgin before, he was not certain if her distress was only the result of the major change that had just occurred in her life, or if she actually did think she ought to be punished. When she pulled away from him he let her go, until she picked up her coif and shook it out. Moving swiftly, he tore the cloth out of her fingers and tossed it aside. "Don't cover your hair. It's too beautiful to hide. Now, what is this about punishment? Come on, Merin, don't hide your face from me, either. After what we have just enjoyed together, I deserve an explanation."

"I am forbidden to tell you. Herne, please, please, don't try to make me reveal what I must not. You have taken—no, I will be honest about this. *I have given* you something I should not give to anyone, given it willingly and joyfully. What we have done together I will do again if you ask me. Having begun as we did, I know I could not refuse you. But I implore you, do not pry into Oressian affairs. If you do, it will destroy what is between us. Let me bear the burden of blame. It is my responsibility."

"All right," he said, wanting to reassure her. "For the moment, because we are in strange and unusual circumstances, I will ask no more questions. But I make no promises for the future. There will come a time when I will want some honest answers."

Chapter Eleven

Tula was a plump little man with an honest, open face, a shaved head, and twinkling blue eyes. He wore a blue robe similar to Dulan's, with the hood thrown back.

"The news of your arrival has spread through all of Tathan," Tula said when Dulan introduced Herne and Merin to him. "No doubt by now even the quarry workers have heard the tale. Everyone is asking the questions I now put to you: Where is your home? How did you come here? I need not inquire if you mean us harm, for I can sense that you are merely confused and curious, as well as a bit frightened."

"Tula's special talent is the ability to perceive the emotions of others without the deliberate use of his telepathic powers," Dulan explained.

"We have been friends since we were young." Tula placed a hand on Dulan's shoulder. "It often happens that telepaths just leaving babyhood form a close and unbreakable bond. They need not be of the same gender, and it matters not at all whom they marry, for nothing can destroy their telepathic closeness."

"It was Tula who cared for me after I was released from a Jurisdiction prison," Dulan added quietly, indicating that they should all be seated in the chairs arranged by the fireplace. "For that kindness I owe him my life. I believe he can be trusted with any secret."

"So do I," said Merin. She remained a little unsure about Dulan's character, because of the hood covering the mystery of a scarred and disfigured face and her uncertainty as to whether Dulan was man or woman, but she had liked Tula on sight. She believed there was no guile in the man, and no violence, either. She thought Herne was still undecided about either telepath. She noticed him regarding Tula with hard, disbelieving eyes.

"You are doubtful," said Tula to Herne. "Will you tell me what troubles you?"

"I'm still not certain that you and Dulan, or any of Tathan, for that matter, really exist," Herne responded.

"Do you believe we may be an elaborate illusion?" asked Tula. "What an interesting concept. Have you any idea how much telepathic power would be necessary to create and maintain such a complicated image? Dulan and I would have no energy left to use while conversing with you."

"You would if you were part of the illusion," Herne stated. "Or if you had planted the fantasy in our minds instead of using a physical construction."

"An even more delightful idea." Tula laughed. "I wish it were possible. Like so many in the Jurisdiction, you seem to have an exaggerated notion of the capabilities of telepaths. I doubt if even Saray allied with the entity Ananka could do what you suggest."

"What about Ananka alone?" Herne asked. "Could she do it?"

"I do not know," said Tula, meeting Herne's eyes with obvious honesty. Herne held that gaze for a while.

"All right," Herne said, making up his mind to trust Tula. "Until something happens to convince me otherwise, I will accept your claim that Tathan and everyone in it are real. I would like to meet this Saray."

"Dulan, I think we ought to arrange it." Tula turned toward his friend. "Perhaps tomorrow morning? She will not refuse a request from her old teacher."

"If, as I suspect, she is responsible for the presence of Merin and Herne in Tathan, she will not dare to refuse," Dulan agreed.

"You think this is another of her experiments?" Tula shook his head. "Oh, dear, this matter of Saray and Ananka grows more difficult by the day. Merin, Herne, I must insist that you answer my original questions."

"Tell him how we came to be here, Herne," urged Merin. "Or I will."

Faced with that choice, Herne gave Tula the same story he had earlier told Dulan, letting them believe that he and Merin had been the only explorers to visit the ruins of Tathan, and that the *Kalina* was a small ship.

"I sense concealment," Tula said, "which you believe is for our benefit. Very well, I will accept as much as you want to tell us, while hoping that when you know us better, you will confide all. Your problem, as I perceive it, is to find a way to return to your own time and place. The only telepath I know who has power strong enough to help you is Saray."

"Can't we see her right away?" Herne asked. Tula shook his head.

"Arrangements must be made. Morning is soon enough. In the meantime, let us enjoy Dulan's hospitality, which is famous throughout Tathan."

They ate at a well-scrubbed wooden table in the kitchen, sitting upon wooden chairs with woven rush seats. The dishes and cutlery were simple, handmade shapes. There was a poached fish fresh from the sea, served with vegetables and homemade bread. They drank more of the beerlike beverage, which Dulan told them was called batreen.

"It is made by fermenting our excess grain after we have stored all we need for the winter or for seed in the following spring. Batreen is a means of preserving the leftover harvest rather than wasting it," Dulan said. "Those who drink too much too quickly do become inebriated for a short time, but there are no aftereffects and the brew itself is healthful."

Merin wondered if the cups of batreen she had drunk earlier in the day had helped to lower her inhibitions, thus allowing her to accept Herne's embraces. The place where he had entered her body still ached, but it was not an entirely unpleasant feeling. In fact, each time she looked at him she thought of what he had done to her and she wanted him to do it again. She wanted to rise from Dulan's table, to take Herne's hand and lead him back to their room, there to lie naked on the bed with him while he kissed and caressed her. She wanted to feel him moving deep inside her, thrusting, thrusting. . . . She picked up her cup of batreen and drained it.

It was not surprising that Oressian laws were so strict if this was the result of lovemaking, this almost uncontrollable desire to do it again and again. She saw Tula looking at her and remembered that he could sense emotion. He would know how much she wanted Herne. To protect her disgracefully lascivious thoughts from discovery, she forcefully banished Herne from her mind while pulling about herself the tattered barriers of her Oressian training. When she saw Tula's startled look she knew she had been successful. Thereafter she paid strict attention to the conversation, refusing to allow her mind to wander again.

Dulan and Tula talked about the founding of Tathan, the building of the settlement they proudly called a city. It was a peaceful place, they said, productive and self-sufficient, as all isolated colonies must be.

"Peaceful except for the disruptions caused by Saray," Herne said, returning to the subject that most interested him. "I gather you both feel her experiments could permanently divide your people."

"A problem with which we must deal soon, before Saray becomes so powerful that no one can stop her," said Dulan. "Perhaps it is our good fortune that you have come to us at this particular time. We can help each other. Tula and I will do all we can to assist you in your efforts to leave Tathan, while in return we ask you to add your voices to ours as we try to make Saray understand that what she is doing is wrong, and that she is causing serious conflicts among our citizens."

"Those of us old enough to recall the terrors inflicted upon telepaths by the Jurisdiction know that we must always stand together," Tula put in. "It is the younger folk, born here in peace and safety, who now would join Saray's experiments against the advice of their elders. We old ones know how divisive—and how dangerous to all of us—those experiments could be."

"Saray is not a wicked woman, but she is woefully misguided by Ananka," Dulan added.

"Your plan sounds reasonable to me," Herne said.

"Saray must know we are here," Merin remarked. "Why hasn't she come to see the results of her latest experiment?"

"It is my belief that the experiments exhaust her. She will need time to rest and recover her strength," Dulan replied.

"'Exhaust her,'" Merin repeated, thinking. "If that is so, perhaps we can make her see that these experiments could be physically dangerous for people who are not as telepathically strong as she. If she has any sense of responsibility at all, she won't want to lead others into harmful practices."

"Tell her that. Tell her whatever you think will help our joint cause," Tula urged. The meal finished, he rose to leave.

"May I walk with you?" Herne asked. "I don't like being confined. I want some exercise."

"You are not prisoners," Dulan said. "You may go wherever you wish. But the evening grows cold. You will need some covering."

"I'll go too," Merin said, not wanting to be parted from Herne.

"I will remain here, to make contact with one of Saray's servants and request an appointment. Tula will explain to you how to find your way back to this house." Dulan produced a woven jacket for Herne to wear and a striped shawl for Merin.

Merin was wearing her treksuit and had donned her coif before dinner, over Herne's objections. As soon as she stepped through the door she wrapped the shawl around her shoulders. The wind was surprisingly strong. She remembered that while they had been exploring the ruins of Tathan with Tarik a similar wind had swept down from the plateau every evening.

The streets were deserted, lit only by the silver glow of the twin moons.

"Doesn't anyone go out at night?" asked Herne.

"Dulan lives in a particularly quiet neighborhood," Tula said. "The central square is a lively place, especially on the night of a Gathering, as you will see tomorrow."

"How will your people react to our presence at the Gathering?" Merin asked. "When we walked through the city earlier today everyone ignored us as if we were invisible."

"They would have recognized you at once as Jurisdiction personnel," Tula said. "Even after a century in a safe place fear of the Jurisdiction remains. They were probably trying not to antagonize you. By tomorrow night all will know you have not come to Tathan with violent intentions.

"Now, here is my house, and I thank you for your escort. If you wish to return to Dulan's home by another route, walk to the end of the street and turn right. The path there will take you along the land that rises above the edge of the salt marsh. Dulan's house is the last one just before you reach the Gathering Hall. Good night, my friends. I will rejoin you in the morning."

They found the path with no difficulty. On their right as they walked were houses, each with wide windows or terraces arranged to take advantage of the view, each with an extensive garden. Lights shone in many windows, and here and there a torch flamed to illuminate a garden. Occasionally, they could hear the murmur of voices or the sound of laughter. With the houses sheltering them from the northwest wind that had gusted through the wide city streets, the air seemed warmer.

To their left and a little below the path lay the salt marsh, its grasses bending in the wind, an occasional pool or water channel touched with silver by the moons. Silver, too, were the distant sand dunes, which ran straight across the horizon till they merged into the sandbar that marked the eastern end of Tathan harbor.

"This is a nice place." Herne was walking beside Merin. "I like it here. Too bad it will all be destroyed soon."

"Nothing we can do will change that, Herne. The Cetans *will* come. At least we know Dulan and Tula will escape."

"I don't want to talk about any problems right now," he said. "I'm tired, and still not certain exactly what happened to us to bring us here. All I want to do for the next hour or so is enjoy the quiet and peace, and the view, and being with the woman I love."

He took her hand and they walked along in silence. Merin could think of at least half a dozen subjects they ought to be discussing while they were in the open with little chance of being overheard so long as they kept their voices low. But there was a magical quality to the night, with the moons riding high in a cloudless sky, the mingled scents of flowers and salt in the air, and the warmth of Herne's fingers enclosing her hand.

"I believe this must be happiness," she murmured, just before she tripped over a clump of grass. Herne caught her around the waist.

"You've had too much batreen," he accused her, laughing.

"I have no way of judging whether what you say is true or not. I have never been the least bit inebriated before," she admitted. "Will I now disgrace myself by singing or hiccuping?"

He gave a low chuckle, which ended when his mouth captured hers. The idea of kissing in the open air, where anyone might see them, would not have occurred to Merin. She found the experience shocking, exciting, and totally wonderful.

"From what Dulan said," Herne murmured a few minutes later, "the effects of batreen are pleasant, but they don't last long."

"That's a pity. I was beginning to enjoy myself." She was startled at her own words. She, who did not know how to tease anyone, was teasing Herne. With a sense of delicious freedom, she began to laugh. Herne laughed back at her. They stood a moment longer in the moonlight, with their arms around each other and laughter still on their lips, until he kissed the tip of her nose. Merin decided she wasn't inebriated at all. She was just a little light-headed and ridiculously happy to be so close to Herne.

He took her hand again and they continued walking. Now she became aware of an unfamiliar hollowness in the area of her stomach.

"Are you hungry?" she asked.

"Ravenous." He paused to lean toward her and nibble at her earlobe.

"Herne, I'm serious." She stopped walking, pulling back a little and looking up at him.

"I ate a lot more food tonight than I usually do. Every mouthful tasted delicious, a fact I noted with surprise because I ordinarily don't pay much attention to what I eat. But at this moment I feel as if I haven't eaten at all."

"Now that you mention it," Herne said, "I am hungry. Kissing you distracted me from my rumbling stomach."

"I don't think there was much substance to the meal we consumed," she told him. "Nor do I believe it was too much batreen that made me trip. I drank it because I was thirsty, and it did quench my thirst, but that was the only effect I noticed. However, I have had bouts of lightheadedness and dizzy spells ever since we were hit by lightning while we were still aboard the shuttlecraft."

"Perhaps it wasn't lightning," Herne said. "Perhaps that was the moment when we were transported to another time and place. I've experienced the same feelings of lightheadedness, but apparently not as severe as yours, and it does seem to be occurring less often. Do you think the dizziness made you trip, not the batreen? It's possible. The spells will probably fade away, as mine are doing."

"It would be a relief." They were walking once more, this time with Herne's arm around her. "I don't like the feeling of not being in control of my own body, not even for a minute."

"No?" There was laughter in his voice. Merin knew at once what he meant.

"That's different." From the sudden heat flooding her face, she felt certain she was blushing. She said what was in her heart. "Here in Tathan, the laws I have obeyed throughout my life don't seem at all important."

"I know. On Sibirna I would never dare to tell a woman I loved her. It would be a fatal admission of weakness. But here, I have told you, and will doubtless tell you again before the night is over. Whatever has happened to us, it's not all bad so long as we have each other."

They had reached Dulan's house. Behind it they could see the long white shape of the Gathering Hall. Dulan had left a lamp burning for them, and the door unlatched. The sitting room was empty.

"You said earlier that we should take turns standing watch," Merin reminded Herne.

"Right." He moved toward the guest quarters, Merin following him. "We ought to close the door too."

"Your tone of voice leads me to believe you are not entirely serious about our need to stay on guard," she chided.

"I am, but at the moment something else interests me more. You." He threw the bolt on the guestroom door. "I want to make love to you again. I think you want it too."

"My existence has been turned upside down," she said. "Everything I was taught now seems wrong to me. It's difficult to think clearly, especially when we touch."

"It's the same for me." He reached toward her, to draw her closer. She put her hands on his upper arms, keeping their bodies apart for a little longer while she tried to understand the sudden differences in her thought patterns.

"Herne, when we came together before did it hurt you? Please be honest."

"I wouldn't call it pain," he said. "It was a little uncomfortable for me at first, because you were obviously untouched and your entrance was unusually tight. Believe me, there is no man in the universe who would consider it a fault in his woman that she came to him completely innocent. You can also trust me when I say neither of us should feel anything but pleasure from now on."

"Am I your woman, now that we have lain together?"

"For as long as you want to be. I hope forever."

Once more Merin felt as though everything she knew had been turned around. She had always been taught that the forbidden act she and Herne had committed was hideously painful, that there would be great loss of blood along with permanent, debilitating damage to the bodies of both partners. But Herne had apparently suffered only a moment of discomfort, while her own pain, though sharp and prolonged and accompanied by some bleeding, had ended in unexpected delight. And they were both obviously still healthy. It was easy for her to reach the only possible conclusion from all this.

For reasons she did not understand, she and everyone else on Oressia had been told lies about the act of love. If her teachers had lied about one subject, they might well have lied about other matters also. She had been betrayed by those whom she had trusted completely. The realization made her feel ill. It also made her determined to deal honestly with others, especially with Hernc, who was dearer to her than anyone else had ever been, and who had not lied to her.

"I sat at Dulan's table tonight," she told him, "thinking about what we had done together, and wanting to do it again."

"Then we had identical thoughts." His quiet voice ignited a fire inside her. She offered him the one gift she had left to give.

"Would you remove my coif?" He could not possibly know that no one was ever allowed to remove an Oressian's coif, to look at another person's hair, not even in death, but he seemed to understand the solemnity of her request.

"I would be honored." He unfastened the chinstrap, then lifted the stiff white fabric off her head. Beneath it her hair was tightly coiled and pinned. She bent her head so he could loosen it. He combed through it with both hands, releasing it into curls and delicate tendrils, till her face was like a pale flower set in a mass of gleaming dark brown and gold. Herne caught his breath at the sight.

"My dear love," he said, "thank you for trusting me enough to let me do this."

With her hair freed from its strict restraint, Merin was able to answer the question he had asked when they first entered their bedchamber.

"Make love to me, Herne." Smiling at him, she opened the neck of her treksuit.

Solemnity suddenly gone, he tore at his own suit, pulling his arms out of the sleeves. Wanting the sensation of his skin against hers, she turned her back and quickly removed all of her clothing, then went to the bed. He moved behind her to run his hands up along her spine and down her sides. She leaned back against his chest to let him reach around and play with her breasts and stroke her abdomen and down between her thighs, while he kissed the nape of her neck, her shoulders, her throat. His hands moved further, pressing, probing, exciting her beyond endurance. He was doing the most incredible things to her, and she could tell by his quickened breathing that his passion was growing as fast as her own, yet when she pulled away he let her go. She lay down upon the bed and stretched out her legs. To her surprise, it did not embarrass her to have him watch her movements with devouring eyes. The need that had been growing within her all during the evening could no longer be controlled. Innocent as she still was, she did not know how to indicate what she wanted, except to simply say the words.

"Come." She opened her arms to him. "I want you inside me right now."

He was as gentle as he had been the first time, which was a good thing, for Merin knew an instant of jabbing pain—but only an instant and then all was soaring delight. Her tongue was in his mouth, his manhood was deep inside her, and the exquisite madness was upon her again. She went rigid, poised at the brink of an ecstacy nothing could prevent, then sailed bravely out into empty space with him, fearing nothing so long as Herne was with her.

Afterward she slept deeply, lying on her side with her hands at her face like a child. Herne pulled himself up to sit with his head against the wall, keeping watch, protecting his love in case of danger. Moonlight shone upon her through the open window. Even in the silvery light her hair showed brown and gold, with glints of red. Herne picked up a strand, twisting it around his finger.

She had been so innocent that she hadn't entirely understood exactly what they were doing the first time they had made love. Still, for all her innocence, she was the most passionate woman he had ever known. He wanted to cherish her, to guard her and keep her safe for the rest of their lives. His chronic anger, his constant irritation with the daily frustrations and difficulties of life, had vanished, absorbed into the vast expanse of his growing love for her. It was as though there had been a gaping, ugly wound in his soul, and Merin had healed it. He felt completed by her, a whole man for the first time in his life.

He knew they might not be able to return to their own time. They might both die here at Tathan when the inevitable Cetan attack came. If necessary, he would give his life to protect her. Whatever finally happened to them, he would always be grateful to her for the happiness and the new peace she had brought him. And nothing could ever make him stop loving her.

Chapter Twelve

"We are to meet Saray at midmorning," Dulan told Merin and Herne when they gathered for the first meal of the day. Tula, who was to go to Saray's house with them, arrived soon after. He had brought their transportation, a wooden cart painted bright blue and yellow, drawn by paired black Denebian ixak.

"So this is where you get your leather." Herne appraised the prancing beasts with a knowing eye.

"Ours is not so fine as true Denebian leather," Tula said, "but it is adequate for our needs."

"How many ixak did you bring with you?" Herne asked, adding to Merin, "It's no wonder Denebian leather is so expensive. The

Denebians have a near monopoly on it because ixak are notoriously difficult to transport. When I was a boy there were only a dozen ixak on all of Sibirna."

"We lost fifty out of eighty animals during our travels," Dulan informed them. "Fortunately, most of the survivors were female, so we were able to mate them to the remaining males as soon as we arrived, and the herd has grown steadily. They provide meat for those of us who choose to eat animal products, their hides are tanned into leather, as Herne has noted, and their sharp-edged horns make excellent cutting tools. We turn their hooves into glue and grind their bones into a powder that is used to make both pottery and mortar. There is little in the ixak that is not valuable to us."

"Best of all," said Tula, holding the reins tightly to keep the animals under control, "is their willingness to pull heavy loads over long distances."

Dulan and Tula climbed into the front seat of the cart, with Tula driving. Merin and Herne sat in the back seat. They were comfortable enough while moving slowly along the paved streets of Tathan, but once they had left the town and were heading northward across a treeless plain, Tula urged the ixak into a faster pace. It was a bumpy ride over a rutted country road. Merin held tight to the side of the cart to keep herself from being thrown about, and Herne did the same on his side. The two telepaths, accustomed to this form of transportation, did not seem to mind the lack of springs or of padding for the wooden seats.

"There is the River Tath on our left," said Dulan, waving a hand in that direction. "North of the city the land begins to rise as we approach the cliffs. Half a day's journey beyond Saray's house is the quarry where all our stone is cut. The stone is floated down the Tath to the city on barges."

It took about an hour to reach Saray's house, which was built on a slight rise overlooking the river. A servant was waiting for them at the entrance, to show them to Saray.

The rooms through which they passed were decorated in white, pale green, and silver. All were open and airy, sheltered from sun and wind by the surrounding garden, planted with trees and white flowers. They came out of the house onto a sun-dappled terrace, where a small fountain played. In the pool beneath the splashing water blue and black fish darted, searching for food. White stone benches were set about the terrace. On one of them sat a black-and-white cat, and a woman with long black hair. The woman rose as her visitors approached.

"I am honored that my old teacher comes to me for help," she said, looking toward Dulan. "What is it you wish of me?"

"I think you know," said Dulan.

"Good day to you, Tula." Saray smiled at him. "Who are these strangers?"

"Merin and Herne." Tula sounded annoyed, as if he thought Saray was playing with him. "Thanks to you, they arrived at Tathan unwillingly, out of time, out of place. It is your duty to return them at once, after which we expect you to cease these outrageous experiments."

"Gently, Tula." Dulan put out a restraining hand. "Saray is not one to be forced into anything."

"Dear Dulan," said Saray. "Always patient, always slow to change."

"Some changes are best not made," said Dulan.

With the black-and-white cat trailing after her, Saray approached Merin and Herne. She was a gracefully slender woman, but older than Merin had first thought. Seen from a nearer perspective, there were fine lines about her dark eyes, and a softness to the outline of chin and throat that suggested approaching middle age. But there was no gray in the straight black hair that hung almost to her waist, and her white gown was fastened at her shoulders with round gold brooches in a style that made it clear how firm and smooth her upper arms still were. Her feet were bare. She wore twin bracelets of gold strands twisted together to look like rope and tied into a knot at each wrist.

Merin glanced at Herne and saw that he had noticed too. Saray's jewelry was more finely made, but in style it was identical to the twin bracelets of a High Priest that Osiyar had worn when he had first arrived at Tarik's colony.

"Do you call yourself a High Priestess?" Herne asked.

"Others do." Saray responded with a look of astonishment at the abrupt question. "I do not. I am but a conduit for the power of Ananka."

"From what I've heard and experienced," Herne told her, "you have great power yourself."

"Why do you ask if I am a High Priestess?" Saray inquired.

"We count among our friends a telepath who was a High Priest in a different settlement on this world. He wore bracelets like yours."

"I am pleased to hear you say this." Saray flashed a triumphant look in Dulan's direction. "Will you believe me now, old teacher, that my efforts will have meaning far beyond your lifetime or mine?"

"What I believe or do not believe is not the issue here," Dulan replied. "Your thoughtless experiment has harmed these good people by removing them from their friends and all they know. What you and Ananka do that does not affect others is not our concern. But now you have begun to harm the innocent and the unwilling. That we cannot allow."

"Do not threaten me, Dulan. My power is greater than yours."

"While you were my pupil," Dulan told her, "I tried to instill in you a sense of moral obligation as well as telepathic strength. Talent such as yours carries with it the responsibility to balance it against the temptations of unbridled power."

"You accuse me of immorality, of irresponsibility?" Saray looked stunned. "I have merely followed the dictates of my teacher, who advised me always to test the boundaries of my skills."

"To every skill there are limits beyond which it is unwise to reach," Tula said.

"I would expect that from you," sneered Saray. "You, who cannot control your own detection of the emotions of others, who have but minimal telepathic talent."

"Tula had talent enough to cause him to be banished from the Jurisdiction along with your parents and the rest of us," Dulan snapped. "Saray, we are not here to quarrel, but to find solutions to mutual problems. We ask your help for Merin and Herne."

"I am aware of no problems that we have in common," Saray said disdainfully. "And what you call a request sounded more like a demand to me."

"Saray." Seeing the flash of rising anger in the woman's dark eyes, Merin decided she ought to make her feelings known instead of letting others speak for her. "Herne and I do not belong in Tathan. We want to go home."

"And you believe I can send you there? How flattering." Saray transferred her attention from Dulan and Tula to Merin.

"You brought us here. Only you can see us safely back again," Merin insisted, boldly meeting Saray's gaze.

"I did not do it alone," Saray admitted. "I needed Ananka's strength to carry out this most daring of all my experiments."

"Now that you have proven your ability to overcome the barriers of time, it seems to me that the necessary next step would be to reverse your experiment. You can have no other use for Herne and me." Merin kept her eyes on Saray's and held her breath, hoping.

"An eminently reasonable scientific proposal. I will consider your request," Saray said. Then, looking at Herne, she asked, "Does Merin speak for you? Do you wish to leave Ananka and the delights she has to offer in order to accompany Merin?"

"I love Merin." Herne replied without hesitation, his prompt and sincere words ending a moment of anguish for Merin, making clear his preference for her over the mysterious attractions of Ananka. "Wherever Merin is, I will be at her side."

"I think Ananka will not be pleased." The corners of Saray's mouth pulled downward. "Still, because Merin has made a polite request of me instead of commanding me as these two who claim to be my friends have done, I will confer with Ananka on the matter."

"When may we expect an answer from you?" asked Tula with more than a little impatience.

"The answer will not come from me, but from Ananka. When I have learned it I will convey it to you," Saray responded. "May I offer you food and drink after your journey?"

The question was a rhetorical one, for servants had already appeared bearing trays of fruit and delicate pastries, pitchers of cool water, and the ever-present batreen. Feeling desperately hungry in spite of having eaten a large morning meal, Merin eagerly accepted several pieces of fruit, some pastry, and a goblet of water. She saw that Herne was eating heartily too.

"Will you attend the Gathering tonight?" Saray sat down next to Merin.

"Dulan has offered to take us," Merin said.

"A Gathering is always an important and formal occasion," Saray noted. "Have you anything else to wear?"

Merin suppressed an impolite urge to remind Saray that, thanks to her efforts, both Merin and Herne had arrived in Tathan with only the clothing they wore.

"Since I see by your coif that you are an Oressian, you will want a head covering as well as a gown." Saray stood, holding out a hand. "We will find something more fitting to the occasion than that uniform."

"I see nothing wrong with my treksuit." Stubbornly, Merin remained seated on the bench.

"If you intend a deliberate insult to all those who will be present in their finest garments, then wear it."

Saray did not enter Merin's mind. There was nothing like the prickling sensation that had accompanied Osiyar's joining with Merin's thoughts. Still, she felt the compulsion of a powerful will. It was irresistible. Without a backward glance at her companions, Merin followed Saray into the house, to a bedchamber of white and pale green like all the other rooms she had seen, lit by silver lamps, with gauzy white curtains blowing across wide-open windows.

The cat had prowled silently behind Saray. Now it jumped into the middle of the spotless white bed, where it sat upright, watching the women. Merin felt herself released from the power Saray had exerted over her movements.

"Why did you do that?" she asked Saray. "There was no need to compel me."

"You would have wasted time in a foolish argument, which I would have won in the end," Saray said, "because if you think about it in a reasonable way, you will agree that I am right about this. It would be inexcusably rude of you to greet all of Tathan in that outfit."

"I have no intention of greeting all of Tathan," Merin said. "I will stand quietly at one side of the hall to watch what happens."

"And vanish into the background? Is that how you protect yourself? I wonder that Herne ever noticed you." Saray looked her over from head to foot with an expression that was not at all unfriendly. "You aren't bad-looking. You just need a little help. Now, let me see what I can find that you might wear tonight."

"Saray, I am not interested in this frivolity. Herne and I have one concern only—to return to our ship and to our own time."

"I am not being frivolous. Love is the most serious subject there is. Do you want to keep Herne interested in you or not?" Saray laughed. "I have just the thing, and it has a matching headdress, so you cannot refuse to wear it." With that, she vanished into the next room.

Having made up her mind that she was absolutely not going to wear clothing chosen for her by Saray, Merin walked to the window, pulling back the curtains a little to look out at the green-and-white garden and the river. She could hear the sound of Herne's voice coming from the other side of the house, followed by Dulan's low, scratchy tones.

A sound behind her made her leave the window, thinking that Saray had returned. It was not Saray. The cat was gone, and in its place on the bed sat a woman, her eyes fixed on Merin. She was almost transparent, the edges of her shape wavering a little.

It was like looking into a slightly clouded mirror or the surface of still water. The woman wore a flowing white gown, a short gold cloak was wrapped across her shoulders, and her face was Merin's face. In three details only did this apparition differ from Merin. Her curling hair was a light golden brown. She had no scar on her right cheek. And though Merin could not clearly see the color of her eyes, she had the impression that they were some other shade than her own.

There was the sound of something dropping in the next room and a muttered exclamation from Saray. Merin looked toward the door, then, not seeing Saray, looked back to the bed.

The woman was gone. Where she had been, the black-and-white cat sat once more. Merin took a step toward the bed. The cat arched its back, hissing at her, then leapt off the bed and ran out of the room.

Shaking, Merin sank down onto a corner of the mattress. There was continued clatter from the next room, along with disjointed comments from Saray, indicating that she was having difficulty finding what she wanted. Merin was glad for the delay. It gave her a few minutes to compose herself. By the time Saray appeared once more, Merin was the very picture of Oressian reticence, eyes lowered, emotional barriers firmly in place. But behind the facade she was still so upset that she meekly accepted the costume of shining green and glittering jewels that Saray now pressed upon her, and promised she would wear it.

"It's lovely. Thank you." Merin scarcely glanced at the outfit.

"And these cosmetics too." Saray was so concerned with deciding how Merin should look that she seemed completely unaware of Merin's distress. "Use just a little of this powder on your cheeks, the cream on your lips, and paint around your eyes with this brush. The dress has been stored in khata wood, so you won't need perfume." Saray was packing all of these supplies and the dress into a wooden box as she spoke.

"You are very kind." Merin rose from the bed, relieved to find her legs would support her. She took the box Saray handed to her. "Will you also attend the Gathering?"

"I will appear. I am certain Dulan will have admonishing words to speak about my experiments. I will want to answer them in a way that will calm my friends. It seems I have become the cause of much dissension in Tathan." Saray's hand touched Merin's shoulder. "I am not your enemy. I am truly sorry for what has happened to you and Herne. For reasons of her own, Ananka deliberately chose the two of you to be the subjects of our most ambitious attempt. I will do what I can to convince her to help you, but you must exercise patience. Tula and Dulan seem to think I can simply order

Ananka to do something and it will be done. It's not that way at all. We work together, by merging our different abilities, and we cannot do it often, because for a long time afterward we have no power left. The experiments Dulan fears so much are rare events."

"I wish they had been rarer still," said Merin.

Chapter Thirteen

They had almost reached Tathan on their return trip before Merin could bring herself to speak about what had happened in Saray's room.

"You were more right than you realized, Dulan," she said. "Saray told me the experiments exhaust not only her, but Ananka as well."

"I hoped when you went off alone with her," Herne said, "that you would discover just this sort of useful information."

"I was compelled to go with her, but I don't mind," Merin told him, "because I saw Ananka."

"You what?" Herne stared at her. Dulan turned completely around on the front seat. Tula dropped the reins in his astonishment, thus allowing the ixak to run free. They immediately broke into a fast trot, perhaps scenting their stables and evening food. Before Tula had them under control again they were racing down the main thoroughfare of Tathan. It was not until both cart and ixak had been returned to the stable and Tula had rejoined his companions in Dulan's sitting room that the others began to question Merin.

"Where did you see Ananka?" Herne asked.

"If I am correct," Merin told them all, "you saw her too. I believe the cat was Ananka in disguise."

"Tell us everything," Dulan urged, taking the chair nearest the fire.

"Saray left me alone while she found clothing for me," Merin said. "When I turned around instead of the cat sitting on the bed a woman was there. When Saray made a noise the woman vanished and the cat reappeared. It hissed at me and ran away."

"What did the woman look like?" Tula regarded her with wide eyes.

"Like me," Merin told him, "except her hair was lighter."

"Remarkable," Tula breathed.

"Exactly what I would expect," said Dulan. "Herne, you have mentioned before that when you first saw Ananka she looked much like Merin."

"I only noticed the resemblance later," Herne amended the story, "after I had looked more closely at Merin. I didn't really see her in those days."

"When Ananka first appeared to you," Dulan asked, "had you been thinking of Merin?"

"Yes." Herne spoke slowly, recalling that now remote scene by the campfire. "I was wishing she would remove her blasted coif so I could see what color her hair was."

"Did you have a mental image of her hair?"

"I thought it must be light brown," Herne said. "But I was wrong. It is actually much darker."

"Ananka did not know the real color of Merin's hair, either," Dulan pointed out, "because Ananka took the image of Merin out of your thoughts, and showed herself to you as the Merin you imagined."

"No wonder she looked so familiar. But when I went to her in the grotto later that night— when I—we—damnation!" Herne stopped, his face growing red. "Was it a real creature I saw and touched, or was it all an illusion?"

"We do not understand Ananka's full powers," Dulan said.

"That answer is no help to me at all." Herne looked so miserable that Merin reached out to take his hand.

"You could no more have stopped what happened in that grotto," she told him, "than I could have refused to go with Saray today. There are some things humans cannot resist."

"I thought I wanted her," Herne said, "because I wanted you without knowing it. I understand that now, but still, what I did—"

"It's all right." Fortified by the way he had told Saray it was Merin he loved, she was able to smile at him. "It doesn't matter now. I understand. I'm not angry."

"Tarik said it must have been an illusion." Herne's eyes were locked on Merin's face. He was totally concentrated on her, forgetting the others in the room. "Tarik was so sure of it that he made me certain too."

"Tarik?" Dulan's sharp voice made them both jump. "This is the second time today you have mentioned other people. Herne, you two were not alone on this world, were you?"

"No." The stark word brought a gasp from Tula and a stiffening of Dulan's robed figure.

"You led us to believe an untruth," accused Dulan.

"We were trying to protect our friends," Herne said. "We weren't sure you could be trusted, and we didn't know how extensive you power might be. I wasn't even sure you were real."

"And now?" asked Dulan.

"I still don't know what to think about how we found ourselves here," Herne admitted. "But I do believe that you are honestly trying to help us, so I will tell you that there were ten others with us, two of them descendants of your own people who joined our colony after we arrived.

We are all living in your building far north of here, on an island in a lake. We call it Home."

"At Lake Rhyadur? You have moved into our private retreat, the place most truly my home on this planet?" Dulan paused, apparently overcome by strong emotion.

"In their time," Tula said to Dulan, "we are dead for hundreds of years, old friend. Should we care if someone else lives in our rooms after we have gone?"

"You are buried there," Merin said. "Both of you."

"How do you know this?" Dulan asked.

"By your own words." It was Herne who answered. "You kept a notebook. Our leader, Tarik, found it. Your mate is there too. It seems you all died of extreme old age."

"Well, then." Dulan's head was bowed. "A peaceful death, with loved ones near. A final resting place at Rhyadur, where my heart lies. Thank you for telling me."

"There's more," Merin said. "We call this world Dulan's Planet. That is the official Jurisdiction name."

There was a laugh from beneath the blue hood, a hoarse, choked sound that broke suddenly into a clear peal of pure mirth. On Tula's round face a look of startled delight appeared.

"Fair enough," said Dulan. "In the Jurisdiction I lost a world that should have been mine to rule because I was born a telepath. It's only fitting for the Jurisdiction to give me back a world. What matter if it's a posthumous honor?"

Merin insisted on dressing in private for the Gathering. She waited until Herne had bathed and donned the robe Tula had brought for him to wear. It was a soft gray-brown in color, trimmed in silver, and loosely made like the robes worn by Tula and Dulan, with long full sleeves and a hood, which Herne wore thrown back into a cowl. His ash-brown hair was still a little damp from his bath. Without a supply of the pills that kept his beard from growing, he had been forced to shave with a razor. There was a tiny nick on one side of his jaw. To Merin he was remarkably handsome, even if he looked pale and tired, with the harsh planes of his face drawn and tense.

"I hope there are refreshments at this Gathering," he said. "I'm hungry."

"We just ate with Dulan." She laughed at his words, dismissing the hollow feeling in her own stomach.

"Nothing I eat seems to fill me," he said. His hands were at the chinstrap of her coif, unfastening it. "Aren't you hungry?"

"In all of Tathan there is only one thing that fills me," she murmured, reaction to his touch stirring deep inside her, "and leaves me satisfied too."

"You, my dear, are rapidly becoming a

galaxy-class tease." He grinned at her. "Who would have thought the cold and self-controlled Merin of just a few days ago could turn into such a passionate woman in so short a time?" The coif was off now and his hands were stroking through her hair, pulling it down out of the tight coils and over her shoulders.

"I don't understand what has happened to me." She sighed. "I never dreamed of feeling like this, of wanting another person so badly that I can't think about anything else."

He had unfastened the opening of her treksuit down to her waist. His hands were on her breasts. Merin felt the passionate heat begin to rise in her. In another moment or two she would not be able to stop what was certain to happen between them, and neither would he. She pulled away.

"There isn't time for this," she protested. "I have to bathe and dress."

"Are you refusing me?" He sounded stern, but when she met his gray eyes they were filled with laughter.

"Never," she promised, sliding her hands along his chest, down toward his thighs, pausing at a crucial spot, smiling into his eyes all the while. "It's only a postponement. Later, after the Gathering is over, when we are in this room again with the rest of the night before us, then we will taste passion and I'll make the waiting up to you. You won't regret the delay."

"I was wrong," he said. "You aren't a tease at all. My dearest, you rank as one of the great seductresses of all time."

"An Oressian seductress?" The idea made her laugh.

"That's one of the reasons why I love you so much," he told her, turning serious. "You are a mass of fascinating contradictions. You could even forgive what I did with Ananka. I don't know of another woman who would excuse that stupid mistake."

In a gesture that was rapidly becoming familiar to her, he kissed the tip of her nose. She watched him walk to the door, her eyes filling with tears of love. He had enlarged her heart with tenderness and joy beyond anything she had ever imagined was possible. He paused at the door to look back at her.

"While we are at the Gathering we ought to be watching and listening for any information that might help us to find our way home," he said. "But even while I appear to be concentrating on other subjects, I won't stop thinking about you for a moment, or fantasizing about the things we'll do when we are alone together. Now, get dressed. And as you put on each garment, imagine what I'll do as I remove it later."

She almost called him back. She almost told him to forget about the Gathering, the waiting telepaths, Saray, Ananka, everything but their love. All she wanted was Herne in her arms, kissing her, his hands on her skin, his rough voice speaking passionate words. She had to force herself not to tear open the bedchamber door and go after him. Instead, she made herself walk into the bathing room and pull off her treksuit while the water ran into the tub. And when she sank into the warm, fragrant suds she thought about sinking onto the bed in the next room, with Herne on top of her and his hot love surrounding her.

She rinsed in the coldest water the pipes could produce. She reminded herself over and over again that she had a duty to perform this evening. For Herne's sake, as well as her own, she had to be prepared to seize upon any fact that would help them return to their own time.

The gown Saray had given Merin was made of a green so dark it was almost black, a floor-length, long-sleeved column of tiny pleats that clung to her figure, swaying and rippling when she moved. The only decorations on the dress were the golden band set with green and blue jewels that edged the high, round neckline, and a matching sash that wrapped just below her breasts. It was a design as demurely covered as any Oressian robe, yet because of the way the pleats folded and unfolded with every breath or motion, it was scandalously revealing. The tantalizing fragrance of khata wood that wafted from the fabric only added to the seductiveness of the gown. The headdress was made of golden fabric thickly sewn with jewels of blue, green, and purple. It was uncomfortably heavy, but it did cover all of Merin's hair.

She applied the cosmetics Saray had provided, using a narrow brush to paint a silvery-black line around her eyes, rubbing pale pink on her cheeks and a darker shade on her lips. She had not planned to use these artifices—they were entirely unnatural to an Oressian—but when she looked into the bathing room mirror her face stared back at her as pale and tightly drawn as Herne's had seemed to her earlier. Her spells of lightheadedness had diminished somewhat, but she felt tired and listless, and oddly weak. And hungry. Always hungry, ever since she had arrived at Tathan. She was used to eating little. Gluttony was not a vice permitted to Oressians, and she had always been even more abstemious than her Oressian companions. Yet now she constantly craved food. She wondered if vigorous lovemaking could create such an unceasing need to eat. She decided to ask Herne about it later.

When she appeared in Dulan's sitting room Herne's reaction to her costume was all that any woman could have wanted.

"Spectacular. Glorious. Beautiful," he said, walking around her slowly, to take it all in. "Best of all, beneath that glitter is my Merin. I'm almost afraid to touch you for fear I'll disarrange something or smear the paint, but later,

234

my dear—" His glowing eyes completed the sentence he had left unfinished. His hand was warm when it enclosed her fingers.

Dulan arrived, robed and hooded in severely plain dark red, and Tula, in bright green trimmed with gold embroidery. Both paused to consider the appearance of their guests.

"Most appropriate," murmured Dulan.

"My dear friend, I protest," said Tula, laughing. "This is something more than merely appropriate. Merin, Herne, you look splendid. I am proud to escort you to our most important event."

"You haven't told us yet what will happen tonight," said Herne.

"The Gathering Hall is the place where the telepaths and the Chon meet, to communicate with each other," Dulan explained.

"Do you mean the birds will be there?" asked Merin, glancing toward the windows. "But it is almost evening. I thought birds went to sleep at sunset."

"Every thirty-two days, on the single night when both moons are completely full," Dulan said, "we mingle with the Chon in memory of our first meeting. We were newly arrived on this world then, living in tents or sleeping in the open, still weary after our long journey and uncertain of our ultimate destiny. That night, just as the sun set and the full twin moons rose, changing a dark world back into almost daylike brightness, the Chon who live in the

cliffs north of Tathan came to us. I can still see
the scene in my mind, still recall the brilliant
colors flashing in the last rays of the sun. All
that green and blue, dazzling the eye. Then
came the joyous knowledge that these were
creatures with whom we could communicate.

"We built the Gathering Hall," Dulan told
them, "so we would have a permanent location
in which to meet the Chon, who after that first
night have come to us in large numbers whenever both moons are full. We meet individually
or in small groups at almost any time, but the
Gatherings are special occasions."

"You still haven't explained what will happen
this evening," Herne protested.

"But I have," said Dulan. "We gather with the
Chon."

"Is that all? Just gather? Then why do you
need us to be there?"

"Tonight your situation will be discussed,"
Dulan said.

"We hope," Tula added, "to convince certain
of our friends to add their voices to our appeal
to Saray, to beg her to return you to your
home."

"It is time," Dulan said. "We mustn't be late."

Merin and Herne followed the two telepaths
out of Dulan's house and along the alley to
the small door that led to the Gathering Hall.
Behind the door the garden lay green and
fragrant. Merin had paused to exclaim over a
particularly lovely white blossom when Herne

236

touched her hand, then pointed upward.

The sky was pink and gold with sunset. A few brilliant streamers of gold-tinged clouds drifted across Merin's line of vision. She thought at first that her eyes were reacting to the combination of bright color and concentrated light, until she realized the dots she was seeing were not a visual distortion; they were birds.

The Chon came silently, on softly fluttering wings, filling Gathering Hall and garden, their jewel-like blue and green bodies seeming to shine with an inner light.

The huge double doors to the Gathering Hall had been thrown wide open. From where she stood Merin could see the interior, where more Chon mingled with brightly robed telepaths. She was not frightened; she knew the birds were friendly creatures. But she was dazed by color, movement, the rustle of feathers, the footsteps of the many telepaths, and she sensed a vibration in the air, which she believed was caused by the telepathic communications now going on between the birds and their hosts.

"How beautiful," she murmured as Herne's hand clasped hers, drawing her toward the doors. They entered the Gathering Hall directly behind Dulan and Tula.

"Now we know why it was built so large," she said, "and why half of it is open to the sky."

"I have seen this before," Herne told her. "Once, at Home, when a Chon touched me for a second or two, I saw this scene. And you were

237

the woman who stood beside me."

"Remarkable." Tula had heard him. "We know the birds have long ancestral memories, which are passed from generation to generation, but you have no telepathic ability."

"I was unhappy," Herne said. "Perhaps the bird wanted to comfort me. Osiyar thought so."

The crowd had separated to make way for their little group. As they walked toward the center of the Hall, Merin could see that Dulan, born to be a ruler on another world yet banished from it because of an involuntary and perhaps unwanted talent, had become a respected and important person on this planet. Following in the wake of Dulan and Tula, she noticed polite bows, heard pleasant greetings exchanged between their escorts and the other telepaths. She quickly became aware of the intense curiosity directed toward herself and Herne.

Ordinarily, she would have been frightened to be the object of so many direct and assessing looks. But Herne's fingers curved around hers. With him next to her she felt safe, and she was learning to trust Dulan and Tula. Thus she was able to look back at telepaths and at birds with as much open interest as they displayed toward her.

She was amazed at the racial diversity represented within the Hall. She turned her head at the sound of a hissing breath, to meet the triangular, milky eyes of a scaly-skinned female

Styxian, who politely acknowledged her look. Merin bowed back in wonder. On any other world a Styxian would have torn out her throat before asking her name.

After that encounter it came as no surprise to her to see a pale gray Denebian, or even a stiff, antennaed Jugarian, who actually smiled at her. A Demarian who looked remarkably like Tarik, with pale skin, black hair, and midnight blue eyes, moved aside to let Dulan's party pass. It was then, as those around them changed position, that Merin saw a one-armed Cetan.

He had dark brown hair, worn long in the Cetan style, and an unruly brown beard that could not entirely hide the terrible scar disfiguring his face. Merin could easily imagine that a telepathic Cetan would have to fight again and again for his very life among his fiercely warlike fellows, and he probably had finally fled his homeworld in order to save that life. He stood now with his single hand resting upon the bosom of a blue Chon. The two were obviously in deep communication, for they took no notice of anyone near them, and the Cetan's attitude was one of profound peace.

Merin's fascinated study of the crowd filling the Hall was interrupted when Herne tugged at her hand, pulling her forward to stand beside him at the pedestal of the golden Chon statue. The Hall grew still, those present turning toward them.

"We welcome to our company tonight," Tula

began, raising his voice to be better heard, "visitors from a far world, who have come to us in friendship."

"There's no friendship from the Jurisdiction for telepaths," called a voice from the crowd. Merin could not see the speaker.

"Drive them out!" shouted someone else.

"No, kill them so they can't tell anyone where we've settled," cried another voice. This idea was roundly cheered by a small group on the far side of the Hall.

"Those are Saray's friends," Tula murmured to Merin. "They are few in number, and most of us do not agree with them." But when he tried to speak again the angry shouts of those few drowned his words.

"Stop this at once!" Dulan's voice, that peculiar scratchy sound that gave no indication as to gender or age, carried above the clamor. "This is a peaceful Gathering, not a place for dispute. How can telepaths, who are victims of a terrible persecution, who have been forced to find safety in a dangerous and uncharted part of the galaxy, condemn lost strangers simply because they are unknown to you?"

"Did you think we wouldn't recognize them if you put them into familiar clothing?" demanded a dark-haired young man who now strode forward out of the crowd. "Any true telepath can smell Jurisdiction blood from a light-year away. I say, kill them now, before they bring the Jurisdiction Service here to wipe us out."

"Your enthusiasm does you credit, Hotan." Saray stepped around the corner of the pedestal. "But enthusiasm is not a sufficient excuse for murder."

"Saray. Saray." The crowd began to separate, leaving a widening space near the statue. The Chon moved with the telepaths, like them splitting into two groups.

"There before you is the division in our society," said Tula to Merin.

It was easy to see what he meant. On the one side, ranged with Tula, Dulan, Herne, and herself, were most of the telepaths. Some of the older ones had missing limbs or obvious scars and a few were hooded like Dulan, most bearing mute witness to the brutality of the old Jurisdiction law prohibiting telepathy. Apparently, the persecution to which they had been subjected and their long journey to this world had produced odd combinations, for the one-armed Cetan, his hand still resting lightly on the blue Chon's breast, stood next to the Styxian, seemingly on friendly terms with her.

On the other side of the Hall was a small, unruly faction made up mostly of young people, including several argumentative Jugarians, their antennae bristling and bright red with excitement. Within this group there was a knot of brawny males of several Races, all rather dusty looking, whom Merin thought were probably the quarry workers, and another group in bare feet who wore what looked like sailors'

241

outfits. Quickly, Merin assessed them all with a professional eye.

"So it has been throughout history," she said to Tula, responding to his remark. "In every dynamic society there are always divisions between generations and professions. As we see demonstrated here, frequently they clash."

"That may be excellent historical theory," Tula replied in a nervous voice, while pressing himself more firmly against the stone pedestal at his back, "but it won't help us if they become violent. Let us hope Saray can control her adherents."

Into the empty space left when the telepaths drew apart Saray now stepped, and those in the Gathering Hall grew quiet to hear what she would say. She created a dramatic picture, gowned in glittery black-and-silver fabric draped upon one shoulder to leave the other shoulder and both arms bare, her only jewelry the gold rope bracelets on each wrist. Her straight black hair streamed down her back. Her face was pale, her dark eyes large.

"These strangers are not to be harmed," Saray declared. When an angry muttering began among the younger faction she raised both arms, silencing them once more. "Only fools resort to violence before they understand a situation."

"We are wise enough to rid ourselves of Jurisdiction agents before they can harm us," objected the dark young man who had called for immediate death for Merin and Herne. He took a menacing step toward Saray. "Who is going to protect us when the Jurisdiction Service arrives, fully armed? Will these old men and women on the other side of the Hall help us then, or will they bow their heads and let themselves be killed, and we, their children, too?"

"Hotan, my friend, you do not understand," Saray said. "It was I who brought Merin and Herne to Tathan."

"You have conducted another experiment?" Hotan regarded her with awe. "Is it possible then? What you have been promising us is true?"

"You see these two here as proof of my success," Saray told him, flinging out an arm toward Merin and Herne. "No longer need we remain bound to one time or place. Anywhere in the universe that we desire to visit, any time past, present or future, is open to us. All we need to do is strengthen our powers."

Now the scaly Styxian stepped forward to face Saray.

"Thisss isss wrong," she hissed. "You know it. Not every telepath hasss your skillsss. Desist, SSSaray, before you destroy us all by tearing apart the very fabric of time!"

"You may be content to live bound by the ancient rules of telepaths," Saray said. "Younger and braver folk are not."

"Imra is right." The one-armed Cetan had moved to stand beside his Styxian friend. The blue Chon came with him. "We all know there are limits beyond which even the most skilled telepath cannot go. Repeated experiments of the kind you have attempted can only result in madness and death."

"Does Saray look mad to you, Jidak?" asked Hotan, who was now standing with Saray to confront the Cetan and the Styxian. "Her experiment has succeeded. That is all the proof we need."

"Saray has admitted to Dulan that she required the help of Ananka," Jidak replied.

"It seemsss," put in Imra the Styxian, "that despite her claimsss, SSSaray isss incapable of stretching her skillsss as she would have you believe."

"One day," Saray told the assembled crowd, "you will all believe in what I am doing."

"I already know what I believe in," said Jidak, "and it's not a ball of light that lives in an underground cave that no one can find."

"You will regret those words, Cetan," declared Hotan.

"There isss no Cetan here," hissed Imra, "nor Styxian, nor Jugarian, nor any other Race. All are telepaths and we have no help but each other. In a galaxy ruled by the Jurisdiction, you would do well to remember that."

"Saray!" Dulan stood alone, a straight figure in dark red. "Long ago, in my own youth and arrogance, I attempted what you are now doing. Thus I can warn you out of my own

244

knowledge. There will come a time when your mind can no longer bear the terror or the strain of repeating these experiments. I was fortunate to have friends with telepathic abilities equal to my own to help me back to health. But who among us is equal to you? Who could aid you in repairing your mind and talents? Nor is the danger only to yourself. With each experiment you will distort time a little more for those who are physically near you, and that distortion will drive them toward the same madness that will claim you. Do you want to bring such an end to your friends? I tell you unequivocally: these experiments are unethical and they must stop!"

"Think before you command me, Dulan," cried Saray. "Dare you order anyone to cease learning, to allow superior telepathic skills to stagnate because of an ancient tradition?"

"I plead with you not to destroy yourself. These others agree with me." Dulan indicated the telepaths on one side of the Hall, who held up their hands in affirmation of that plea. "We are your friends. Let us help you. I myself am willing to work with you to the limits of my ability, to repair the damage already done to your mind."

"She doesn't need you," yelled Hotan. "She has Ananka."

"Saray," said Dulan, ignoring the young man, "warn your friends not to harm Merin or Herne. After what you have done to them it is the least you owe."

245

"She owes no one anything!" shouted Hotan, but Saray's hand on his arm stilled any further rudeness.

"In this Dulan is right," Saray announced. "Merin and Herne are to be treated with respect until Ananka has decided what to do with them. No friend of mine is to raise a hand against them. I want your word on this, Hotan. The others will listen to you."

"I'll do it for you," Hotan said. "Not for strangers, and certainly not for these old ones who have forgotten what it is to be young or energetic, or ambitious and eager for life."

"Hotan," said Jidak dryly, "it is my dearest wish to live long enough to see you when you are your father's present age, so I can repeat those words to you. Saray, like Dulan, I offer my assistance if you will but accept it."

"And I," put in Imra.

"I thank you for your concern," said Saray, but she did not say she would accept the offer.

"On behalf of all the folk of Tathan, who truly care for you," Jidak said in formal tones, "we implore you to end your unhealthy alliance with the alien entity you call Ananka, before you, and we, are destroyed."

But Saray seemed to be unbending on the question of her controversial attachment.

"Ananka does not intend anyone's destruction," she said, leaving Jidak and Imra shaking their heads in sadness at the obduracy of this most talented of telepaths.

"We are gathered here," Dulan now reminded them, "to commune with our dear friends the Chon. I wonder that they have not left us in distress at the anger and dissension filling this Hall. Please, my friends, for this evening at least, let us have peace in Tathan."

"To this I can agree," Saray said. "Hotan, Imra, Jidak, separate in peace, I beg you."

Slowly the telepaths and the birds broke into smaller groups and the tension began to ease.

"That foolish young woman," Tula grumbled to Merin, "is stubborn enough to destroy herself and all those who love her rather than admit she could be wrong."

"Tula speaksss truth," hissed Imra, joining them. "If this situation continuesss, it will be the end of Tathan. I fear a future in which we disperse across this world and live in isolation. To prevent that possibility, SSSaray's experiments must stop, and soon."

"She won't stop voluntarily," said Jidak. "She's too strong-willed to bow to any pressure we can exert, and Hotan will always back her, no matter what she does."

Herne had been watching and listening with great attention. Now he voiced his opinion.

"What I have seen tonight has made me realize that Saray needs a shock to convince her. There may be a way," Herne said, his eyes on Saray, who was talking to Hotan. "It is just possible that I could bribe her with a piece of valuable information."

"Yesss," breathed Imra. "You know the future, don't you?"

"What will you tell her?" asked Jidak.

"First, I am going to insist on meeting Ananka again," Herne said. "I'll begin by confronting that ball of light."

"If you need a friend to stand with you—" Jidak offered.

"Or a second friend," put in Imra.

"Don't try to speak to Saray this evening," Tula advised. "On the night of a Gathering she stays with Hotan, and he will dispute any attempt to confer alone with her. I will send a message in the morning, asking her to join us at Dulan's house before she goes home tomorrow."

"Be sure she meets with us early in the day," said Herne. "There may not be much time left."

"You are a brave man, yet you are afraid. But it is not fear for yourself," Tula murmured as Jidak and Imra moved away from them. "This is what I sensed in you the first time we met. You have been concealing something of deadly importance."

"I'll tell you soon," Herne promised. "Don't worry, Tula, there is no danger to you, or to Dulan."

"I never thought there was." Now that Hotan and his band had been stopped by Saray, Tula was able to smile again and to leave the protection of the pedestal. "You are free to speak with anyone here, though I know you cannot communicate with the Chon. You may retire to Dulan's house whenever you wish. After Hotan's promise to Saray no one will bother you." With that, Tula bowed to them, leaving to join Dulan and a group of Chon. On the far side of the Hall, Saray and Hotan stood talking to a few of the rougher-looking men and the two Jugarians, until Hotan took Saray's arm a bit roughly and led her through the main door.

"There is a soundless murmuring in the air," Merin said to Herne, "a constant vibration. It's like overhearing a conversation that is just too far away for me to be able to catch the words. I know it's there, but I can't understand it."

"I don't think anyone would mind if we left," Herne said, giving her a look that made her heart pound. "Come with me now, my love."

Chapter Fourteen

The hidden light source that illuminated the Gathering Hall did not extend to the garden behind it, where there was only moonlight and the pale gleam of hundreds of white flowers. Herne paused, his eyes searching the shadows.

"The entrance to Ananka's grotto has to be here somewhere," he said, "and in that grotto we'll find the answers we need."

"If Ananka is capable of appearing at Saray's house, then she isn't confined to one place," Merin pointed out. "In any case, you won't find those answers in the dark. The moons are lower now, and will set soon."

"Which means we are free until daylight." Merin saw a flash of white teeth as Herne's arm slid around her waist. She stiffened, fearing they might be seen. Much as she welcomed his caresses when they were alone, she still could not adjust to demonstrations of affection when others were near. She was relieved when he did not try to kiss her, but instead hurried her through the door and into the alley between the Gathering Hall and Dulan's house.

His arm was still around her waist, and now he drew her near, his free hand tilting her face upward. Her eyes had not yet grown used to the almost total darkness in the shadow of the wall, so she could not see his face.

"All evening," he whispered, "every moment, I was aware of you. I could almost feel your skin beneath my hands. I could remember the look of your hair all undone and falling over my arm. And I remembered the way you cry out in pleasure when I make you mine."

"Oh, Herne." His fingers cradled her chin, and she knew his mouth was almost on hers.

"You are part of me now, Merin, part of my mind and heart and in every cell of my body. No matter what happens, I promise I won't let anything separate us."

His kiss was meant to be gentle, to seal that tender oath, but the meeting of their mouths lit a fire in Merin that was out of control in an instant. Had Herne not retained a bit of common sense, she would have lain down upon the hard stone paving of the alley and let him take her there, not caring who might come upon them, for she was beyond embarrassment, beyond the reach of any discipline she had ever known. She burst into frustrated tears when he pulled away from her to urge her toward Dulan's house.

Once they were indoors she reached for him again, and now Herne did not resist the temptation she offered. A moment later they were in their bedchamber, where a dim lamp burned, and they were tearing at each other's clothing. From Merin's gown rose the rich fragrance of khata wood, filling their nostrils, heightening their desire. They fell upon the bed together, naked limbs entwined, Merin nearly attacking him with her greedy kisses and the most unabashedly erotic caresses she had ever bestowed upon him.

At first Herne reveled in this unleashing of repressed passion, but she would not stop— not until he caught her hands in a tight grip, holding them at either side of her head while he thrust into her hard, harder, harder still. She began to moan and writhe. Herne forced himself to control his own need so he could watch her lovely, tormented face dissolve into ecstasy. But that sight, together with the thrashing of her legs and the swiveling of her hips had had their effect on him. With a loud cry he burst into a passionate climax that seemed to extend Merin's, for she continued to move and throb beneath him. It was not until her wild cries of passion had eased into soft sobs that he withdrew and lay beside her. When she turned toward him he saw the tears upon her cheeks.

"I don't know what's happening to me," she choked. He put his arm around her, pulling her against his shoulder. "Never in my life have I lost control like that. I couldn't think, I only *wanted*."

"Perhaps it's something to do with the telepaths," he said, kissing her forehead.

"Oressian minds are not suited to telepathy," she reminded him.

"Nor are Sibirnan minds," he responded. "But close contact with many telepaths in communion with the Chon made us aware of what you called 'vibrations in the air.' That must have affected us. And don't forget, we are suffering from a severe dislocation. I haven't really felt like myself since we arrived in Tathan."

"I'm hungry all the time," Merin said, sitting up. "At this moment I am absolutely starving. I have to find some food."

"I'll go with you." He found their towels in the bathing room. Wrapped within them, they explored Dulan's kitchen, discovering bread, ixak cheese, fruit, and a small jug of batreen. All of this they piled onto a tray, which they took back to their room, where they sat upon the bed to eat. Merin cut the cheese, laying the pieces neatly on small slices of bread before feeding them to Herne.

"Do you think I'm so hungry because of our lovemaking?" she asked.

"I wouldn't be at all surprised. Just a moment there!" he cried in mock anger. "For every one you give to me, you eat two yourself." He snatch a slice of bread and cheese out of her hand and ate it.

"I can't help myself. This tastes wonderful. In fact, all Tathan food tastes marvelous. Could I have some of those little orange berries before you finish all of them?" When Herne popped the fruit into her mouth she caught his finger in her teeth.

"Will you eat that too?" he teased.

"Possibly." Still clenching her teeth around his finger, she circled it with her tongue.

"Woman." Herne pulled his finger free. His voice sank to a husky whisper. "I hope you are aware that I haven't finished with you yet."

"I'm so glad." She ran her hand across his naked chest, then tugged at the towel still twisted around his waist. Her eyes met his, and in their purple-brown depths Herne saw all the love that had gone ungiven throughout her lonely life. "I hope you never finish with me," she said. "I know I will never be finished with you."

Not taking his eyes from hers, Herne piled the few remaining crumbs of food and the empty batreen jug onto the tray and set it on the floor. Then he took her into his arms again.

This was a less frantic loving, but still passion flared hot and bright between them. Merin was an apt pupil, always willing to learn more, and Herne found her endlessly fascinating. She was exquisitely sensitive to his every caress, so that he felt as if her body sang beneath his searching, probing hands and his eager mouth. Their coming together was a delight so intense, he almost lost his mind.

"I love you," he said, looking into her wondrous eyes. He waited, poised above her, his manhood deep inside her, hoping, secretly praying to all the ancient Sibirnan gods for the answer his heart longed to hear.

"I love you," she whispered, and moved in exactly the way he wanted her to move. Then he did lose his mind, and every vestige of self-control, in an explosion of happiness that went on and on until he was drained and weak and they were both completely, blissfully satisfied. This was his woman, his love, in this time or any other. And he knew with absolute certainty that for him there could be no other love.

"Whether we ever get home again," Herne said during the darkest reaches of the night, "or whether we are forced to spend the rest of our lives in this time, I want everyone to know that you are mine and I am yours. Will you marry me tomorrow? And if we can go home, or if we find a way to escape the Cetan attack, will you have my children? Will you live with me until we both grow old and die?"

In Merin's mind a blot of fear began to grow, canceling out the indescribable joy she had just experienced with Herne. She was going to have to tell him the truth about herself. His insistent love would compel her to speak. She could not say she would marry him, or even refuse him, without explaining.

"I don't know how to have a child," she began, fighting back tears.

"We have just been practicing." Laughing, he laid a hand on her abdomen. "As a doctor, I will be happy to provide the intimate physiological details. The child will grow in here. Shall I demonstrate again how it enters?"

His teasing manner did not disguise how much he wanted her to say she would agree. Suddenly, she wanted it too. For all of her carefully regulated existence the idea of pregnancy had been a horror in her mind worse even than contemplation of the act of love. Now a new thought occurred to her. The Oressian Elders had lied about the pain and physical damage caused by lovemaking. Could they have lied about childbearing, too? Was it possible that she might be capable not only of carrying Herne's child inside her body, but of surviving its birth? A real child, a natural child, conceived in hot passion, born of love . . . Herne's child inside her, growing . . . a child. . . .

"I wish it could be," she whispered, covering her face with both hands, knowing that once she had told him everything he would want that miracle no longer. Not with her. Never with her.

"I know we're in danger, and it's probably foolish to talk about having a family," he said, "but knowing it's what we both want will give us something to hang on to. We'll find a way out of here, Merin. I'm almost certain I can convince Ananka to send us back."

"If you can't . . ." she began.

"If I can't, then we'll leave Tathan anyway. We'll go to Dulan's retreat at Lake Rhyadur, where we know the Cetans won't find us, and we'll live there. We can leave a message there for Tarik, so he'll know what has happened to us."

"It's a dream," Merin said. "It can never be. You won't want it."

"It *can* be," he insisted. "Whether here, or in our own time, I'll make certain you are safe."

"I cannot marry you."

"Why not? You can't deny that you want me." When she tried to get off the bed he reached for her, but she eluded him. "Merin, answer me. Why won't you marry me?"

"I cannot tell you." Tears were running down her cheeks. She knew he would insist upon knowing everything, and the thought of telling him was breaking her heart. She made one last effort to stop what was inevitable, taking refuge for a final time in the stock Oressian phrase of denial. "I am forbidden to tell you."

"I thought we had finished with those old excuses." They were both standing now, Herne holding on to her hands so she could not cover her face again or try to run away from him. "Merin, I have just asked you to be my wife. For a Sibirnan, that is no small thing. I deserve a better answer than just 'I am forbidden to tell you.'"

For a long time she stared at the floor rather than at him, trying to gather her courage while he held her hands as if they were tethering him to life itself. Then the weight of the terrible secrets she had been carrying since leaving Oressia became too great for her to bear the burden any longer. Her shoulders slumped. She took two steps backward and lifted her head to look directly at him.

"You are right, Herne. You do deserve an explanation. Your honest proposal, the love we have repeatedly made, and the emotions you have made it possible for me to feel, all have negated my oath never to speak of Oressian customs, just as my telling you the truth of my origins will dissolve all the promises you have made to me, all the sweet and gentle oaths you thought would bind us together forever. Let me cover my nakedness first; then I'll tell you whatever you want to know, for when I have finished you won't want to look at me any longer."

"Wrap yourself in this." He handed her the towel she had used earlier. While he was searching for his own towel, she disappeared into the bathing room. He found her standing with her back to him, in the doorway to the enclosed garden. She looked at the plants instead of at him while she spoke. Winding his towel about his waist once more, Herne walked across the room to stand beside her.

"Long ago," she began, "Oressia was a world of profligate and violent passions. Wars were fought for foolish reasons or for no reason at all except the love of killing. Rampant lust led to diseases and unhappiness. Oressian culture seemed doomed because the people would not control their simplest desires. Every wish must be gratified immediately. There are vast resources on Oressia, including metals needed for the manufacture of spaceships and their propulsion systems, but the companies formed to mine and export those metals were ruined by the greed of their owners and the indolence of the workers.

"Then arose our great leader, Olekan." Merin sounded as if she was declaiming the lines of some ancient epic poem. "Many were the battles, terrible the bloodshed. Entire clans were exterminated before Olekan brought peace to our world. Once he had conquered all of Oressia, Olekan established stern laws and named a Tribunal of Elders to enforce those laws. All forms of violence were strictly forbidden, the slightest infringement punishable by death. But that was not enough to prevent future wars, or a return to our old decadent ways under a new leader after Olekan had died. He understood this, so he made still more laws for our protection. Oressia became a closed planet. No outsiders were allowed to set foot on it, and any Oressian who left could never return to contaminate our newly peaceful society with alien ideas. Exportation of our products was from that time conducted by mechanized ships and robots. The only importations allowed were foodstuffs and the few raw materials we lacked, which came to us on the returning unmanned ships."

Here Merin stopped, considering how to explain the rest, how to make Herne understand without despising her. Knowing her hope was a futile one, she continued.

"Under Olekan's laws, marriage was forbidden. Families were forbidden because they generate ambition. Friendship, greed, hatred, social status, all were forbidden, for these had once been the temptations that led Oressians into near extinction. The few children left alive after the wars ended were educated to hate and fear those temptations." Another pause. Merin swallowed hard. "Lovemaking was forbidden. Even mention of it was against the law. We are taught from our earliest days how dangerous it is to feel any emotion. We are strictly trained from childhood to repress all disruptive feelings."

"What you are describing is totalitarianism of a particularly insane kind," Herne protested.

"For your people, perhaps," Merin returned. "But those Oressians who had survived the

261

great wars understood that for us there could be no other way. It was strict regulation or certain extinction, and my ancestors made the only choice that would allow their society to continue. For centuries, Olekan's system has worked well, proving the wisdom of this great leader. Oressia is now a peaceful and prosperous world. Poverty no longer exists. The metal mines are profitable once more, and those profits are dispersed for the good of all our people. Where once we were disreputable outlaws, now we have become valued members of the Jurisdiction."

"No lovemaking. No families. No friends. A lonely price to pay for social stability," Herne said. Then, "Without lovemaking, how do Oressians reproduce? And how are the children raised if no families are allowed?" ·

Merin was silent, trying to decide how best to explain this difficult matter to one who had been raised in a world vastly different from her own.

"We do not reproduce," she told him. "Not in the way you mean. What you and I have done together is strictly forbidden because it is the vilest of crimes, leading to terrible social ills. Until your body entered mine, I did not even know exactly how it was done. From early childhood each Oressian is taught to avoid any activity or any situation that might give rise to illicit desires. Disobedience of this law is punishable by immediate extermination."

"By Oressian law, you and I are criminals?" Herne looked as if he could not believe what she was saying.

"From the first moment you touched me in the grotto all those weeks ago, my life was forfeit," Merin said, "and rightfully so, for from that moment my discipline has been dissolving until now it is completely gone and I am lost forever."

"Only on Oressia," Herne said. "Not here, not on Dulan's Planet."

"We carry our homeworlds with us, wherever we go." Her voice was filled with sadness.

"You still haven't explained how Oressians reproduce," Herne noted. "Obviously, you do reproduce, since the system you describe has been in place for centuries. As a doctor, and as a man, I find the question intriguing."

"Olekan decreed that the population of Oressia should remain stable at the level best suited to our resources," Merin said, evading a direct answer. "And so it has been done, since that time."

"How?" Herne demanded. "I doubt that even your Olekan could abolish all diseases, or accidental death, or the ravages of old age. How, then, can a stable population be maintained? Answer me, Merin, and tell me the truth, because I have a terrible feeling that what we are discussing here is against Jurisdiction law."

"Oressia became a member of the Jurisdiction on condition that our planetary isolation and our ancient laws be preserved," she reminded him. "The Jurisdiction needs Oressian metals. Our conditions were accepted."

"And every Oressian who leaves the planet is sworn never to reveal anything about Oressian culture," Herne prompted softly, trying to encourage what was obviously going to be a difficult admission for her to make.

"It is a rule I never broke until I came to Dulan's Planet," Merin said. "Great Olekan and the Elders were right. It took only the sight of your naked body and one kiss to lead me into moral degradation. I fell further from discipline and honor each time you touched me. See me now, unclothed, my hair unbound, my body repeatedly opened to yours, unable to deny you anything you want of me, even to speaking our deepest secrets. By loving you, I have betrayed everything I was ever taught." She stopped on a sob.

"You are a perfectly normal human female," Herne said, "capable of great passion, able to conceive and bear a child. I ask you again, Merin: Would you bear my child? Would you want to?" He saw in her face wonder, hope, joy—and horror. It was that last emotion, unconcealed and painful, that decided his next words. He had to know. He made his voice hard. "No more delaying, no more evasions. Tell me now how Oressians reproduce. Do they use artificial insemination? Or have they discovered a means to induce parthenogenesis, like the Riothans do? Is that it? Do your women not need the male seed; do they literally get themselves pregnant?"

For a long time he thought she would not answer him. He watched her struggle with this last, deepest restriction, watched tears fill her eyes while she gathered her courage to defy the final Oressian law. And he felt pride in her and a love so wide and deep it was beyond measuring when she began to speak again. But only until he understood what she was saying. Then his heart went cold.

"We are grown from tissue stored in the BabyCompLab," she said. "By Great Olekan's order, fifty males and fifty females were chosen to be the progenitors of all future Oressians. The choices were carefully made for diversity of physical characteristics, for strength, endurance, lack of inherited diseases, and for comeliness. Olekan saw no reason to create an ugly race."

"Create? BabyCompLab?" Herne was shaken to his core. What Merin was explaining was absolutely forbidden by Jurisdiction law. No wonder Oressians were so secretive. He could not keep the distaste out of his voice. "When you once told me you had no mother you were speaking the truth. You are a clone."

She bowed her head under that condemnation, and Herne thought his own heart would break with the pain of it. This woman he came near to adoring was the product of a practice so abhorrent to all the Races of the Jurisdiction that he could not yet comprehend the horror of her confession. But then she raised her head and looked him straight in the eye.

"I am a member of the five hundred and sixty-fifth generation of my original parent," she said, with an almost defiant air that touched him through his revulsion and disgust, and told him that whatever else Olekan's laws had achieved, they had not entirely eliminated familial pride.

"Tell me about your childhood," he commanded.

"We are raised under laboratory conditions, in isolated cubicles, where the master computer teaches us what we need to know at each stage of our development. At the age of ten, we are given our first clothing, removed from First Cubicles, and turned over to advanced education. At the age of twenty those needed to replace dead Oressians are sent into society."

"What about the extra children?" Herne tried to keep his voice calm, tried to hide the repugnance and anger he felt at what Merin was telling him. "Olekan must have provided for extras to be produced, in case they were needed." It made him sick to talk about humans in that way, as if they were components in a factory, waiting to be used on an assembly line to manufacture a product.

"Those who are not needed as replacements on Oressia, who have displayed exceptional abilities, are permitted to leave, to live on other worlds. I have an unusually retentive mind for details. That is why I was sent to the Archives at Capital."

"So variations appear as you are trained. Interesting." Herne stopped, aghast at his own words. "What about those who are not needed on Oressia but do not rate placement elsewhere? What happens to them?"

"They are exterminated."

"But they are sentient beings!" This was too much. Herne was furious. "Willful destruction of intelligent life forms is forbidden by all the worlds in the Jurisdiction, and by overriding Jurisdiction laws!"

"There are those who believe that life forms, sentient or not, that are produced by methods other than the natural manner for their species, have no souls and therefore are not protected by those laws," Merin said quietly. "Which is one of many reasons why Oressians are bound to secrecy when they leave their own world. It is for our protection, Herne."

Herne staggered to the bench beside the tub. There he sat down and put his head in his hands. He could not blame Merin for what she was. The way she had been born—or rather, created in a laboratory—was not her fault. Nor could she be blamed for her acceptance of one way of life when she had never been given the opportunity to know another. None of this was her fault. *None of it,* he told himself again. She was a victim of the Oressian system.

His reaction to what she had revealed was physical. His head ached from the awfulness of it. He wanted to vomit. He wanted to leave her and never see her again.

He loved her. He had repeatedly made love to her. To a clone.

But she was a normal human female in every respect. His diagnostic rod had told him so each time he had examined her. His body had told him the same thing whenever he had held her in his arms, when he had made her his while they made love. She was human, real, a courageous companion in their strange predicament. He admired her intelligence and her learning. She was a valuable contributing member of Tarik's colony.

She was a clone.

He loved her.

"I'll need some time to digest all of this," he said, his face still in his hands. He heard a movement, then saw her feet in front of him, delicate bones covered by creamy skin, with opalescent nails. She knelt, and he saw her hands, slender and beautiful. He felt like crying. She took his hands in hers, pulling them away from his face.

"Please look at me," she said.

"How many times have I begged you to do the same thing?" he countered, unable to meet her eyes.

"Herne, I know I have shocked you beyond your ability to accept what I am. I wish it had not been necessary, but I could not agree to marry you and then live a lie. I love you too much to lie to you about something so important. If there is anything I can do to make acceptance easier for you, please tell me."

"Easier?" He gave a bitter laugh. "Nothing in my life has been easy, but this is the hardest thing I've ever had to deal with. I'm not angry with you; I want you to know that. But I do need to be left alone until I think through everything you have said."

"I understand. I know my revelations have made it impossible for you to continue our intimate relationship." Her voice was amazingly cool, perfectly calm, like the Merin he had first known. And every word she said tore at his heart. He wondered how she could speak without breaking into tears. "Thank you for freeing my emotions. I will cherish the memory of our lovemaking for the rest of my life, though I know those same memories must disgust you. Nevertheless, I hope we will still be able to work together to achieve our mutual goal of a safe return to our own time."

Mutual goal? Cherish the memory? Herne nodded, unable to speak for the emotion now choking him. She left him, going into

269

the bedchamber, where he heard her moving about. After a few minutes he heard the door open and close. He assumed she had gone out, perhaps to walk alone along the path by the salt marsh, to breathe in the salty air that reminded her of her homeworld—her home!

What kind of home was it that could treat its children so impersonally, so brutally? Though his own childhood had been anything but happy, still Sibirnan parents did see their children into the teen years with some show of concern for their welfare. It hurt him to think of Merin as a small, delicate-boned girl with dark curls, not running free and playing as children ought to do, but confined in a miserable, isolated cubicle, being fed information and food at predetermined intervals, by a computer. No human contact, no loving mother's arms, no brothers or sisters or playmates. Nothing but a machine to tend to her needs. No machine could be programmed to care if a little girl cried.

That thought broke him. The picture in his mind of a tiny Merin, alone and weeping with no one to comfort her, brought him to the first tears he had shed in more than thirty years. He wept for what had been done to her, for her loveless childhood and her lonely life since leaving Oressia. And he wept for himself, because no matter how much he loved her, he was not sure he could ever accept what she was.

Chapter Fifteen

While Merin and Herne had been talking, night had faded into a misty dawn. The dull red of the sun's disk moved steadily higher until a bank of heavy clouds obscured its heat and much of its light. The scene across the salt marsh matched Merin's mood as she watched the fog roll in from the ocean beyond the dunes.

"For one who is not a telepath, there is nothing to see," said a quiet, scratchy voice.

"I find the fog comforting," she responded, not needing to look around to know who the speaker was. "On my homeworld it is often foggy, and there are many marshes at the edge of the sea."

"From what I know of Oressia," said Dulan, falling into step with her on the path, "there is little on that world to comfort its citizens."

"Little?" Merin gave a harsh laugh. "There's no comfort at all, Dulan, nor on any other world either, for an Oressian."

"It takes no telepathy to recognize a troubled heart," Dulan said. "Would it help you to confide in me? I keep secrets well, and you may find it easier to speak where there is no visible face to show emotion in response to your words."

"I have already said to Herne every word that I can bear to speak," Merin replied. "He is struggling now with my terrible truth."

They walked a little farther along the path, not talking.

"I wish," Merin began, then stopped. They walked a few paces more. "If only—" She stopped again, uncertain how to ask for what she wanted. Dulan paused, waiting. Merin went on a step or two, then turned, looking hard at the blue-robed figure.

"Speak freely and without fear," said Dulan.

"You have heard Herne mention Osiyar, the telepath who lived—will live—in our own time," Merin said. "Osiyar found it necessary to enter my mind. Thus, he was the first non-Oressian to learn the truth about my origin. He knew everything about me and still accepted me. He was my first friend."

A profound silence lay between Merin and Dulan. The incoming fog bank had covered the marsh as far as the path, and pale gray scarves of mist drifted around them. Merin felt moisture on her face and brushed it away, unsure if it was fog or her own tears.

"Do you want me also to enter your mind?" Dulan's voice was so soft, it might have been a verbal extension of the fog now surrounding them.

"Please." Merin's own voice, not much louder than Dulan's, cracked on the single word. The rest of her thoughts came out in a whispered rush. "Herne knows now, so there's no point in hiding it from you or anyone else. And, oh, how I need someone to understand the truth, yet not turn from me in disgust as Herne has done. I thought if Osiyar could manage to be so tolerant, perhaps you could too."

"Give me your hands," said Dulan.

"Don't you have to look into my eyes?" For all she had asked for this, Merin was as frightened as she had been when Osiyar had touched her mind.

"Not all telepaths must do so," said Dulan. "I require only your consent. I will hold your hands to steady you should you grow faint, and because I sense a debilitating change in you. Physical contact will make recognition of any ailment easier."

Perhaps it was telepathy already working in her mind, but at Dulan's words Merin became absolutely calm and fearless, certain that whatever Dulan might learn of her, she would not be left without friendship. She put out both her hands and felt those pale, slender fingers fold around them.

She experienced once again the unique prickling sensation in her mind, but far more gentle, far more subtle than Osiyar's entrance had been. Because she was unafraid this time she was fully aware of the instant when Dulan's thoughts merged completely with her own. Trusting Dulan without reservation, she willingly allowed the blurring of her own self, until she knew Dulan as Dulan knew her. She sensed a power far beyond her comprehension, a power disciplined and channeled for the benefit of others, as great power ought always to be used. She touched memories of unbearable physical pain and emotional loss, followed by recollections of a broken life courageously rebuilt into dignity and usefulness. For one second of heartstopping joy she saw what Dulan really was, and heart and mind both overflowed with gratitude for the honor that had been granted to her with that revelation. Then, slowly and delicately, the connection between them was broken.

"Thank you," she whispered, knowing full well that words were unnecessary, and in her thoughts Dulan smiled at her.

"There was a time in the history of mankind," said Dulan, still holding her hands, "when men believed the females of their species had no souls, and therefore women were not people as men were. They know better now, but the learning was not an easy process. Telepaths have more recently been called soulless monsters and persecuted because of their abilities. You have told me that in your time the laws against telepathy have been repealed. Like women in ancient times, like telepaths in my own lifetime, clones are called by many pejorative terms: soulless, abominations, monstrosities, hideous aberrations. But you have a mind, a heart, a spirit. You have a well-trained intelligence that you have placed at the service of others. I observed you closely in the Gathering Hall last night and saw how you respect other life forms. You have courage, you love, you fear, you hope. You dream of the future. If all of those qualities do not make you a true human, then what will?"

"A natural birth," said Merin, knowing it was the one thing she could never claim.

"No. Humanity lies here." Dulan's hand touched Merin's bosom, then moved on to rest upon her bowed head. "And here."

"Herne does not think so."

"Ah, Herne." Dulan sighed. "Sibirnans have their own problems in accepting unsimilar others, though Herne is more advanced than most. He will need time."

"Time." Merin shook her head.

"Time is not an enemy," said Dulan, "but a healer, as I have learned."

They were walking back along the path now, heading toward Dulan's house.

"My friend," said Dulan, the simple words

touching Merin deeply, "I ought to meet with Jidak and Imra. We have a large computer system safely installed underground, and they are searching through the files there for any data that might be of help to you. I want to consult with them on a puzzle that has only now become clear to me. I believe you would benefit from a little time spent alone while you consider what we have done here. Can you find your way to my house through the fog?"

"Of course." Merin lifted her head, smiling, watching while Dulan vanished into the mist.

She found Herne lying naked on the bed, with his eyes closed. When she touched his cheek he did not respond. She decided he was either asleep or he did not want to speak to her.

"Oh, Herne," she whispered, looking down at his pale, harsh features, "you said you would always love me no matter what, and I believed you. I broke every law of Oressia for your sake. Because of you I learned to trust and, finally, to love. I could accept anything you might tell me about yourself. I wouldn't care if you were a clone, or an android, or a Jugarian crab in disguise, or even a Styxian! If I could go on loving you no matter what your outward form or origin, why can't you love me? If Osiyar and Dulan can know me and still be my friends, why can't you?"

There was no answer. Herne slept on. Watching him, Merin became aware of her own fatigue. Between lovemaking and her confession to Herne, she had not slept at all the previous night. She was emotionally drained and physically exhausted. Without removing her treksuit or coif, she lay down on the opposite side of the bed from Herne. When she found her thoughts running over and over everything she had said to him she made herself think instead about her communion with Dulan and what she had learned when their thoughts had joined. If that kind and wise telepath could rebuild a useful life after dreadful torture and forcible separation from home and family, after the ruin of health and reputation, then Merin of Oressia ought to find in Dulan's example the inspiration to go on with her own life. With thoughts of Dulan on her mind, and the fresh memory of friendship freely offered, she fell asleep.

She wakened at midday to find Herne gone. When she tried to sit up she discovered she was almost too weak to get out of bed. It was hunger that drove her upright, that sent her to the bathing room to splash cold water on her face, then lured her to Dulan's kitchen. She had to find something to eat.

There were two large round loaves of still-warm bread on the table. Merin tore at one, breaking it into pieces and chewing on the crust. With half a loaf in her stomach, the relentless, empty gnawing eased. She looked around for some other food.

"Would you like batreen or just water?"

"Dulan, I'm sorry I demolished your bread. It's just that I'm so hungry."

"I understand." Dulan handed her a pitcher of foaming, freshly brewed batreen. "I left the food for you and Herne."

"No matter how much I eat, I'm never filled." The batreen smelled of the grain used to make it. Her hunger returning, not caring what effect the intoxicating drink had upon her, Merin filled a cup and drained it with greedy relish. "Where is Herne?"

"He has gone to try to convince Saray to take him to Ananka," Dulan said, refilling Merin's cup. "Since Saray is still with Hotan, who is intensely jealous of other men, I doubt if Herne will be successful."

"You're right about that." Herne walked into the kitchen, looking wan and tired. With his eyes on the bread, he added, "Saray says perhaps tomorrow Ananka will see me."

"Eat," said Dulan. "I know you are hungry."

Herne snatched up the half loaf Merin had left and began to chew on it.

"Do you think we could find Ananka by ourselves, without waiting for Saray?" Merin asked him. "I'll search with you if you want."

"No thanks." Without looking at her, Herne took the cup of batreen Dulan offered him. "I'll search the garden by myself later today. But what I'd like to do before then, Dulan, is return to our shuttlecraft. We were badly shaken up during our flight, and not thinking too clearly after we landed. It's possible that we missed something important when we went over the ship the first time."

"I'll go too," Merin said.

"It's not necessary," Herne began.

"It *is* necessary!" she blazed at him, angered by the way he was trying to ignore her presence. "I piloted that ship. I know it as well as you do. I am going with you."

"As will Tula and I," said Dulan, putting an end to the quarrel. "We are both curious about the ship in which you came here, and we may be of some help."

"It's a long walk," Herne protested.

"Which is why I will have Tula bring his cart and ixak from the stables," said Dulan. "I do not think it wise for either of you to waste your strength on the walk."

Dulan left them. Herne picked up another chunk of bread. Merin laid her hand on his wrist. Herne looked at it with so cold an expression that she immediately removed it.

"I am still the same Merin I was yesterday," she said.

"True, but yesterday I didn't know the real Merin, did I?"

"I wish you would not hate me."

"Hate?" He put down the bread untasted. "I don't know exactly what I do feel for you, but it's not hate. It will take a while for me to get used to the idea that you are a—that you are what you are. In the meantime, there is the problem of how to get back to where we belong. If I could just find Ananka."

"Did Saray give you no help at all?"

"I had the impression that she might have provided some information, but Hotan was there. I think Hotan wants to keep Saray to himself, perhaps in hope of using Ananka's power in some way, while Saray wants to keep Ananka to herself. I also think Hotan and Saray are sleeping together. Whatever intrigue is going on in that trio, you and I are caught in the middle of it."

"Meanwhile, the Cetans may attack at any time," said Merin.

"Which means I have to get to Ananka fast," Herne told her.

The shuttlecraft appeared to be untouched since they had left it. They crowded inside, Dulan and Tula expressing great interest in the workings of the ship, while Herne and Merin tried unsuccessfully to start the engines.

"We do have a few mechanics who maintain our air transportation vehicles," Tula said. "If you think they will be able to help you, I will call upon them."

"I'm no mechanic," Herne admitted, "but these are relatively simple engines, and I can find nothing wrong with them that any mechanic might fix."

"Nor can I," said Merin. "I think the problem

isn't mechanical at all; it's something to do with our movement through time."

"Then it is possible that only Ananka can repair the ship," said Dulan.

"We always return to Ananka." Herne sounded resentful. "Let's go back to the city and demand that Saray take us to Ananka immediately."

"Saray is not amenable to demands," said Dulan, climbing out of the shuttlecraft.

"I don't care what she's amenable to," Herne responded rudely. "I'll threaten to kill her if I have to. I'll do anything so we can clear out of this cursed place."

This was the Herne Merin had first known, irritable, abrupt, seeming not to care whose feelings he hurt. She knew him better now. She was able to see beneath the hard surface. She could tell he was in pain, and it was her doing. Her heart ached for him, but still she could not allow him to insult their two best friends in Tathan.

"You know you don't mean that," she protested. "You wouldn't harm Saray."

"Give me a fair chance to reach Home again," Herne snarled, "and see what I'll do to make it happen."

"You are right," Dulan told him, much to Merin's surprise. "It is absolutely essential that you leave Tathan as soon as possible."

Herne and Dulan walked away from the shuttlecraft, toward the cart in which they had come. Tula jumped out of the hatch to the ground with unexpected grace, considering his rotund shape. Merin began her downward jump, but was overtaken by a wave of dizziness. She fell out of the shuttlecraft onto Tula, who attempted to hold her upright. Neither of them had made a sound, but as if a warning shout had been given, Dulan spun around, tugging at Herne's sleeve. By the time Merin's head had cleared, she was in Herne's arms and he was carrying her toward the cart.

"This cannot go on," Tula said. "My friends, this affair must end before irreparable damage is done to your health."

"Stop babbling and help me get her into the cart," Herne snapped. "And this time see if you can make those star-blasted ixak move at something more than a slow walk. I know they can run; they did it yesterday."

"You need not swear at me, nor at my ixak," Tula responded with injured dignity.

"I don't care how you do it; just get us back to Dulan's house so Merin can lie down and rest," Herne ordered.

Merin did not care how long the return trip took. Herne had laid her across the backseat of the cart. He sat at one side of the seat, holding her in his arms to brace her against the bumps and rattles of a hasty journey across rough ground. She let her head rest on his shoulder, allowing him to think she was ill, when in fact her head had cleared within a few minutes. It was wonderful to be so close to him again, to know he did care if she was sick.

"Don't worry," he murmured, his cheek against hers. "Just a little longer and we'll be at Dulan's house. I'll give you something to eat and put you to bed. I'm not feeling any too healthy myself. I think it's the food. We have to get out of here."

She must have fallen asleep, or possibly she fainted, for the dizziness came once more and she was not fully aware of her surroundings again until Herne was setting her down on the bed in Dulan's guest quarters. She let him remove her boots and even her coif, but when his hand reached for the fastening of her treksuit, she caught it, holding it against her bosom.

"Take this off," he said, "and get beneath the covers. You'll sleep better."

"I can't sleep. I have to help you. Let me talk to Saray."

"You aren't going anywhere until you've had some rest." With the cool professionalism of a well-trained doctor, he removed her treksuit, then eased her back on the bed. The harsh, angry Herne was gone. He ran a hand across her rib cage. It was a doctor's touch, not a lover's caress, but still it awoke a warmth in her. "You are much too thin, Merin. You're fading away a little every day."

"I'm frightened." Her fingertips brushed his lips. "Hold me. Make me feel safe."

"Neither of us is safe." But he sat on the edge of the bed to pull her close. She craved the touch of his body so strongly that she thought she would melt into him. She could tell by the quick tightening of his arms that he was not unmoved by her nearness. She let her hands work their way around his waist. His lips touched her ear, the side of her jaw, her cheek. He would kiss her mouth next. She knew he would. He moved backward a little, staring hard at her. "I can't do this," he said.

She was no longer a complete innocent. Her hands were still at his waist, and now she brought them forward, lowering them to fondle his hardness in the way he himself had taught her. She saw by the immediate closing of his expression that she had lost the chance to convince him there was still hope for them. He leapt off the bed, not stopping till he had reached the door.

"After we get back to headquarters," he said, "assuming we ever do, then we can talk about what is between us, and what you are. Then, and only then, can we make a sensible decision on the kind of relationship we might have in the future. If there *is* a future for us."

"If love were sensible," she cried, "I never would have fallen in love with you."

She would have gotten up to follow him but the dizziness assailed her again. She collapsed onto the pillows, closing her eyes to shut out the spinning, darkening room. When she had recovered enough to open her eyes Herne was gone.

"I think it's the food," Herne said to Dulan. "It doesn't agree with us in some way. That's why we don't feel well."

"You have come close to the truth of your situation," Dulan replied.

Merin joined them in the sitting room, not taking a chair but crouching on the raised hearth, as near to the fire as she could get. The chill and the dampness of the wet day had seeped into her bones. Herne did not look at her, but kept his attention on Dulan.

"I have learned something unexpected from my direct physical contact with Merin earlier today," Dulan said. "I discussed my findings with Jidak and Imra when I met with them, and they agreed that my conclusion must be correct."

"What conclusion?" Merin held her hands out to the fire, trying to warm them. Her treksuit, with its thermal adjustment properties, should have kept her warm or cool, depending on the temperature of her environment, but the cold she felt was inside her, the product of too many unfamiliar emotions and an ever-growing weakness.

"You are both starving," said Dulan. "Because you are in the wrong time, your digestive functions and our food are not compatible. You eat constantly, but only a small portion of what you consume provides nourishment to your bodies. For the most part, it is as though you were not eating at all."

"But water quenches my thirst," Merin said.

"We do not fully understand the metabolic process involved. In this respect, water may be an immutable substance," Dulan said. "We believe there may be other effects of the temporal displacement you have suffered. Merin, I know you are aware of a significant change in your ability to control your emotions."

"Are you saying," asked Herne, "that what we feel for each other is only the result of where we are? That if—when—we return to our own time, our feelings will change?"

"I do not know," Dulan replied. "No one has ever moved through time before."

"It would help," Herne said with ice in his voice, "if we could return emotionally to where we were when we first came to this planet."

Merin caught her breath. There it was, laid out for her so that she could no longer deny the truth. Herne found her so repulsive and his desire for her so painful that he wanted to feel nothing for her. It would be better for her if she could arrange to feel nothing for him, as well. She wondered if it would be possible for her to achieve the same control of her emotions that she had once maintained, and knew, with a sense of rising despair, that she could not.

"I'm going to see Saray." His expression

fierce, Herne stood, heading for the door. "I'll force her to contact Ananka."

"Force won't help," said Dulan. But Herne had gone. Dulan's head was bowed. "He is in terrible pain. He loves and hates at the same time, fears and hopes in the same moment. Hourly he grows weaker, but he will strive for your safe return until he dies."

"If he dies," Merin whispered, "I will die too. If he is gone, it won't matter to me."

"You should rest. I have an appointment with Jidak, who believes the Chon may be able to help you."

Left alone, Merin wandered into the kitchen in search of food. She found bread and ixak cheese laid out together, and a bowl of fruit, but she did not eat. She was too angry. Rage against the circumstances of her life, against the lies she had been taught throughout her youth, fury toward Ananka and Saray for their heedless experiment that had brought Herne and herself to Tathan, a sense of the unfairness of it all, filled her, giving her a desperate strength.

"I won't lie down and die," she swore. "I won't let Herne die, either."

She ran out of Dulan's house, along the alley and through the door into the garden at the rear of the Gathering Hall. She climbed the steps, where she stood with her back toward the Hall, facing the garden, trying to recall every detail of the investigation she and Herne had once undertaken through the ruins of Hall and garden while they explored the site with Tarik.

"Now," she said, suiting action to her muttered words, "we walked down the steps and across the garden to this spot. There was a tree just here, and another here, and then a steep slope. I tripped and rolled to the bottom."

Pushing through the shrubbery, she came up against the garden wall. She knew Herne had done the same thing many times in his own futile search for Ananka's grotto. Frustrated, she beat at the wall with both hands, but it remained solid, with no sign of a break or crack in its smooth white surface. On the other side of the wall was a house similar to Dulan's, one of a series of buildings that clustered near the Gathering Hall.

"Where are you, Ananka?" Merin shouted. "Stop hiding. Come out and show yourself. *Ananka!*"

There was no response. Merin leaned her back against the wall, mentally going over every step she had taken through the garden.

With a fluttering sound, a green Chon settled a short distance away from her. At the same time, Saray stepped from behind a bush, giving the appearance of having materialized out of air.

"Herne is looking for you," Merin said.

"I know. Jidak has told me of your illness. He blames me for it."

"So do I." Merin had never dared to use such a challenging tone to anyone before, but her anger was with her still. "What are you going to do about it, Saray? Will you just let us die?"

"I am afraid there is nothing I can do," Saray replied. "Let me explain. I want you to understand. I did not want this new ability. My life was planned to be a simple one spent perfecting my talent. We all knew it was exceptional. There is no special merit attached to it. I was born with it, as I was born with dark hair and eyes, but like intelligence or an inborn skill in music, telepathic ability exists to be developed for the benefit of all. For the sake of that development, I married an elderly man who became my tutor after I left Dulan's schooling.

"Ananka approached me; I did not seek her. At first, my husband encouraged me to experiment with time as Ananka wanted, in order to expand my powers. I did not question his urging. I believed myself safe because I had his experience and strength to guide me. But he died, leaving me with no adviser, for I would not listen to Dulan any more. I thought Ananka was mentor enough, and I had become completely immersed in our experiments.

"More than a year after my husband died, Hotan came to my home to make some repairs. He is a carpenter, a man young and vigorous, while I am approaching middle age. I had never enjoyed physical love until Hotan lay with me.

Merin, do you know what it is to want a man you should not desire, a man who can bring you only pain? Have you ever loved so deeply that you cannot stop what you know should not happen?"

"Yes," said Merin, "I know." The all-too-familiar dizziness struck her, and she put out a hand toward the nearest solid object, steadying herself on the Chon. The bird did not move; it did not even look at her. Its soft black eyes were on Saray, but as Merin's hand rested on the green feathers, strength returned to her shaking arms and legs, and her thoughts began to clear.

"Of course you understand," Saray said. "You love Herne."

"Herne does not love me," Merin said sadly. "Not anymore."

"Nor does Hotan love me," Saray told her. "What he wants in me is my telepathic power. While I am for the first time in my life enthralled by the pleasures of a man's body." She put her hand on the Chon's breast, laying her head against it in a gesture of profound sorrow.

"And now I will lose everything dear to me," she said. "My truest friends have forsaken me because of what I have done. Ananka has drained my power for her experiments until it barely exists anymore. Once it is gone, it cannot be replenished. When Hotan learns how weak I have become he will leave me.

There will be other, younger women for him, but I will live the remainder of my life alone, without the talent that gave the deepest meaning to my existence. Dulan was right about the experiments: They are wrong. Worse, they are morally dangerous. In my pride I believed for a while that I could change time itself. Now I know the power Ananka promised me was an illusion, and as Dulan warned, I feel madness gradually overtaking my mind."

Merin could think of no response to this confession. She doubted that even Dulan could do anything to help Saray. The two women stood linked together by their mutual contact with the Chon, each leaning upon it, each drawing strength from the great bird. As the minutes passed, Merin became aware of the energy vibrating between the bird and Saray. With a start, she realized what was happening. In her intense interest in what Saray was telling her, Merin had almost forgotten that the Chon had telepathic power as well as intelligence. Now it seemed to her that the bird was not only lending its physical strength to Saray, but in addition it was feeding telepathic energy to her. Merin, with no telepathic powers of her own, could not partake of this generous offering, but for her physical fortification was enough.

"I will do whatever I can for you," Saray said at last, in a much firmer voice than before. "Return to Dulan's house and wait for me. Tell Herne to wait too."

* * *

It was late evening before Saray appeared, looking fragile but triumphant.

"Ananka will see you at sunrise," she said.

"It's about time." Herne glared at her. "You have been hiding from me."

"I will conceal myself no longer," Saray said, taking a seat. "Dulan, may I stay with you until morning? I don't want to see Hotan just now, and my house is far away."

"You can sleep in the guestroom with Merin," Herne said before Dulan could answer. "I'll sit up here. I won't be able to sleep."

Nor did Merin or Saray sleep, though they dutifully retired to the guest chamber and lay down on the bed. In spite of having eaten heavily during the evening, throughout that long night Merin could feel her strength seeping steadily away. With every hour that passed she was weaker, and she knew that no food in Tathan could adequately fill her empty stomach. When Herne knocked on the door, calling out that it was nearly daylight, Saray had to help her to stand, and it took all of Merin's strength to pull on her boots and adjust her coif. She slung her useless recorder over her shoulder, then picked up her own kit along with Herne's, which she gave to him when they met in the sitting room.

"In case we are able to go home at once," she said, trying to smile at him. "We ought to have all of our gear with us."

"Your handweapons too," Dulan said, returning them. "I know now you would only use them in self-defense."

Herne looked as sick as Merin felt, but he stood resolutely upright and followed Saray toward the garden with determined if slightly wavering steps. Dulan walked beside him as if to lend support. In the gray light of early dawn they found the green Chon waiting for them among the bushes and white flowers.

"Well?" Herne demanded with a touch of his old energy. "Where is she? Where is the entrance to her grotto?"

"Ananka will appear when she is ready," said Saray.

"We can't stand here all day," Herne objected, swaying a little.

The Chon cocked its head and made a soft clucking sound. The rear garden wall disappeared in a blaze of light. As the light faded, Ananka stood before them.

Chapter Sixteen

For this appearance, Ananka had once again assumed her image of Merin's face and body, but still with light brown hair. Her golden cloak swirled above her white gown, and a few locks of loose hair rippled as if a breeze blew, though the air in the garden did not stir.

"Herne," Ananka said, "I knew you would come to me."

"Come to you?" Herne exploded. "We have been trying to find you for days. What in the name of all the stars do you think you are doing to us? Are you deliberately trying to kill us? And if so, why? We've never done you any harm."

"I need you," Ananka said. "I need your love."

"Well, this is no way to get it." Herne was

weaving on his feet, trying to stay upright.

"You are ill," Ananka said with a look of pained surprise.

"Ill?" he shouted at her, unable to contain his rage. "We are dying because of you and this deluded telepath you have been using for your cursed experiments."

"You should not be ill."

"They should not be *here*," Dulan said. "Wicked creature, you have forced them into the wrong time and it is killing them."

"I want to know why you have done this to us," Herne declared. "Why me? Why Merin?"

"I also want to understand your motives," Dulan said, "because this kind of interference in the lives of others is prohibited by telepaths."

"It was not forbidden to Saray," sneered Ananka.

"Yes, it was, and I am deeply at fault here." Saray stood before Ananka with clenched fists, looking as angry as Herne at his most fierce. "Moving simple objects through space and time was questionable enough, considering the disruptions such acts can cause. Moving simple living creatures was worse still. Moving intelligent life forms was immoral beyond all forgiveness. *And I helped you.*"

"It was only an experiment," Ananka protested, shrugging her shoulders and laughing.

"If you were as all-powerful as you would have us believe, instead of a foolish and mischievous spirit," said Dulan, "then you would need no explanation of something so simple as the moral obligation to use your power responsibly, to do no harm with it."

"You can discuss ethics later." Herne cut across Dulan's measured words with angry abruptness. "Now that we are all together, Ananka, I want to know who or what you are, and what you intend to do with us. Make your explanation fast and basic; we don't have much time."

"I recall a night when I found your impatience charming," Ananka said, smiling at him until he took a step toward her. When she saw by his frozen face and menacing posture that he meant to have some answers she sighed dramatically "Very well, since you insist, I will explain. I am one of an ancient race of entities who journeyed to this world eons before insignificant creatures like you came into existence. There were hundreds of us then. We were happy and confident in our strength because we had brought with us lesser beings who ministered to our needs and respectfully honored our great powers. But as time passed the race of servants died, until there was no one left here but ourselves. It was then we learned we were not immortal. Deprived of the close relationship we had once enjoyed with our servants, my kind began to weaken, and one by one we ceased to exist. There were but three of us left on this world when the ones with open minds settled here."

"The telepaths," Herne murmured.

"They treated us with respect," said Ananka, "and in the beginning their presence renewed our hope, for we saw in them a new race of servants. But the telepaths have proven to be uncontrollably independant of mind and remarkably diverse in their attitudes toward superior beings. Only a few of them, young rebels all, have shown any willingness to honor me as I should be honored. I had begun to fear for my own life when you and your friends arrived at Tathan.

"Long, long ago, on another world," Ananka said, looking at Herne with a wistful expression, "there was a Herne who served me well. I thought one with the same name would serve again, and I knew from your careless throughts when first I saw you that you were curious about Merin. I decided to separate the two of you from your close companions in order to discover if you would dare to make your idle dreams come true. You have become lovers, as I hoped you would. Now you will settle here among the telepaths, to breed and increase in numbers. Your descendants will provide me with the servants I require."

"You want worshipers," Merin said. "You want to become a goddess."

"In another part of the galaxy, before you humans existed," Ananka replied, "I *was* a goddess, and a great one. So I will be again, before many more centuries have passed."

"You haven't been listening to us. We won't live long enough to provide you with worshipers. We are dying," Merin cried, but Herne stopped her despairing words.

"It is obvious from your talk about the future," he said to Ananka, "that I hold a vital piece of information you don't have yet."

Ananka looked at him doubtfully.

"I'll make a bargain with you," Herne offered. "Send Merin and me home and I'll tell you what I know."

"There is no need for a goddess to bargain with lowly beings like you," Ananka said with regal scorn. "I will simply take your knowledge from your mind."

"You will not! You have done enough harm. You have used me and my abilities most shamefully. I will help you no longer." Saray moved to stand next to Herne. She put one hand on his shoulder at the same time that Dulan placed a hand on Merin's shoulder. Behind them the green Chon moved closer, spreading its wings. A humming sound filled the air, while a vibrating shimmer rose like a barrier between the little group and Ananka, who began to fade into near transparency.

"Stop!" Ananka had become almost invisible. "Stop that infernal noise. I won't hurt anyone. I'll listen to your bargain."

The humming stopped. The shimmering barrier vanished. Ananka became substantial once more.

"It's that vile bird," she said. "My kind never could master them."

Merin was oddly invigorated by what had just happened. Believing that the bird had transmitted some of its strength to her, as it had done on the previous day, she glanced at Herne to see if he had been similarly affected. She was glad to see that he looked much healthier too. The wan, taut look was gone from his face, and he stood more easily, as though the mere act of keeping himself upright was no longer a test of his will. Merin straightened her shoulders and faced the would-be goddess with new hope.

"You have made a promise," Dulan reminded Ananka.

"Only to listen, not necessarily to agree to what is proposed," Ananka responded, smirking.

"Throughout history, goddesses were always capricious and frequently treacherous," Merin noted.

"She's a poor excuse for a goddess," Herne said, his eyes on Ananka. "She's just a peculiar entity with specific but limited powers. She may be an alien to us, and unimaginably long-lived, but she's not supernatural. If she were, the Chon would have no power over her."

"Excellent," said Dulan. "You learn quickly, Herne."

"Ananka," Herne said, "I want to know exactly how you brought us here. I very much doubt if you are capable of creating the solar storms."

"But I could take advantage of the electro-magnetic changes the storms caused," Ananka said with undisguised pride in her achievement.

"Then you can use the same electromagnetic changes to return us," said Herne. "You can send us back to a moment when we were still aboard the *Kalina*."

"I could," Ananka told him, "but I don't want to."

"Listen to Herne voluntarily," said Dulan, "or the bird and I will force you to listen. The secret Herne would tell you is all-important, to you and to the people of Tathan."

"You know what it is?" Herne stared at Dulan in amazement.

"Dulan learned the secret yesterday, when our thoughts merged," said Merin. "Ananka, you must promise to send us home."

"It seems I have little choice," said Ananka ruefully, looking at the Chon.

"Swear to it," Dulan insisted.

"If I swear a lie, how will you know it after your friends have disappeared?" asked Ananka.

"I will know. The Chon will tell me," said Dulan, the words making Ananka take a deep, gasping breath.

"I swear," she said, looking frightened.

"Tathan will be attacked," Herne said, not wasting any more time or words. "We don't know the exact date, but in our own time there is a record, in Dulan's hand, of Cetans destroying the city a century after its founding. Since the settlement is one hundred years old, it follows that the attack will come soon."

"All will die?" That was Saray, her face white with shock. "Every telepath dies on that day?"

"I have read Dulan's record several times," Merin said. "We know from it that twelve telepaths made their way safely to the island retreat at Lake Rhyadur, where they lived out their natural lives in peace. From my friend Osiyar, I have learned of another group of telepaths who escaped into the forest and later founded a village beside the sea in the northeastern part of this continent."

"Where one of my kind still lives," put in Ananka.

"I believe so," Merin said, "for Osiyar spoke of a mysterious entity who lived in a sacred grove."

"*She* was properly worshiped, no doubt," snapped Ananka.

"You will not be forgotten. Osiyar knew your name."

"I suppose I shall have to be content with that." Ananka did not sound at all content.

"It's more than you deserve," said Dulan.

"Herne, you could still stay with me," Ananka coaxed. "I will protect you from the Cetans, and I'll show you pleasures beyond human knowing."

"Since I am only a human, how could I know them?" asked Herne, with remarkable patience for him. "Thank you, but I want to go home. Send both of us back."

"I wish I hadn't promised." Ananka sighed. "You remind me so much of that earlier Herne. He was stubborn too. Very well, then. When do you want to leave?"

"Now," said Herne. "Just tell us what to do."

"Return to the little ship in which you arrived. You will find that the engines will start. Rise into the air, hover over Tathan, and I will do the rest."

"There are to be no tricks," Dulan warned, and Ananka sighed again.

"No tricks, Dulan. I promise." But then she smiled with a sweetly poisonous glance at Herne.

"No," cried Saray. "We must tell them everything, Ananka. How cruel you are! I can't believe I ever thought you were my friend. Merin, Herne, once you have returned to your own time, you will remember nothing of what has happened while you were in Tathan. In your time, only a few moments will have elapsed. There, the last four days have not happened."

"But we have made friends here," Merin protested. "You, Saray. Tula. And most of all, Dulan. Oh, my dear, dear friend Dulan, I don't ever want to forget you and all you have given to my heart and my spirit. I don't want to forget any of you."

"Stay and remember," said Ananka lightly. "Or go and forget. The choice is yours. By the way, once the change is made, they won't remember you, either, and you will no longer be aware of what you now feel for Herne. It will be as though you never were in Tathan."

"Dulan. Saray." Merin put out a hand to each of them.

"If it is truly love you feel for Herne, and he for you," Dulan said, understanding her deepest grief, "then your hearts will remember and find a way to join again. As for our friendship, it will endure through the centuries that separate us. I know it, and you know it too."

"You ought to leave Tathan at once," Herne suggested to Dulan. "Warn Tula, and the three of you start for Rhyadur."

"And what are we to do," asked Dulan, "when you are gone and we suddenly cannot recall why we are headed northward? No, we must wait here until the moment is right."

"I will not go to Rhyadur," Saray said. "I must atone for my crimes. Because of my close association with Ananka, I *will* remember what has happened. When the attack comes Hotan and I will lead the resistance against the Cetans. It is a role Hotan will relish, and I, at least, can be by his side until the end comes."

"You will die," said Ananka, sounding surprised at Saray's decision.

"So be it," Saray replied calmly.

"You are all mad," Ananka told them. "I don't think I want to be worshiped by your kind after all."

"It's just as well," Herne told her, "since you aren't really a goddess."

"Still, I can see where you are blind," Ananka replied, laughing. "What is the past for you remains the future for me. Time moves in its endless loops, and we will meet again for the first time, Herne. You will find me in the grotto."

"We will go now," Herne said, not responding to Ananka's brazen invitation. "Dulan, thank you for everything you have done for us. Tell Tula I thank him, too, and I'm sorry I was rude to him yesterday."

"Tell him so yourself," said Dulan. "Here he is, and Jidak and Imra with him."

"Your mate has returned," Tula told Dulan, "and is waiting for you in the computer room, where it is safe."

"There isss no sssafety," hissed Imra, her pale, triangular eyes darting around the garden. "All isss lost."

"As you suggested yesterday, Dulan," Jidak added, "we have been monitoring the computer's scanning device, set on its longest range. A Cetan ship has just moved into orbit. It won't take them long to send out shuttlecraft, nor to locate Tathan."

"No doubt they already know of our presence," Dulan said with remarkable calmness. "We know what they will want."

"Pillage, rape, murder, bloodshed." Imra stalked toward Ananka with the swift, smooth movements of her reptilian kind. "Isss thisss the entity Ananka? Will you help us defend our city?"

"I think you will find," Herne told Imra, "that if she gives you any aid at all, she will expect you to worship her in return."

"Styxians have their own gods," Imra told Ananka. "And I would not revere an entity that deliberately harms others."

"Nor would I accept the worship of an insect-eating lizard," returned Ananka with great contempt. "Don't speak to me of hurting others."

"Don't make her too angry," Herne warned. "She has promised to send Merin and me back where we belong, and we don't want her to change her mind."

"Then you had best go at once," Tula urged, "for Hotan and his friends are marching on the Gathering Hall even now. We came here to warn you. Dulan, they are convinced that Herne and Merin called the Cetans here to destroy us, and Hotan claims to believe that you helped them. He says you are all Jurisdiction spies, in league with the Cetans. Listen, you can hear them shouting."

It was more than shouting they heard; it was running footsteps. Hotan burst through the doors of the hall and into the garden. At the same moment when he appeared, the green Chon spread its wings and flew away.

"I knew I'd find you here," Hotan shouted, sprinting down the steps to grab Merin's wrist.

"You and the other spies. We'll kill all of you in the town square and leave your bodies for your friends the Cetans to find."

"They are not spies!" Saray was at Hotan's side. "Here is Ananka. She and I brought them to Tathan, just as I told you, and Ananka will verify that. Merin and Herne have nothing to do with Cetans."

"Nothing?" scoffed Hotan. "Then what is Jidak doing here with them? I'd wager he's a spy too."

"We all know," Dulan said, "what Jidak endured before he left Ceta to join us on our journey to this world."

"We only know what Jidak told us," Hotan declared. "A one-armed Cetan is still a Cetan."

"Have we come to this in our own time of peril?" cried Tula. "What has happened to our dream of a city where all the Races of telepaths could live together in peace?"

"Keep your dreams, old man," Hotan told him. "This is war. I'm going to see these spies dead in the square and then I'm going to fight and kill as many Cetans as I can."

"Wait." Saray caught at Hotan's arm. "My love, only talk to Ananka. She will tell you the truth, and she might even help us."

"Don't look to me," Ananka said, laughing. "I only promised to send Herne and Merin home again. Which I will do, Herne, if ever you are able to reach your shuttlecraft and get it into the air. As for you, Saray, since you refuse to

307

help me any longer, why should I help you? Fight your own battle." With that, Ananka vanished.

Hotan still had his fingers around Merin's wrist. He began to drag her up the steps toward the Gathering Hall. Herne leapt after him, followed by Dulan, Saray, and the others.

"Good." Hotan bared his teeth in a mirthless grin. "I knew I only had to capture this one and the rest of you would follow."

"Hotan, stop this at once." Saray was faster than Herne, and got to her lover and the struggling Merin first. She threw her arms around Merin's waist, trying to pull her away from Hotan by using all the weight of her body. "I won't let you hurt her. Please, Hotan, we have to organize a resistance. Let Merin go and help me rally our friends."

They had all reached the interior of the Hall by now. Ignoring Saray's continuing pleas, Hotan pulled the two women in the direction of the Chon statue. With Saray still clinging to her, Merin kicked and scratched at Hotan, finally bending over to bite his hand. He did not loosen his hold on her wrist but only swatted at her with his free hand as if her struggles were as unimportant as the buzzing of an insect.

The double doors of the main entrance stood open, allowing the roar of noise from the square to reach those inside the hall. Turning her head toward the sound, Merin caught a glimpse of frightened-looking people rushing about. Sud-

denly a group of obviously angry young men
and women surged through the door and raced
across the hall to surround Hotan, Merin, and
Saray.

"Death to the spies!" yelled one woman, a
Denebian by her pale gray skin and hair.

"Kill them, kill all the Cetans too!" shouted a
red-antennaed Jugarian, whom Merin recalled
seeing with Hotan at the Gathering she had
attended.

To Merin's perception, the crowd about them
quickly disintegrated into fragmented bits and
pieces. Someone snatched at the gear she still
had slung over her shoulder. She heard a loud
snap as a strap broke, but she did not have
time to look for whatever she had lost. She
caught glimpses of Herne's furious face as he
bare-handedly pushed through the mob toward
her, with Jidak on his right side and Imra on
his left.

Hotan is right about one thing, Merin thought
wildly, seeing Jidak sweep aside two young men
at a blow, *once a Cetan, always a Cetan. Even
with one arm and no weapons, he fights as a
Cetan should.*

She saw two other opponents pull away
when Imra bared her reptile's teeth and hissed
at them. Behind Imra, Tula was struggling
with a muscular young woman. Somehow,
Dulan had reached Merin's side. Someone
reached out to pull off the concealing blue
hood.

All motion, all sound, ceased at the sight of smooth, colorless skin stretched over the ruined bones of a once-noble face. Dulan stood immobilized.

No, Merin thought, her heart aching for Dulan's sake, *not like this, revealed so rude, uncaring folk can see.* Struggling against Hotan's hold on her with renewed purpose, she stretched her free hand forward. At the same time Saray released her grip on Merin's waist and stepped toward Dulan. Together, Merin and Saray lifted Dulan's hood back into place.

The few moments of hesitation on the part of Hotan's followers had given Herne the opportunity to reach Merin. He landed a well-placed punch on Hotan's jaw. Letting go of Merin's wrist, Hotan staggered a step or two, and Saray went to him.

Merin and her friends were left standing with their backs against the pedestal that held the Chon statue, just as they had stood two nights before. As on that night, Hotan and his group were separated from them. But not for long. With Hotan leading them and Saray dragging on his arm to hold him back, the angry rebels advanced toward the statue.

"Chon. Chon-chon. Chon."

Merin had never seen an angry Chon before. From the frightened reactions of the others in the Hall, she thought no one else had, either. There were three of them: a green one that Merin was certain was the same bird who had been in the garden earlier, and two blue Chon.

"Cho-on. Cho-on." It was a fearful sound. The birds spread their wings wide so they hovered just above the golden statue. Then, with another ear-piercing cry, they extended their talons in a terrifying display of fury while their long beaks opened to show their teeth. The threat was unmistakable. Anyone who harmed those gathered by the statue would be torn to shreds. Hotan's people fell back. A shimmering barrier rose between them and the statue.

"Merin," Saray shouted from the far side of the barrier, "Go! Love Herne till you die, as I love Hotan. Leave now, before it's too late."

"Come," Dulan said to Merin. "The birds will protect us for a few minutes more."

"Saray?" Merin could not take her eyes from Saray's tear-streaked face. Anything they might have called out to each other would be lost in the roar of outrage Hotan's followers now set up as they realized they would be deprived of their intended victims. Merin saw Saray's lips move, made out the single word, *good-bye*, and then Herne was pulling her toward the back door and the garden. Their friends followed, all of them running across the garden and into the alley behind it, where Tula's blue-and-yellow cart stood ready, the twin ixak harnessed to it.

"Get in," Tula ordered, clambering onto the front seat and picking up the reins. "Hurry!"

Herne's hands were at Merin's waist, lifting her upward. Imra, already aboard, caught

Merin's wrists in scaled three-fingered hands, hauling her into the cart. A moment later, she was sitting between the Styxian and Herne on the back seat, with Tula, Dulan, and Jidak in front, and Tula was racing his team through the streets of Tathan. It was no easy task. It seemed that every citizen of Tathan was frantically seeking a safe place to hide, and some were trying to take all of their belongings with them.

"The Chon have warned them," Dulan said, answering Merin's unasked question as to how the alarm had been sounded so quickly.

"Herne," Tula called over his shoulder, "we are heading toward our own safe place, the underground computer room. Once there, we will seal it against detection and do what we can to resist the coming attack."

"But you two must go to your shuttlecraft," Dulan added, "as Ananka has told you to do. It is the only hope you have of seeing Home again. Tula, it's best that you unharness the ixak and let them ride the beasts. It will be faster than taking the cart, and they will have to outrun any pursuit that Hotan might organize."

"But you will need the ixak," Merin protested, "to carry you to Lake Rhyadur."

"We have small air vehicles," Imra hissed. "They are faster and safer than travel by land."

Tula pulled up in front of a red stone building that looked no different from the other houses near it. Herne let Imra lower Merin to the ground while he went to help Tula free the ixak from their traces. Merin put her hands on Imra's shoulders and the Styxian swung her downward.

"Do not fear for Dulan," Imra hissed softly into her ear. "Or for Tula. Jidak and I will guard both of them with our lives. They will reach Lake Rhyadur in sssafety."

"I'm certain of it." Merin smiled at Imra, at a fierce, supposedly untrustworthy Styxian reptile, knowing she could depend on Imra to keep her promise.

"Go in sssafety yourself," said Imra. "You are brave, for a human female."

"Dulan." Merin turned to her dearest friend.

"We have no need for words, or for an embrace," Dulan said. "We understand each other's hearts."

"I thank you all," Merin said, looking at each of them.

"And I," said Herne. "I haven't always been polite, but I appreciate everything you have done for us."

"You should hurry." Tula's voice was rough. "The attack could begin at any time."

Merin had never ridden an animal before. With Imra holding the ixak steady, it took Herne and Tula both to boost Merin toward its back. They would not have succeeded without Jidak's help. He caught the seat of her treksuit in his single hand and raised her into the air. Merin was terrified. She clung to the reins with her right hand and clutched the ixak's mane with her left. She wanted to tell Herne that she could not possibly ride this huge beast, but Imra caught her eye. If a Styxian thought she was brave, then she would try to show courage. She straightened her spine and sat proudly. Imra nodded, hissing her approval.

"After you reach your ship," Tula advised, "turn the ixak free. They will be safe enough, and may even find their way back here when all is peaceful again."

"Farewell, my friends." Dulan's head was bowed. Tula waved to them. Imra raised her left arm high in the ancient Styxian salute. Jidak's clenched fist thudded against his broad chest in a gesture of great respect. Then Herne urged his mount forward and Merin's ixak followed it. They rounded a corner and the telepaths were lost to view.

Swallowing her tears, Merin looked about her at the chaos engulfing Tathan. The streets were jammed with carts, with other ixak, with lost pets howling, screaming children and anxious mothers of numerous Races. Many males brandished weapons in protective gestures if anyone came too close to their loved ones. Above them, the Chon circled endlessly as if to guide the fleeing. The single bridge across the Tath was impassible. Herne pulled the reins out of Merin's hand.

314

"Hold on tight," he said. "I don't know how strong the current is, but we'll have to go through the water. It's the only way. From what I know of Ananka, I don't think she's going to allow us much time before she reneges on her promise."

Now Merin had renewed reason to be grateful for the added vigor the Chon had imparted to her and to Herne. Through every moment of the next half hour she knew that without that fortification they would have been unable to survive.

The water of the Tath was far from cold, and the seaward current not strong, but Herne had reckoned without the tide. They were halfway across the river when the incoming bore caught them in a rush of churning, salty water. Merin was submerged by it, nearly torn from the ixak's back. Closing her eyes against the stinging wetness she wound both hands through the ixak's mane, clinging to it as hard as she could. When her head was above water for a few seconds she gasped for air before she was pulled beneath the surface once more. She did not know where Herne was; if he still had hold of her reins or if he had been swept away by the tide. She could only trust to the ixak's instincts and hope the animal would reach the farther shore before they both drowned.

Without any warning she felt the heat of the late summer sun on her face. She opened her eyes just in time to be tossed to the ground when the ixak collapsed under her. She lay where she had fallen, only a foot or two from the water's edge, breathing deeply of the clean, hot air and watching the ixak struggle to its feet. Before she could get to her own feet, Herne was pulling her upright.

"You've lost your coif," he said, pushing her wet hair back behind her ears. "It took a Cetan attack and a raging river to get that thing off your head in daylight, out in the open."

"You're alive," she cried, placing both hands on his chest to make certain it was true.

"So are you," he replied, grinning at her. "In case you haven't noticed."

"Where are all these people going?" she asked, looking about. The fields surrounding Tathan were filled with folk hurrying away from the city. More were pouring across the bridge and onto the only road, while a few, perhaps inspired by the success of Herne's bold decision, were trying to swim or to ride their ixak across the river.

"Who knows where they'll go?" Herne replied. "They are just hoping to find shelter before the Cetans arrive. Come on, help me get the bridles off the ixak. After that swim they are too exhausted to carry us any farther. We owe it to Tula to give his animals a chance to get away."

It took only a moment or two. The ixak gave no trouble, nor, when Herne slapped each on the rump, did they move off at any great speed.

316

"Got your breath back?" Herne caught her hand. "Can you run?"

"I'm sure of it. I'm fine now. Thanks to the Chon, I feel healthy again."

"Me too," he said, pulling on her hand to urge her along.

"I've lost my recorder," she told him. "I think it happened during the struggle at the Gathering Hall."

"Never mind that. Just concentrate on reaching the shuttlecraft."

They set off at the fastest pace they could manage while weaving their way among the hordes fleeing Tathan. Herne held tightly to Merin's hand so they would not become separated.

"There it is," he said. "We've moved off the common track now, which is good. We don't want to have to fight off terrified refugees who might want to go with us. I don't know how I could tell anyone to stay behind, but I believe Ananka's promise applied only to the two of us."

Freed of the press of so many people, they picked up speed, running as fast as they could toward the ship. Herne unbolted the manual latch and pulled the hatch open. As soon as they were inside, the hatch automatically slid shut again.

"That's encouraging," Herne noted. "Let's hope Ananka keeps her word about the engines too."

"I'll pilot." Merin took her familiar seat. Across the aisle, Herne strapped himself into the navigator's position. Finished with her own safety harness, Merin lifted her hands to the controls.

"Wait." Herne stopped her. He spoke in rapid, disjointed phrases, but to her ears, and to her heart, he made perfect sense. "When Hotan grabbed you—might have killed you—river— could have been lost. If we don't get out of this alive—want you to know—in spite of everything—I don't care what you are. I love you. *You*, Merin. Everything about you."

"I love you too," she said. Frightened as she was, and uncertain that Ananka would keep her promise to them, Merin had never been so happy. "In this time or any other, I don't think it's possible for me to forget what I feel for you."

"Nor I for you." He loosened his safety harness so he could lean across the aisle to kiss her. A long, blissful moment slid by while they reveled in tender emotion.

"All right," Herne said, laughing a little. "I'll finish proving it to you later. For now, let's go home."

"Aye, aye, sir." She laughed back at him.

The engines started on the first try. On his side of the aisle, Herne flicked a switch.

"Viewscreen and all navigational instruments working," he reported, then swore a rough Sibirnan oath. "The Cetans are here."

Chapter Seventeen

The viewscreen came to life as Herne spoke, revealing small, rapidly moving ships. Merin recognized them as an earlier version of their own craft.

"Cetan shuttlecraft coming in fast," Herne noted. "More of them than I expected, considering the size of the mother ship. Poor Tathan. Poor telepaths. If only we could help them."

"Perhaps we can, once we are airborne." Merin went to work at the controls. Their craft rose off the ground. "Ananka said to hover over Tathan until she does whatever she plans to do for us. We have weapons, Herne. We can distract the Cetans as long as we are in this time."

"Every moment we can keep them occupied in the air is that much longer the people on the ground will have to reach safety." Herne nodded his agreement. "Let's try it."

Just as Merin brought the shuttlecraft into position above Tathan, a burst of light on their starboard side rocked the little ship.

"Nasty people, the Cetans," Herne grunted, concentrating on their own weapons. "Give the word when you're ready."

"Fire." Merin's voice was cool. "Fire again."

"Got one! Will you look at that!" Herne pointed to the viewscreen. "We've got help. Those are Chon, maneuvering to confuse the Cetans, who probably don't even know the Chon exist. Are they going to be surprised! They'll think the birds are a whole fleet of small shuttlecraft. And now there's some fire coming from Tathan. Our friends aren't as defenseless as we thought. Our scanning instruments show hidden weapons placed all around the city, and from what I can see they are using them well. I'm sure it's Jidak's doing. He will know how other Cetans would plan an attack. It's just possible that more telepaths than we believed will survive this battle."

"I doubt if they can hold off this kind of all-out assault for long, though," Merin replied. "We're in position again, Herne. Fire when ready."

A bright flash on the viewscreen showed that Herne's weapon had found its mark. From the spot where a ship had been debris rained downward.

"Six Cetan shuttlecraft closing on us," Herne announced. "At least they're after us and not those people on the ground."

"Two more to port," Merin said, her eyes alternately on the viewscreen and the control panel. "Fire. Fire again."

A sudden blast from a Cetan ship sent the shuttlecraft spinning. Merin fought to regain their position above the city.

"Damnation," Herne muttered. "Where's Ananka? If she lied to us, I'll—"

"If she lied to us," Merin responded, "there is nothing we can do but die bravely."

"I think you're enjoying this." Herne spared her a quick glance before resetting his sights and firing at an oncoming Cetan ship.

"I was thinking how much Jidak and Imra would enjoy it," Merin answered. "They both come from warrior races. I wish they were in another ship, fighting with us."

"Watch out! Dive!" Herne's warning came too late. The Cetan ship fired straight at their bow. A stream of white fire ran along the control panel, searing Merin's hands. Screaming with pain, she fell backward. Herne was out of his seat in a heartbeat, burning his own fingers to put out the fire and set the damaged controls on automatic.

Merin lay senseless, sagging out of the pilot's chair into the aisle. Herne unclasped her safety harness and pulled her into his arms. Another bolt from a Cetan ship struck them. Herne fell

321

to his knees, still holding Merin.

In the center of the viewscreen a globe of greenish white light formed.

"Ananka?" Herne's voice was hoarse. The globe of light grew larger and brighter, more purely white.

"Come on, Ananka," Herne whispered. "You promised. Don't let her die. We haven't much time left. Do it now. Please. *Please*, for her sake."

The white light filled the shuttlecraft. Herne looked down at Merin's peaceful face, so thin and pale, and felt her fragile weight in his arms.

"Until later, Herne." Ananka's laughing voice came from the dazzling globe.

Herne looked into the light again, staring at it without flinching, until his head began to spin and his ears rang with the sound of a thousand bells. He stared until the universe went black.

Part IV
Home

Chapter Eighteen

Herne came onto the bridge just as Tarik's voice sounded over the speaker.

"The solar flares are too frequent and powerful for safe travel in the shuttlecraft," Tarik said, his words accompanied by much interference from static. "Stay aboard the *Kalina*, where you will be better shielded. Merin, do you hear me?"

"Heard and understood," she responded.

"Narisa calculates it will be two to three days more before it's safe to send Carlis and Alla to relieve you, and for you to come home. I'm sorry about this, but it can't be helped. Is everything going well there?"

"As you know, we've had one or two minor problems, but they've been repaired."

"How are you getting along with Herne?"

Well aware that others at headquarters might be nearby to overhear whatever she said, Merin replied, "Herne is always professional. He was most helpful when we had that trouble with the disconnected cable."

"I'm glad to hear it. I know he doesn't enjoy being confined on the ship. We'll talk again later." Tarik signed off.

"So we're to stay a few days longer." Herne came toward her, smiling in a way that was not at all usual for him. "Tarik is wrong, I don't mind at all. Do you?"

"Not really. I like the *Kalina*." Merin started to rise in order to yield the science officer's chair to him while she made her end-of-watch report. She hesitated, struck by sudden dizziness.

"Are you sick?" Herne had seen her waver. He put out a steadying hand, catching her at waist level. Instead of backing quickly away from him as she ordinarily would do, Merin leaned toward him, placing her hand on his upper arm. They stood thus in a half embrace while she marveled at the absence of supressed anger in him. There was a calmness about him that she had never noticed before. He was regarding her with serious concern, so it was possible that quiet competence was part of his medical persona when dealing with a patient.

"I have been light-headed for the last few

minutes, but there is no reason for it," she told him.

"I've been feeling a bit queasy myself," he admitted. "Perhaps it has something to do with the solar storms. But there is another reason why you should be dizzy. You haven't been eating. Sit down."

His hands on her shoulders made it impossible for her to resist the order.

"Put your head down." He pressed her forward till her face was touching her knees. "Now stay there for a minute."

She could hear the soft whirring of his diagnostic rod.

"You are constantly examining me," she complained.

"That's because I worry about you." He took her wrist between his fingers. She straightened a little, not enough to give him cause to scold her for lifting her head before he had given his permission, but far enough to be able to watch him counting her pulse.

"Isn't that method a bit primitive?" she asked.

"These things aren't infallable." He pocketed the rod. "You pulse rate is rapid, but otherwise you check out as perfectly normal. Do you have any aches or pains I should know about?"

"My hands still itch, but you said they would till the lacerations heal. Today, there is a burning sensation in my fingers, too."

"That's not unusual." Herne turned her hands

palm upward to look at them. "They're healing normally, although your fingertips are a bit red. It could be a minor burn. Have you been getting too close to the heating element in the galley?"

"Not that I remember. May I stand up now?"

"Only if you promise to eat something. You are much too thin."

"As a matter of fact, I'm hungry." She sounded as surprised as she felt. She was never hungry, she simply ate when it was time to do so.

"I'm hungry, too." He put his arm around her waist to help her rise. She did not protest the gesture. She went to the hatch, where she paused, looking back over her shoulder with a quirk of her lips that Herne thought might have been the beginning of a smile, except that Merin never smiled.

"In that case, I had better prepare enough food for two," she said. "Vegetable stew, bread and fruit for both of us, with a double serving of pastry for you."

"Merin." His teasing tone stopped her exit from the bridge. She saw the harsh lines of his face softened by amusement. "It is still your watch for another hour. I am the one who should prepare the food."

"I forgot." She put one hand to her head. "I wasn't thinking. I guess it's because I'm so hungry."

"Then I had better bring your meal quickly,

and make it enough for four."

When they passed each other, Herne heading for the galley, Merin back to the science officer's chair, he patted her shoulder in a light, friendly touch. She stared after him, wondering why she was not offended by what he had just done.

The light-headedness washed over her again, leaving her with a distinctly unsettled feeling, as though some fundamental aspect of her being was in the process of shifting position. She sank into her chair, rubbing at her itching, burning hands. By the time Herne returned with their food the dizziness was gone.

"I have never seen you eat like that before," he said, leaning back in his chair in a relaxed posture and smiling at her. "I take it as a healthy sign."

"You're different," she told him.

"In what way?" He had been reaching for a third piece of pastry, the kind he especially liked, stuffed with juicy red berries. His hand stopped, hovering over the plate, while his eyes flashed a sharp look at her that said all she needed to know.

"You are confused, too, aren't you?" she said. "Upset, unsettled, a little dizzy. And very hungry. You have eaten twice as much as I have."

"What of it?" He was trying to hide what he thought was a weakness with his usual abruptness, but it wasn't working. She knew him too well for him to fool her in that way.

Knew him too well? Why should she think that? She didn't know him at all.

"We are not sick," Herne told her. "I have checked both of us thoroughly. There is nothing wrong with the air supply, the water, or the food on this ship. There are no toxic substances affecting us."

"And yet?" she encouraged, more confused than ever.

"And nothing." He popped the third pastry into his mouth and began to chew.

"There is something hovering around the edges of my memory, but I can't get it back," she said. "I wish I could remember."

Herne swallowed the last of his qahf, watching her. She knew he was watching her because she was looking straight at him. She was looking right into his eyes without the least twinge of embarrassment or shame. It seemed perfectly natural to do so. His answering gaze warmed her, lifting her spirits. In the blink of an eye, as she sat there looking at him, she saw herself going into his arms, felt his naked body against hers, his mouth scalding her own. She felt him inside her.

With a gasp she leapt out of her seat and across the bridge. How could she imagine something so dreadful, so completely foreign to her training? What was wrong with her, to make her feel this way, to make her allow passionate emotion to suddenly take such strong

No Other Love

control of her mind? She knew as well as anyone else that the coming together of male and female was the most terrible crime of all under Oressian law.

Her thoughts reeled in confusion. Her body was telling her something her mind dared not accept. She knew, *knew* absolutely, that union with Herne would bring with it not pain and physical destruction but an intense, sweet joy, and the beauty of their joining would endure for the rest of their lives. Her certainty of that heretical belief was so strong that it was as though her body understood something her mind did not know, or had rejected, or had forgotten.

For one long moment of nearly unbearable conflict, Merin's strict Oressian training fought against her knowing body, and against her deep, complicated feelings toward Herne. She wanted him. She could *not* want him. It was impossible, vile, unnatural. She wanted to be a good Oressian. *She wanted Herne.*

She clamped her mouth shut on a groan, refusing to express by any sound her terrible inner turmoil. Unaware of Herne's reaction to her stiff posture or her tense, withdrawn expression, she was completely focused on the battle taking place inside her deepest self.

It was a painful struggle. For a time it seemed her sanity would be utterly destroyed by the strain of it. But at her weakest moment, when any hope of integrating two totally antagonis-

331

tic desires seemed impossible, there rose into her thoughts the image of a blue-robed figure with an ageless face. From the figure radiated so much affection and strength, so much pure friendship, that Merin, her courage renewed, was able to set herself once more to find a way through anguish and uncertainty back to reality.

Finally, as if a thousand tiny clenched fists had opened themselves in her mind to set her emotions free, the complex web of Oressian laws and rules and training that had held her bound for her twenty-five years of life drifted into the back of her consciousness. She knew that web would never be entirely gone from her. She did not want it gone. There were valuable qualities she had gained from her childhood: her respect for order over chaos, for peace over violence, her love of learning. But there were advantages to other ways of life, and strong emotions were not necessarily destructive. Miraculously, she could now accept those revolutionary ideas. She could accept Herne, and her need for him.

"Merin, speak to me."

She realized that Herne had been talking to her for some time, while she had been silently undergoing the most amazing internal transformation. He was holding her shoulders, as if he thought only his strength could keep her upright. She laid both of her hands flat upon his chest and lifted her face to his.

"Please," she whispered, with the oddest sense that she had said the same words before, "please kiss me."

"Don't ask unless you mean it," he growled, stepping back a pace. She took one of his hands and laid it over her breast. He made a sound in his throat, a low primeval moan of rising male passion.

"Kiss me, Herne."

"If this is some weird aberration of Oressian hormones caused by the solar flares," he groaned, pulling her toward him, "I don't want to hear the scientific explanation."

"It's no aberration," she whispered, her mouth against his. "It's me. It's what I want."

His mouth was hot on hers, his arms held her tightly. Her lips parted to let his tongue surge into her. Merin put her arms around his neck, raising herself on tiptoe, and gave herself completely to his kiss. It was wonderful; it was everything she had known it would be. It ended too soon.

"We are supposed to be watching the ship," he said, his voice a little hoarse.

"Could we put the instruments on automatic for a few minutes?" she asked.

"A few minutes?" He shook his head. "More like a few hours."

He did not let go of her. Perhaps he was afraid she would change her mind if he did not continue to touch her. He kept one arm around her waist while he transferred all the *Kalina's* instruments to automatic.

"Our cabins are too far from the bridge," he said. "It's not that I'm unromantic, but I'd like both of us to stay alive through any emergency that might occur. We will have to use the conference room."

Still holding her at the waist, he led her toward it. The rest of the ship was black and gray, and the conference room had gray walls, but during the refitting at Capital new furniture had been installed. The conference table was ebony artificial wood, the chairs around it covered in darkest maroon. To one side of the room were two armchairs and a couch, all in dark maroon upholstery. The couch was narrow for two people to lie on it, but the bunks in their cabins were not much wider.

Merin went toward the nearest armchair. There she paused, one hand at the neck of her treksuit.

"Let me." Herne's fingers brushed hers aside, then slid along the pressure sensitive opening. The front of her suit fell apart. He peeled it off her shoulders and down the length of her body. Soon treksuit and boots were removed and she stood before him in the thin sleeveless undershirt and low-cut briefs that were standard Jurisdiction Service issue. His fingertips lightly touched her breasts, circling her nipples until they stood up hard and obvious through the semitransparent fabric.

Merin caught her breath. She was trembling in eager anticipation, but she was surprised at her own lack of fear. She touched Herne's treksuit.

"It's my turn," she said and opened it from throat to crotch. He did not wait any longer for her. Within a second or two he had pulled off the suit, his boots, and his underwear. He looked as he had in her dreams, a large-boned, hard-muscled man, with thick ash brown hair and gray eyes. His manhood stood out stiff and proud from a cluster of brown curls.

Merin licked her dry lips and reached for the chinstrap of her coif. Now that his body was revealed to her in all its masculine glory, she could see how much he wanted her. It was time for her also to show her most intimate secrets. She unfastened the chinstrap, pulled off her coif, and dropped it onto the armchair where he had laid her treksuit. With both hands she began to remove the pins that held her tightly coiled hair. She bent to lay the pins neatly on top of her coif, then straightened to find him staring at her in awestruck wonder.

"I swear by all the stars that I have never seen anyone or anything as beautiful as you," he whispered.

With her eyes locked on his, she pulled off her undershirt. She reached for her last remaining piece of clothing, but he stopped her.

"My turn again," he murmured. He slid his

hands around her hips, beneath the top edge of her briefs and over her buttocks. Slowly, deliberately, he eased the flimsy undergarment down along her legs to the floor, kneeling as he moved lower. His face was against her thighs, his hands still caressing her ankles and calves. He began to kiss her thighs while he stroked upward with both hands. Merin cried out, her knees buckling. She caught at his shoulders to keep herself from falling.

He must have heard the alarm in her voice, for he stood at once and lifted her, carrying her to the couch. He bent over her, looking deep into her eyes.

"You have always been so reluctant," he said. "Are you absolutely certain this is what you want?"

"Could you bear it if I said no?" she responded, smiling at him. "I know I could not bear it if you were to turn away from me at this moment."

"What has changed you so radically in so short a time?"

It would take too long to explain what had just happened to her and she did not want to lose this precious moment. She would tell him everything later, but for now she answered almost flippantly.

"Perhaps the solar flares had something to do with it." She laughed a little, then saw him looked startled, as though she had never laughed before. But she had laughed, and he

had laughed back at her. Where? When? The
faint trace of a lost memory faded. She tried a
more rational approach. "Perhaps the change
occurred when you tried so desperately to rescue me from that awful shaft, and kissed me
afterward. Perhaps I just didn't recognize the
change until now."

"You have never been with a man before." It
was a statement, not a question.

"Oressians don't—" She stopped, unsure how
much to say. She saw him frown and shake his
head a little as if to drive away an unwelcome
thought.

"No, of course Oressians don't," he said.
"You did tell me that once. It may hurt a
little when we first come together. I'll be as
gentle as I can."

"I'm not afraid." Smiling, she raised both
hands to catch his face and pull it close
enough for a kiss. She met his mouth with
her lips open.

Any barriers that might have remained
between them disappeared in an instant.
Herne's passion engulfed her like a raging
flood, his hands and mouth and tongue
driving her to near madness. She felt as
though her body remembered him, but that
was obviously impossible. Still, every touch,
every caress, every kiss evoked a familiar
physical reaction. And she knew how and
where to touch him so as to give him the
greatest possible pleasure. As her excitement

mounted, she cried out shamelessly, begging him not to stop what he was doing. She saw him poised above her, his face tense.

"Please," she whispered, as earlier she had begged him to kiss her. "Please, Herne."

He pushed against her. Smiling into his eyes, she pushed back, offering him all she had to give. Being gentle as he had promised, he moved into her. There was no pain, there was only a long, slow, beautifully sensuous slide until he filled her completely. She sighed with pleasure. This was what she wanted. Herne made a slight movement, joining them even more closely. Passion rose in her with great naturalness, as if she and Herne had been together like this many times in the past.

That notion was nonsense, of course. It was just the memory of his previous stolen kisses that had inflamed her senses, making her want what he was doing now. She moaned when he moved again. She saw him looking at her in amazement.

"I know you," he whispered. "My body knows yours."

He withdrew from her completely, then drove into her with fierce passion, again and again, harder and harder. Merin wrapped her arms and legs around him, crying out with mounting desire at each vigorous thrust until finally they shuddered together into a great, gasping climax that met the unfulfilled need secretly waiting within her and released it into quivering beauty.

Nor did he leave her at once, but held her still, his mouth upon hers, through a long and quieter resolution, while their hearts gradually stopped racing and their breathing steadied. Passion completely spent at last, he gathered her tenderly into his arms again.

"I once read," he told her, wiping the tears from her face, "that when a woman weeps at the climax of lovemaking, it's because her soul has been touched."

If the woman has a soul. She could not speak for fear she would begin to cry in earnest and blurt out what she knew she soon had to tell him. She had made her peace with her past, but she was not certain Herne would be able to accept it. She caught his caressing hand and kissed it instead of using words to describe her feelings.

"I love you," he said. "With all my heart and for all time, I love you."

Still she said nothing. She only held his hand to her lips.

"I suppose an Oressian can't say it." He sounded wistful.

"An Oressian." She sighed, knowing she could not put revelation off much longer. "There is much I need to tell you. When I do, you will turn from me in disgust."

"There is nothing disgusting about you," he

said with great firmness. "Didn't you hear me, Merin? I love you."

She sat up, the sudden action almost pushing him off the couch.

"We are neglecting our duties," she said. "I will dress and check the instruments."

He was beside her, taking the treksuit out of her hand, tossing it back onto the chair.

"For a virgin who has just had her first experience of lovemaking," he said, "you are behaving with remarkable coolness."

"First?" Confused, she wrinkled her brow. "Yes, it was my first experience. How could it be otherwise?"

"Then I guess Oressian women are made a little differently from other women."

"What do you mean?" She tensed, all too aware of what she had to tell him in the next hour.

"Only that it didn't hurt you. In fact, it was as if we had made love before."

"I will dress now." She wanted to delay the painful subject, at least until she was decently covered again. Then his rejection wouldn't hurt so much.

"If you must, then just your underwear," he said. "It's warm enough, and with only the two of us aboard, it doesn't matter what we wear. Besides, we may want to come back here in a little while."

"Not after you hear what I have to say." Nevertheless, she put on only undershirt and briefs. Herne pulled on his own briefs and they went out onto the bridge.

"There, you see, everything is as it should be." Herne flicked the switches, turning part of the instruments back to manual control. "I'm hungry again. Will you make some food or shall I?"

"I cannot eat until I have told you the truth about me. Please stop looking at me like that, and stop touching me until I have said what I must."

"Sorry. I like to touch you. It seems natural now that we have become lovers."

"We are not!" She stopped, one hand over her mouth. "Yes, we are. I want to go on being your lover till we grow old and die. My body and yours, my heart and yours. My soul and yours. But you may not think I have a soul. Oh, Herne, let me speak before my heart breaks from the weight of this guilt I carry. I have allowed you to imagine things about me that are not true. I have deliberately led you to believe falsehoods."

He sat down in the navigator's chair and spun the science officer's chair around to face him.

"Sit here," he ordered. "Say what you want, and never believe I'll stop loving you."

She told him everything.

"So you are a clone," he said quietly when she had finished. Then, with a hint of anger, "How many other Merins are there, back on Oressia?"

"We are not named, we are numbered. I chose the name of Merin for myself when I was told I had to leave Oressia. I had read it in a history book."

"So on Oressia there is a society of identical people, created to certain specifications, functioning like living machinery." His disgust showed in his face. "No wonder the Jurisdiction forbids that kind of artificial reproduction."

"If the Jurisdiction ever learned the truth about Oressia," she said sadly, "the planet would be destroyed, with no compunction whatsoever, because we are considered, as you say, identical, soulless, subhuman creatures."

"Not long ago," Herne said, "I think I would have been unable to accept what you have just told me. But something inside me has changed. I don't know how or why it happened. Perhaps the change occurred as I learned to love you. Whatever the cause, I'm not the same man I used to be, and I know you are not a soulless creature. If ever anyone had a soul, you have."

"You don't know me well enough to say that."

"I do know you. You are a physically normal, exceptionally beautiful, intelligent, warm-hearted woman, though you try to disguise most of these qualities. You are courageous and inventive in a crisis, you are tolerant of personal differences, and a wonderful friend. I know you here." Herne struck his chest. "You spoke earlier of the two of us, body to body, heart to heart, soul to soul. That's true. You and I, together. I don't care if there are a thousand others back on Oressia who are just like you. You are the Merin I love."

"But there are not a thousand others," she exclaimed. "That is the greatest mystery of Oressia. We are alike when we leave First Cubicle, but after that, changes occur in each of us that make us distinctive individuals by the time we are twenty. It should not happen, but it does. No one knows why. There are theories linking the differences to Oressian water, or to the soil in which our food is grown. Others claim the changes occur during the maturing process that takes place at age fifteen. The mystery remains unsolved. All we know is that by the time we are twenty, we are more like very similar brothers and sisters would be on some other world than like identical clones.

"You can understand," she went on, "why Oressians are bound to strict secrecy about our way of life. But it seemed right to me for you to know. I cannot swear you to silence; I can only ask you not to reveal this truth to anyone who would find me repulsive as a result of the knowledge. This is not something I had control over, Herne, any more than you could control the hair color you were born with or the shade of your eyes."

She fell silent. Herne was staring at his hands, which he had clenched into fists. He did that sometimes, when he was trying to control his anger, but she had not seen him do it since—since when? He himself had admitted that something had happened, something important, that had changed him, had taken away his inner rage. But what? And when? Had her story so revolted and angered him that the rage was back?

"Have you ever killed anyone?" he asked suddenly. "No, don't bother to answer. It was a stupid question after the tale you have just told me. You have been trained not to be violent. Merin, I was fifteen when I left Sibirna. Before my fifteenth birthday I had killed eight men. I had to, to stay alive. That's the kind of place Sibirna is."

"That's horrible," she whispered. He went on talking, his eyes still on his clenched fists.

"The true horror was that no one, not even close relatives of the dead, cared very much. That kind of violence was just accepted as an everyday occurrence, because all Sibirnans should be free to do whatever they want. To my mind, that way of living, without any self-discipline, is as bad as growing children in a laboratory. Both cultures degrade the human spirit, but I think Sibirna is worse than Oressia. *Eight men.* All of them attacked me first, but still, after that what right do I have to call you a horror?"

Wanting to comfort him, she put one hand over his fists. He looked up at her, searching her face.

"I don't usually talk about my past. Do you hate me for it?"

"I could never hate you." Then she thought of an argument that might help him. "Herne, you told me once that you left Sibirna because of the violence. You became a physician because you wanted to help people, not hurt them. How many lives have you saved?"

"I don't know; I've lost count. I was in the Service for years during the Cetan wars, and assigned to Riotha during the plagues there. It was hard to keep track of my patients during all that." He rubbed his hands across his face, as if he were tired. "I know what you're trying to say, Merin."

"I'll say it anyway. You are by nature a healer, not a killer. It is certain that you have saved more lives than you have taken."

"I hope so. It would be some recompense for the blood on my hands."

"Jurisdiction law recognizes self-defense. You said those men all attacked you. The death of your opponent in one-to-one combat in which you were fighting for your life is not a punishable offense."

"Eight-to-one combat," he corrected her, "and the Jurisdiction knows about it. I confessed before I entered the Service. They cleared me of all guilt in the incident, but I still can't forgive myself for those deaths. I should have found a better way to end the fight."

"Eight to one? And you think you are to

345

blame for what happened during that cowardly attack?" She went to her knees before his chair, taking his hands in hers. "You must have been terrified. How brave you were, at such a young age, to win over so many. How proud of you I am. How much I love you."

"There can be no question you have a soul," he said, "but there's more than a little barbarian in it. Your ancient ancestors would be proud to claim you as their own. Who would have thought it would take the story of that dishonest ambush to make you say you love me?"

"It's not the first time I have said it to you."

"Really? When did you ever say it before now? In the shaft when I couldn't hear you, when we both thought you were going to die?"

"I said it in my dreams," she told him, knowing there had been another time, another place, when she had dared so much. But where? When?

"Merin," he said, touching her face with gentle fingers, "your watch is over now, and I am suddenly half-starved. Do you think you could prepare enough food for both of us?"

"It will take a while," she said. "But you want to be alone for a time, don't you? You want to think about what we have both said."

"You know me well." He watched her walk toward the hatchway, a tense young woman barely covered by her skimpy underwear. There was one thing he did not need to think about, not for a moment more. "I love you," he said, and watched the tenseness leave her slender figure.

"I have a theory about why sex was the activity most particularly forbidden among Oressians," Herne announced. He paused, noting a flush of rising color in Merin's cheeks, though she continued to eat with every appearance of indifference to what he might say. "I suspect it was because Oressians are an extremely passionate people. I have known a few women in my life, not many, but enough to know that you are unusually responsive."

"We were taught that it is extremely painful to men and women alike," she began, "that it destroys the body."

"Was it painful for you?" he asked.

"Not at all. It was wonderful." Her cheeks were flaming now. She had stopped eating.

"It was more than wonderful for me," Herne told her, "because of the way you reacted to me. Which is probably why the ancient Oressians spent so much time at it, until their promiscuous actions threatened wholesale destruction to their society. It's easy enough to imagine jealous passions causing personal dissension, or family and clan feuds, or even escalating into international warfare.

"I believe that is why your Great Olekan forbade the art of love. That's why he made all those strict rules and laws for daily life, why you were created and raised as you were. Perhaps Olekan's methods were the only ones that would have worked on Oressia. I don't know about that, not being a sociologist or a historian, but it does seem a shame to me to force an entire planet to forego the pleasures of rapturous sex in order to keep peace and preserve the Oressian race. There should have been an easier way." He paused to smile at her. "At least you are freed from that tyranny. On Dulan's Planet there is no punishment for love."

"Freed." Her gaze was thoughtful. "I have noticed that other free women, Suria, for instance, or Narisa, or even Alla from time to time, incite their men, rather than waiting for the males to make the first advances."

"Have you thought of following their example?" He raised an eyebrow at her. "I like that word, incite. It suggests the possibility of a riot."

She stood, the motion pulling her undershirt tighter across her breasts. He looked from her bosom to the tempting curve of her abdomen and then below, to the dark shadow beneath her briefs, where her thighs joined. She shook her head in a seductive motion, making her mane of qahf-colored hair swing forward across her right shoulder.

"Can there be a riot with only two people

present?" she asked with great seriousness.

"I don't know." He reached over to switch all the instruments back to automatic. "Shall we find out?"

Chapter Nineteen

The lake glittered in ice-rimmed winter blue; the bare trees swayed in the cold wind. Dressed warmly against the chill, Tarik and Osiyar had come to the shore to greet Merin and Herne on their return to headquarters. The shuttlecraft appeared on schedule, spiraling downward to settle on the snow-dusted beach.

The main hatch opened and a woman stepped out. She wore a vivid blue heat-conserving jacket over her orange treksuit, but her head was bare. Gleaming hair the color of well-brewed qahf was coiled neatly at the back of her head, controlled except for a few loose wisps caught by the wind. She turned her head, saying something to her companion, still in the shuttlecraft. The sound of laughter drifted toward the watching men.

"Merin?" Tarik gaped at the smiling woman now coming toward him. "Is that really you?"

Herne had jumped out of the shuttlecraft and was following Merin up the beach. When he reached her side he put an arm across her shoulders. She regarded him with open affection.

"She looks different without that cursed coif, doesn't she?" he asked with a big grin. "I convinced her to take it off and dump it into the recycling chamber."

"One must wonder," murmured Osiyar, "exactly how you achieved that notable end."

"Can't tell you." Herne's arm tightened around Merin. "Medical confidentiality, you know." With that, he and Merin headed for the warmth of the building at the center of the island.

"I did say," Tarik noted, watching them, "that they wouldn't mind a few extra days alone together."

"It is as I had hoped," Osiyar mused, also looking after the lovers. "I was not wrong about Merin. She knows, though she has forgotten what she knows. It is enough. She will find her way, and so will he find his."

"I won't pretend to understand what that means." Tarik began to walk toward the headquarters building, toward Home. Osiyar went with him, Jurisdiction officer and telepath together, friends in spite of the cultural and psychical gulf that should have separated them.

Tarik spoke again. "There are more things in heaven and earth than we can know."

"If Narisa could hear you," said Osiyar, "she would doubtless warn you about misquoting poetry."

Tarik's only answer to that was a wicked chuckle.

"I thought you would be interested to learn," Narisa told Merin, "that Tarik and I have finished cleaning and analyzing the recorder you found at Tathan." She gave a copy of the report to Merin, who shook her head in disbelief as she read it.

"What's wrong?" asked Herne.

"I held both recorders at the same time, one in each hand, while we were in Tathan. I know the numbers match," Merin said, "but there must be some mistake. The laws of physics—"

"We have talked about the effects of the Empty Sector before." Tarik had joined them. "Where is your recorder, Merin?"

"I took it with me to the *Kalina,* in case I should need it." She spoke slowly, going over in her mind the last seven days aboard the spaceship. "I put it in my cabin, on the shelf by my bed. I saw it there every day, until three days ago. It seemed to me I had taken it with my other gear when we went to the shuttlecraft to leave. But we didn't leave, we stayed on, and I haven't seen it since. I looked everywhere for it. It's lost."

"Why would you pack and go to the shuttle-craft when you knew you would have to remain aboard for several more days?" Tarik asked.

"We didn't pack," Herne put in. "We just continued with our alternate watches, as you wanted us to do."

"Then why does Merin remember packing to leave?" Tarik's dark blue eyes searched her face. Merin rubbed at her forehead, trying to better focus her thoughts. Her memory was oddly indistinct about the hours in question.

"Perhaps I was thinking of the last time I served on the *Kalina*, with Suria," she said.

"Perhaps." Tarik looked unconvinced.

"May I see the recorder?" she asked.

"Of course. It is yours." Tarik nodded to Narisa, who hurried to the storeroom, returning at once with the instrument. It had been cleaned of the centuries of encrusted dirt. It looked old and well-used, but still serviceable.

"It will work now, but too poorly for daily use," said Narisa. "We tried to obtain any information that might have been stored in it, but nothing made any sense, except for a sentence or two about bolts of lightning."

"That means nothing to me," said Merin. "I don't remember recording anything about lightning. Did you check the data I put into the main computer?"

"We found nothing that matched the phrases on the recorder," Narisa said.

"I'll issue a new recorder to you." Tarik took

back the old one. He held it for a moment, weighing it. Then he looked from Merin and Herne to Narisa. "This represents a mystery we may never solve. Tantalizing, isn't it?" He gave the recorder to his wife.

"Where is the book with Dulan's notes?" Merin asked suddenly. "I want to read it again. I'd also like to review the historical tapes the telepaths left here. And, Tarik, when you make your next archaeological trip to Tathan, I want to go with you. Herne?"

"Yes," said Herne. "I'll go too."

"I see," said Tarik, winking at Narisa. "Will that be as colleagues, or as husband and wife?"

"As both, if you will be good enough to marry us," Herne answered. He turned to Merin, taking her in his arms. She made no resistance at all, but went to him with complete trust and love. "Our hearts have found a way through all the differences and the rigid laws that once separated us."

"'Our hearts have found a way,'" Merin repeated, frowning a little. "I have heard something like that before. I wonder where?"

"Does it matter, so long as we are together?" Herne gazed into her eyes and made his pledge. "Wherever you go, I will go, too, until time ends. And for me, through all of time, there will be no other love."

SPECIAL SNEAK PREVIEW!

COMING IN MAY 1994!

A LOVE BEYOND TIME

Flora Speer

An archeologist by trade, Mike Bailey has had plenty of
practice digging up bones from bygone days. But when a
computer genius's time travel program hurls him to the
eighth century, Mike is thrust into the midst of
Charlemagne's camp. There, an enchanting damsel piques
more than his professional interest. But the Frankish warrior
courting the fair Danise would sooner see Mike become a
lost relic than surrender the love of his intended.

Don't Miss *A Love Beyond Time*—

**Available in May 1994 at Bookstores
and Newsstands Everywhere!**

Chapter One

New Mexico
October, 1992.

"Has anyone ever told you that you are crazy?"

"All the time. But I never pay any attention, because I know I'm right." Henry Adelbert Marsh regarded his visitor with cool arrogance. The man facing him was of average height, with dark hair and nondescript features except for the startling blue eyes that lifted his appearance far out of the ordinary. Hank Marsh wasn't one to be unduly impressed by a person's looks—he wasn't all that handsome himself—but he was annoyed with this man, and he was curious. He met the blue gaze with open defiance. "What I want to know is how you found me. I covered my tracks pretty damned well."

"You did. I'll give you that much. I lost you for a long time. It took me months of searching and a lot of trouble to discover just where you were hiding." Ignoring the woman who was the third person in the room, Bradford Michael Bailey moved a little farther into the back bedroom of the house, his eyes on the computer that filled the better part of the space. There could be absolutely no doubt; he had found his quarry at last, and Hank was up to his old tricks again. "As it happens, I am something of a detective. An historical detective, since I'm an archaeologist. I enjoy the challenge of a difficult search. And I was given a few clues to help me find you. Do you remember Mark Brant? Or India Baldwin?"

"India sent you after me?" Hank's arrogant mask slipped a bit. "I never thought she'd talk. She was so adamant about forgetting what happened last Christmastime."

"You mean about you accidentally sending her far back in time? How could anyone ever forget living through such an experience? No, India didn't talk. My friend, Mark, figured out what had happened. He's the one who sent me after you."

"I knew that guy was trouble the first time I saw him," Hank muttered. "O.K., now you've found me. What do you want with me, Bailey?"

"The name's Mike. I've learned enough about you during the last ten months to put us on a first-name basis. I assume this is your latest machine." Mike took a couple of steps toward the computer, noting the additional components and the power enhancers. He was no stranger to computers. Archaeologists found them remarkably useful. "You have made some interesting changes to this thing, haven't you? Are you hoping to prove some wild new theory, or are you still working on the old one?"

At this point, the young woman who had let Mike into her house when he claimed to be Hank's friend inserted herself between Mike and the computer. From his investigations into Hank's whereabouts, Mike knew her name was Alice. She was small and thin, with dark hair scraped back into a tight ponytail. She wore no makeup and her expression was grimly intense. It occurred to Mike that she would be a lot prettier if she would lighten up a little. But perhaps her interest in Hank was more scientific than romantic. It certainly seemed that way.

"Leave Hank alone," Alice ordered. "And you stay away from his computer, too. Our theories and what we are doing are none of your business. You don't have any right to intrude on our privacy."

"Did you know your friend here is a thief?" Mike said to her. When Alice glanced toward Hank, Mike took another step in the direction of the computer. "Hank has stolen the property

361

of this India Baldwin we've just mentioned. I have been sent to collect and return that property."

"Hank is no thief," Alice protested. "He's a great and misunderstood scientist."

"He broke into India Baldwin's house and took two floppy disks and a notebook that belonged to her. Then Hank left town with those disks and the notebook. If that's not stealing, I don't know what is. But if he'll return her property, India has promised she won't press charges against him."

"You can't interfere with important scientific work," Alice cried, apparently oblivious to the legal implications of what Hank had done. Mike decided he wasn't going to get anywhere with her. Alice was on Hank's side, and she probably wouldn't budge from her position without a good scare.

"Hand over the disks, Hank. And the notebook." Mike put out his hand, waiting. "If you give them to me, I won't call the police. Refuse, and you are going to be in trouble with the local constabulary for possession of stolen property and for trying to recreate a dangerous accident. That is what you are trying to do here, isn't it? You want to repeat the accident that happened to India. You intend to try to send someone else back to the eighth century. Are you going to use your friend Alice as the guinea pig, or are you planning to go yourself this time?"

"He knows, Hank." Suddenly, Alice looked frightened. "I don't want to go to jail."

"Shut up, Alice," Hank ordered. "He doesn't know anything. He's bluffing."

"Wrong," Mike informed him. "I know everything about your theories and your experiments. Now, ask yourself where I got the money to trail you across the country for all these months. Does it begin to dawn on you that I'm not acting solely on my own initiative? There are some very important people who are determined to stop what you are trying to do, Hank. After I leave here, you may have some other visitors, whom I don't think will be as pleasant as I am, or as patient with you. Now, come on, hand over the evidence and you'll be in the clear when other people come searching."

"Are you saying the federal government is after him?" Alice squeaked, backing away from Hank. "I didn't ask for this kind of trouble."

"Last chance, Hank. Hand over the disks." Mike paused for a moment, watching Hank, who stood unmoving and glaring at him. "All right, time's up. If you aren't going to give me the disks, then I'll just have to take them. Here's one. I guess the other's in the machine, isn't it? Now, where have you hidden the notebook?" As he spoke, Mike picked up one floppy disk from the shelf beside the computer and pocketed it. He reached toward the computer to remove the second disk.

"Don't touch that thing!" Hank yelled. "It's all set up and ready to go."

"Then turn it off and give me the disk," Mike demanded. "The notebook, too."

"No way!" Hank shoved at Mike, trying to get him away from the computer, but Mike caught his arm in a tight grip.

"Knock it off, Hank. I don't want to hurt you. Just hand over the disk and I'll leave." Knowing he was the stronger man, Mike released the furious scientist. Doing so was a mistake.

"You aren't going to stop me," Hank declared. "Not you or anyone else, including the government. I can just imagine what the Feds would do with my material. Damn it, I'm sick and tired of uninformed idiots trying to interfere with my work!" With that, he clenched his fist and took a wild swing at Mike, who ducked. Hank was not a fighting man. The punch missed Mike's chin with plenty of room to spare, and Hank's fist slammed into the computer.

"Ow!" Hank cried, nursing his aching hand. "Get out of here. Just leave me alone."

"I can't do that." When Mike did not move, Hank and Alice came at him at the same time, but from different directions. Mike was concentrating on what Hank might do, so he wasn't expecting Alice's attack, and he didn't want to hit a woman. He tried to sidestep Alice while at the same time fending off Hank. As a result of his misplaced chivalry, he was pushed backward until he was up against the computer. He put out a hand to steady himself.

His hand went through the computer screen, vanishing into the solid surface. The computer screen appeared to be undamaged, but Mike could no longer see his own hand and arm.

"Hey! Come back here. You're not the one who's supposed to go," Hank shouted.

But Bradford Michael Bailey was beyond stopping what was happening. He could not *believe* what was happening, so at first he did nothing to help himself. Within half a second it was impossible for him to do anything anyway, because his own body would not follow his commands. Incredibly, he was being pulled into the computer. He saw an orange blur first, then an odd blackness with bright-colored numbers whizzing through it. His head ached and his ears popped as if he were falling fast, which he was.

He came out of the blackness into empty air. Then he was tumbling downward through tree branches. He grabbed at them to try to stop his precipitous fall, but some of the branches broke and his hands slipped off others as he plummeted toward the ground.

He knew he was going to die. Oddly, his life did not pass before his eyes. All he saw was tree leaves and branches, a few rocks below awaiting him, and the too-solid earth on which those rocks were resting.

He hit the ground hard, knocking all the air out of his lungs. His head cracked against one of the waiting rocks. Unable to move or breathe, Mike fell into blackness again, a different kind of blackness this time, a sucking, greedy darkness that engulfed him in an instant, snuffing out his consciousness.

Chapter Two

Francia
Spring, A.D. 779.

At first Danise thought the man was dead. He lay perfectly still, prone on a pile of leaves and branches, and when she turned him over she saw that his face was swollen beyond recognition.

Not that she would have recognized him if he had been in the best of health. She had never seen anyone wearing such strange clothing. His breeches, made of the common dark blue fabric woven in Nimes, had been worn and washed until they were threadbare and faded to near whiteness in places. The knees were torn and bloodstained. She would have thought him a peasant save for the stitching. Danise, no mean needlewoman herself, had never encountered stitches so even or so close together—two rows of them at each seam—and there were little pouches set into the garment near the waist, perhaps to hold the man's personal belongings. His upper body was covered by a short tunic of matching fabric, open down the front. Beneath it he wore a round-necked blue shirt of some soft material. His hair was black and straight. All this she saw in a moment, before her servant Clothilde spoke.

"Is he breathing?" Clothilde knelt in the leaves beside her mistress and pressed a hand against the man's chest. "His heart is beating. He is warm."

"Poor man." Danise let her fingers touch his face softly, so as not to hurt him further. She could see that his nose had been bleeding, but the blood had stopped. In addition to his scraped knees he had scratches on his face and hands and a nasty lump on the left side of his head. Danise could find no open wounds to require immediate stanching of blood. If he had any more serious injuries, they must be internal.

"How could a stranger come so close to the royal camp and not be stopped by Charles's guards?" asked Clothilde.

"I don't know," Danise said, "but he fell from a tree. Those are fresh spring leaves he's lying on, on top of the old leaves from last autumn.

Look up, Clothilde. You can see from the broken branches up there the path by which he came to this spot."

"He was in the treetop, spying on us?" Clothilde gasped. "We must alert the guards at once."

"No." Danise spoke sharply. "We don't know that he was spying. He may have thought *we* would do *him* harm. We can't call the guards. They would think as you do, and be rough with him. He looks too badly hurt to endure such treatment. Clothilde, I think by the fine seams on his clothing that he must be a nobleman. Look at them. No peasant woman could make stitches so small or so straight. I believe he has been traveling for a long time, if such sturdy fabric is so badly worn. Therefore, until he can tell us who he is, we would be wise to treat him as a visiting noble.

"I will stay here to watch over him," Danise went on. "You must find my father or Guntram, who will know where my father is. We will need a litter to take him back to the camp."

"Savarec would not want me to leave you alone," Clothilde protested.

"One of us must go, for we cannot leave him by himself," Danise pointed out. "And, Clothilde, be discreet. Don't talk to anyone but my father or Guntram. Be careful to avoid Sister Gertrude. You know how she loves to make a fuss."

"How am I to do that?" Clothilde demanded,

standing and planting her hands on her wide hips. "That nun has eyes like an eagle."

"You and I together have avoided her eagle eye often enough," Danise responded. "I know you can do it, Clothilde. Just be quick. I fear he must be badly injured, or he would have wakened by now."

Left alone with the stranger, Danise took off her light spring cloak and used it to cover him. Then she sat beside him, gently stroking his hair.

"Why did you climb so high in the trees?" she murmured to him. "Was it to look over the landscape and thus find your way? Were you intending to come to Duren to meet with Charles?"

Since the man remained unresponsive, Danise settled herself more comfortably to await the arrival of help. Despite Clothilde's qualms, she was not the least bit frightened to be alone in the forest. There could be no danger to her there, so close to the Frankish encampment.

Charles, king of the Franks, had called the Mayfield, the great spring assembly of Frankish nobles, to meet at Duren on the River Rur, about two days' journey east of Aachen. The choice of place was deliberate, to demonstrate just how powerful the Franks were to the ever-restless Saxon tribes who lived on the eastern borders of Francia. Still, Duren and the forests surrounding it were safe. If they were not, Charles would never have allowed his beloved queen to accompany him there, for Hildegarde was seven months gone with her sixth pregnancy in eight years of marriage, and she was not at all well.

Nor, if Duren were unsafe, would Savarec have summoned his daughter Danise to meet him at the royal court. Danise had made the journey from the convent school at Chelles, near Paris, to Duren in the company of her usual chaperon, Sister Gertrude, her personal maidservant Clothilde, and two men-at-arms whom her father had sent to protect her along the way. She had seen her father only briefly on her arrival the previous night, before retiring to the tent Savarec had provided for his women-folk next to his own tent.

Duren was but a small settlement, so the Franks had established a town of tents on a broad space cleared between river and forest. There they would live during the weeks of Mayfield, feasting out-of-doors in the fine spring weather, and enjoying the contests of skill in wrestling, weaponry, and riding put on by the younger warriors. Meanwhile, in the huge royal tent or on the open field, the nobles would meet with Charles to decide whether another campaign was necessary against the Saxons. While the men conferred, the women, too, would meet, renewing old friendships and making new ones.

The annual assembly was also the time

when Frankish nobles traditionally arranged marriages for their children, and Danise very much feared this was why Savarec had called her to Duren. At nearly eighteen, she was almost too old to be wed.

The man beside her moaned, diverting her thoughts from herself to him. He raised one hand to his face, then moaned again.

"It will be all right," she told him, catching his hand. "Help is coming soon. We will take good care of you."

He grew still at the sound of her voice, and she thought he was trying to frown. It was hard to tell for sure, since his face was so swollen, but his expression seemed to change and he winced.

"Just lie still," she advised.

He muttered a few words in a language she could not understand, then said a word she did know.

"Angel?"

"*Ange?*" she repeated. "Oh, I comprehend. You think you are dead and I am an angel? I'm afraid not. I am far from being an angel."

He grew still again—listening to her, she was sure—and then he opened his eyes.

They were blue, the deepest, purest, most heart-stopping blue she had ever seen. In his sorely damaged face, swollen and bruised and streaked with dirt and scratches, and smeared with blood from his injured nose, those eyes were like torches in a dark forest. Not even the famous piercing blue gaze of Charles, king of the Franks, had ever affected Danise the way this unknown man's eyes did.

"Who are you?" she whispered, caught and held by light and color and unmistakable intelligence. When she saw the puzzled expression invading the blue depths, she repeated her question, speaking slowly and carefully, hoping he would understand her.

He said something and started to shake his head. The movement elicited a groan of pain. The blue eyes closed and he slipped away from her, back into unconsciousness. Only then did Danise realize she was still holding his hand, clutching it in both of hers, pressing it against her bosom. She let it go, laying it upon his chest and stroking the limp and dirty fingers with her own white ones.

"Don't die," she whispered. "Please don't die. I want to know you. I want to hear you speak again in that strange language."

It seemed a long time before Clothilde returned, leading Savarec, his man-at-arms Guntram, and a third man whom Danise did not know. The black-bearded Guntram carried a rolled-up litter made of two wooden poles thrust through the hems of a length of strong fabric.

"Clothilde has explained what happened." Savarec knelt beside his daughter. "Is he still alive?"

"Yes, he's breathing, and now and then he moans." Danise met her father's level gaze. "He opened his eyes for a moment or two, and he tried to speak, but I could not understand him."

"If he wakened, it's a good sign." It was the third man who spoke, a golden-haired fellow with a pleasant face. He went to his knees and put out a hand, feeling the unconscious man's head and apparently coming to the same conclusion as Danise. "He has a lump here, beneath his hair. From the blood on this rock beside him, I'd guess he hit his head on it when he fell."

"Danise," said Savarec, noting his daughter's questioning look, "this is Count Redmond. I had planned for you to meet him under more agreeable circumstances, but this moment must do."

"On the contrary, Savarec," said Count Redmond, "these *are* agreeable circumstances, for your daughter has shown herself to be both intelligent and discreet. Another maiden might have run into the camp crying to anyone she met that a strange man had been found in the forest, thus leading everyone gathered at Mayfield to imagine we faced a Saxon attack."

"This man is no Saxon," Danise said, certainty in her voice. "I have seen Saxon prisoners and heard them speak. He is unlike any of them. His speech, his clothing, his hair, his clean-shaven face—"

"As I said, Savarec," Redmond interrupted, "an intelligent young woman."

"Father, he will need good care," Danise said. "Will you have him taken to your tent? Clothilde and I can nurse him, and if you think it's necessary, you can easily set a guard there to watch him."

"Yes," said Savarec, "that's what we'll do. We'll keep your cloak over him, Danise, to hide his strange clothing, and if anyone asks who we are carrying on the litter, we'll say he's one of my men-at-arms who met with an accident. That way, we'll cause no alarm. But I will tell Charles in private what has happened, in case he wants to post more guards around the camp."

Guntram unrolled the litter, and he, Savarec, and Redmond lifted the unconscious man onto it. With Savarec and Danise leading the way and Clothilde walking beside the litter, Redmond and Guntram carried it out of the forest and into the Frankish camp. They were not stopped. Savarec was well-known, and his story of an injured man-at-arms was at once accepted.

Inside Savarec's tent, a folding camp bed was quickly set up and the stranger laid on it. Danise sent Clothilde for hot water and cloths so they could bathe the man, and while she was gone, Danise began to undress him. She was not so involved with her patient, however, that she did not hear her father and Count Redmond talking just outside the tent.

"A lovely maiden," Redmond said. "Your daughter is all you claimed her to be, Savarec."

"I knew you would be pleased," Savarec said.

"We will talk again soon, my friend."

"You understand," Savarec said, "she must agree."

"I would not agree myself if Danise did not," Count Redmond responded.

A moment later, Savarec entered his tent and stood behind Danise, watching while she worked.

"Where is Sister Gertrude?" Savarec asked. "Why is she not with you?"

"She has gone to the queen," Danise responded. "Sister Gertrude was of help to Hildegarde during her last pregnancy, while we were in Agen, so Hildegarde asked to see her as soon as we arrived in Duren."

"Which is why you took the opportunity to go off by yourself into the forest?" demanded Savarec.

"I was not alone. Clothilde was with me. I thought it would be peaceful amongst the trees."

"Peaceful?" To Danise's surprise, considering Savarec's overly protective attitude toward her, her father chuckled. "On occasion I have myself wanted to escape to some peaceful place far from Sister Gertrude's sharp tongue. But she does mean well, Danise, and she has your welfare always at heart."

"I know. It's why I am so patient with her.

Father, look at this. I found it tucked into a pouch inside his tunic. What could it be?" Danise held up a flat, square object contained in a parchment-like cover.

"I have no idea what it might be. I've never seen anything like this before." Savarec took the floppy disk, looked at it in perplexity, then handed it back. "Keep it with his other belongings until he is well enough to tell us what it is."

"And this? What could this be?" Danise held up a leather object. Again, Savarec took it to examine.

"It appears to be a folding purse of some kind. These green and white parchments have lettering and numbers on them. Perhaps this man is carrying a message. Now, that is a very strange way to fasten breeches."

Savarec bent to help Danise, who was struggling with the unfamiliar fastenings, and soon their patient lay naked. At once Savarec pulled a quilt over the man's exposed torso and then together they examined his arms, legs, ribs, skull, cheekbones and jaw, noting the many bruises and scrapes he had sustained.

"He appears to have no broken bones and no serious injuries other than the blow to his head," Savarec said, adding, "His body beneath the clothing is surprisingly clean, which suggests you were right to assume he is a nobleman. Here is Clothilde with the water. Bathe his injuries and cover him quickly so he

377

doesn't catch a chill. I am going now to report to Charles what has happened." Savarec paused at the tent flap. "I have posted Guntram just outside. Call him if our guest gives you any trouble. If he wakens, have Guntram send someone to me at once."

The two women worked quickly as Savarec had bidden them, but not so quickly that Danise did not have time to note how well made the stranger was. He was not as heavily muscled as most Frankish warriors, but there could be no discounting the potential strength in his long legs, or in his shoulders and arms. His hands were long, with tapered fingers, and his nails were well shaped, though several had been broken as a result of his fall from the tree.

Clothilde, after an exclamation of annoyance that a young man should be lying almost naked to her mistress's view, made a point of covering his manly parts with a cloth, but not before Danise had rested fascinated eyes on him. She had lived a protected life since her mother's death a few years previously, but her earliest youth had been spent in a freer way, so the sight of unclothed male babies or little boys had been common. She had also, on several occasions, helped wounded men. This unknown man's body should have been no different from any other. But it was. Danise glanced toward the cloth over his groin and blushed.

"Be particularly careful when you wash his face," Clothilde advised. "Those scratches must be painful. I wonder if his nose is broken?"

"My father thinks not, but we won't know for certain until the swelling subsides." Gently Danise wiped dirt and pieces of leaves off the man's hair, taking special care around the lump on the left side of his head. Then, after rinsing the cloth first in warm water, she began to work on his face. He muttered a string of unintelligible words and groaned, but did not rouse from his stupor. When he lay clean and well covered, Danise turned to Clothilde.

"You will have to ask Guntram to find clothes for him," she said. "He cannot go about in his own clothing. He will attract too much unwanted attention."

"I'll see what I can do," Clothilde replied, "but from the look of him, don't expect him to waken soon, if ever. I think Savarec ought to have the physicians to look at him, and then the priest."

"We will leave those decisions to my father." Danise pulled up a stool and sat down beside the bed. She smoothed back the man's damp hair, sighing at the condition of his face, which was turning blue and purple where the bruises were darkening. He was not a pleasant sight, yet in his very strangeness, in his battered form and his helplessness lay a peculiar attraction, while the mystery of his presence alone and unattended in the forest intrigued her.

"You cannot be a Frank," she murmured. "You are from a land far away. When you

379

can speak again, will you tell me about your home?"

"He may never speak again," Clothilde warned. "I'll get rid of this dirty water and wash out the cloths we used on him."

The tent flap had barely closed on Clothilde when the man opened his eyes. Twin pools of brilliant blue regarded Danise with an intensity strong enough to make her hold her breath. He did not speak. When she could bear the silent scrutiny no longer, Danise asked, "Can you tell me your name?"

Still that intent stare, clouded now by a growing anxiety. He moistened his dry lips.

"*Je ne sais pas,*" he whispered.

It took her a moment or two to understand what he was trying to say. The language he used was not Frankish, though it was somewhat similar.

"You don't know your own name?" Thinking she might have misunderstood him, she touched her bosom. "Danise. I am Danise. And you?" She laid her hand on his chest.

"No!" He nearly knocked her over when he tried to get out of bed. "No!"

"Guntram!" Danise did not need to call him; Guntram was with her before the word was out of her mouth. He forced the stranger back onto the bed and kept him there. The stranger put both hands up to his head, holding it tight and groaning.

"He's in pain," Guntram said. "It's the head

wound. Stay there!" he shouted at the man on the bed and shook his finger for emphasis. The man stared back at him, then nodded to show he understood. Guntram released his hold on the man and stood watching him, ready to prevent any threat against Danise.

"He can't remember his name," Danise explained. "My asking upset him."

"His confusion will end when the swelling is gone," Guntram replied. "Don't give him anything to eat or drink until tomorrow. If you do feed him, he may vomit and choke to death."

At that moment Savarec returned with a black-robed physician and the physician's assistant, who carried a basket filled with supplies.

"Charles has sent us the royal physician," Savarec explained. "He said his physician may as well practice on this man, since *he* is never sick enough to give the doctors employment." Guntram and Savarec exchanged manly grins at this statement, acknowledging Charles's famous good health and vitality.

"You must leave," the physician announced, waving them toward the tent opening. His assistant took a pottery jar out of the basket.

"What are you going to do?" asked Danise, unwilling to turn her patient over to anyone else, even the king's own physician.

"Why, I'll put leeches around his head wound to reduce the swelling," the physician replied. "It's the best treatment. He will awaken sooner with my help."

381

"When he did wake for a moment or two, he seemed to have no memory," Guntram said.

"Then he is in dire need of my treatment, and the sooner, the better." The physician waved again. "Go, please, all of you."

"You may need someone to hold him down," Guntram said.

"My assistant is stronger than he looks." The physician turned his back on them and lifted the lid off the jar of leeches that the assistant held out to him.

"He's quite right," Savarec said. "Physician, I'll leave my man Guntram outside the tent in case you need him. Danise, come with me. It's time I spoke with you about my reason for ordering you to join me here at Duren."

Danise knew well that particular note in her father's voice. She made no objection. After a backward glance toward the bed and the physician bending over it, she followed Savarec out of his tent.

"Here is Sister Gertrude, come from the queen," said Savarec, pausing to let a tall, thin nun join them. "How does Hildegarde? Better today, I hope."

"She is as well as any woman can be who is forced to bear child after child with only a few months of rest between each pregnancy," Sister Gertrude told him tartly.

"Hildegarde is not forced." Savarec's method of dealing with Sister Gertrude was always to speak mildly and calmly in response to her verbal provocations, and he did so now. "Hildegarde loves Charles deeply and truly, as he loves her. Their affection for each other is beautiful to see."

"The problem of loving between men and women," said Sister Gertrude with no diminution of sharpness, "is that for the men it is all loving and pleasure, while for the women there is the burden of childbearing and the ills that go with it. Not to mention the trials of motherhood for a woman whose husband is away fighting for half the year, leaving her to attend to his lands as well as his children."

"Sister Gertrude," Savarec warned, "you will turn Danise away from a woman's natural desire to be a wife and mother."

"So I hope to do, and thus prolong her life and her happiness," responded the nun, meeting Savarec's glance with glittering eyes.

"Both of you, please come into your tent," Savarec bid them. "I will not discuss my daughter's future here in public."

"There is precious little privacy in a tent," Sister Gertrude told him. "All the way here from seeing Hildegarde I could not avoid noticing what people were saying and doing in their tents. It is disgraceful the activities supposedly decent folk will resort to in the middle of the day." But she did follow Savarec into the undyed woolen tent she shared with Danise and Clothilde.

Savarec pulled the entrance flaps closed, then

383

turned to face the two women. The tent was small, with barely space enough for three narrow folding cots and a couple of clothes chests. There was no other furniture.

"Sit down, Father." Danise motioned him to one of the beds, then sat facing him, with Sister Gertrude beside her. "I am curious, since you have been content to let me stay at Chelles undisturbed since last autumn. Why did you want to see me now?"

"The time has come," Savarec informed her, "for us to discuss your marriage."

"Marriage?" Danise repeated, looking distressed. "This is what I feared. Father, you promised me you would not force me. You gave me your word."

"And I will not break it. I was too happy with your mother ever to insist that our daughter should wed a man she does not like. But, Danise, if you are to marry at all, it must be soon, before you are too old. Over the past winter I received several offers for your hand. I thought it would be a good idea for you to meet the men who are interested in you, so you will be better able to decide if any of them pleases you."

"What will you do if none of them pleases her?" Sister Gertrude asked. "If Danise decides she wants to return to Chelles to live, rather than marry, what will your response to her be, Savarec?"

"Danise, I will never force you into a decision

384

that will make you unhappy. Because you are so dear to me, I will allow you to decide for yourself whether to marry or to devote yourself to the religious life."

"You know what I will advise," Sister Gertrude said to Danise. "Spend your life safe and comfortable at Chelles, and thus avoid all the problems and heartbreak of marriage to a Frankish warrior. You have heard the story of my youth, Danise, of how I was betrothed to a man who, against all my pleas, left me to go to war, and how he died in battle. He claimed to love me, but he left me. The same fate, the same bitter grief, could easily befall you if you marry."

"No man worthy of the name of warrior would heed a woman's tears and entreaties to stay at home when his honor and loyalty to his king required him to go to war," Savarec said sternly.

"Father." Danise looked at her parent with troubled eyes. "There is something you do not know, which I now must tell you. Last year, when the queen requested my presence at court and you sent me to Agen with Sister Gertrude here, under the protection of Count Theuderic and his men—during our long journey across Francia I became fond of one of those men." She stopped, trying to think how to explain to her father what it had been like during those enchanted spring weeks of riding through the countryside with a man she had loved from their very first meeting.

"Hugo was good and kind and a most honorable man," Danise went on. "When we reached Agen, he told Charles boldly that he wanted to marry me and begged Charles's permission to ask my hand of you. Charles promised he might, when the Spanish campaign was completed, after Hugo had earned rewards to make him wealthy. Charles all but promised him a great estate and a title." Again Danise stopped, this time choked by tears.

"He knows, child." Sister Gertrude's hand touched Danise's. "I wrote to Savarec soon after Charles and his army returned to Agen from Spain. Charles sent my letter along with his own message to Savarec. Your father knows your affection for Hugo was both true and innocent. He knows you did not lie with Hugo. At least my watchfulness was able to save you from that much grief after Hugo's death at Roncevaux. Your body remains untouched, and I believe your heart will heal in time, for you are still young, and there was nothing formal between you, no betrothal vows."

"You knew, all these months, and you never mentioned it in any of your letters to me?" Danise looked at her father. "Is that why you let me stay at Chelles so long?"

"Sister Gertrude thought it would be best for you, and I agreed," Savarec said. "But you cannot dwell forever in the past. Eventually, as

I had to do after your sweet mother died, you must make your peace with what has happened and go on with the remainder of your life. I will leave the choice of wedlock or the religious life to you as I have promised, Danise, but I would not have you remain at Chelles solely because you are afraid to face the world again after Hugo's death. You have had more than nine months in which to mourn him. For the weeks of this Mayfield at Duren and the coming summer at Deutz with me, I ask you to consider what good you may do in the world if you marry and have children and make some noble Frank happy—for any man married to you must be a happy man."

"I need not repeat my opinion on this proposal," Sister Gertrude said.

"Indeed not," said Savarec with unusual asperity. "We know your thoughts on marriage all too well."

"You will give me until the end of summer to decide?" Danise asked.

"I will." Savarec smiled at her. "I have no doubt you would like to hear the names of the men who have offered for you."

"The choice of possible husbands might sway my decision," Danise admitted, smiling back at him. How dear and kind he was. How much she loved him. She knew her happiness was important to him.

"You have three suitors," Savarec said. "First, there is Count Clodion."

"An ancient ogre!" cried Sister Gertrude. "The man has had three wives already and has killed all of them with constant childbearing. He even offered for me when I was younger. That would be thirty years ago at least. I suppose he wants someone young and strong to nurse him in his dotage, though with his history he may yet hope to get more children on a young wife."

"Clodion's offer was honestly made," Savarec said patiently. "Therefore, we will consider it with equal honesty. He is an important nobleman. However, I must admit, I would prefer to see Danise wed to someone closer to her own age."

"Who else asked for me, Father?" It was so strange to sit here in her tent and discuss in this detached way the qualities of men she did not know, one of whom, before the summer was over, might be her husband. Did she want to marry? Danise could not deny to herself certain stirrings of her body, urgings not completely quelled by the tragic loss of her beloved Hugo. He had scarcely touched her and had kissed her only a few times, but his affection for her had been deep and enduring. She would have married Hugo gladly and given him all her heart and soul until she died. But he had died first, while she was young and healthy and of a disposition to embrace life. Chelles had been a place of safety to which she had retreated after Hugo's death to nurse her aching heart and her disappointed hopes. Danise

388

did not think she had a vocation strong enough to keep her contentedly at Chelles until she was an old woman. Still, she was wise enough to know she ought not to close the door on a religious life before she had definitely made up her mind. As for possible husbands, Count Clodion seemed to be favored by neither her father nor Sister Gertrude. "Tell me about the other men, Father."

"There is Autichar, who is a Bavarian nobleman of great note, and who holds lands as vast as Clodion's." Savarec was but a minor member of the nobility and he was perhaps too easily impressed by rank and wealth. Danise could tell he held Autichar in great esteem and had been honored by the offer for her hand.

"Autichar's loyalty to Charles has come into question," noted Sister Gertrude. "Autichar is a known companion of Duke Tassilo of Bavaria, who is no friend to Charles, though the two are close cousins. If a dispute arises between Charles and Tassilo, and from what I have heard of Tassilo's character it is inevitable, on whose side will Autichar fight? Do you want to oppose your son-in-law on a battle-field, Savarec?"

"Is there no man on earth of whom you approve?" Savarec's face was growing red with suppressed anger.

"I want Danise to be happy just as much as you do," Sister Gertrude told him. "But I do not think marriage will make her happy."

"If you will let me finish," said Savarec between clenched teeth, "perhaps you can find one good thing to say about the third man who is interested in my daughter."

"Who is he, Father?" Trying to avert one of Savarec's rare outbursts of temper, Danise said, "I promise I will most seriously consider all of these men, and if they are here at Duren, I will ask you to present me to them, so I can be at least somewhat familiar with all of them before I decide."

"You always were a sensible girl." Savarec appeared to be mollified by his daughter's words. "The third man you have already met, and he is the one I most favor. A man of honorable lineage, with lands near Tournai and also other estates in Burgundy. He is Count Redmond."

"The pleasant man who helped us with the stranger?" Danise tried in vain to recall Count Redmond's face. All she could bring to memory was a thick crop of golden hair and a pair of pale eyes. Was he tall or short, handsome or not? She could not remember. When she thought about the incident in the forest, what stayed in her mind was an instant of shock brought on by the penetrating blue gaze of a sadly injured, unknown man.

"Well, Danise?" Savarec looked at her expectantly. "What is your opinion of Count Redmond?"

"As I said, he seemed pleasant, but I scarcely

had a chance to note him," Danise responded.

"You will have ample time to know him," Savarec told her. "And Clodion and Autichar, too, since all of them are gathered here at Duren. You have my permission to speak to any of them when and as you wish, so long as Sister Gertrude or Clothilde is with you. I do not think any of them will make improper advances to you, but it is always best for a young woman to have a chaperon."

"In so much at least, we are agreed," said Sister Gertrude.

Chapter Three

He did not know where he was. Worse, he did not know *who* he was. His head ached without letup, and his eyesight was totally undependable, ranging from a complete blur to abnormal clarity. Every time he tried to sit up he was overcome by nausea so severe he had to lie down again at once.

People came and went. He knew the man in dusty black robes was a doctor. He knew the leeches the doctor periodically placed at the most painful spot on his head really would help him. Their sucking would diminish the swelling and make his headache go away. How he knew these things he could not recall, but know them he did.

Lying flat on his back, unable to move for

nausea, with the repellent leeches working away at him, he went over the faces he had recently seen, seeking in those faces some clue to his own identity.

There was the portly middle-aged man with gray-streaked dark hair who slept in the other bed in the tent and snored away the long and lonely nights. The others called this man *Savarec*, but to his confused tentmate the name meant nothing.

There was Guntram of the bristling black beard and mustache. He had a fierce expression and wild eyes, but could be gentle enough to turn a patient or attend to his personal needs without causing increased pain. Guntram was Savarec's man, and he loved and respected his master.

A motherly, middle-aged woman, brown of hair and eye and thick of waist, came frequently to change his linen or wash his face and hands. A scrawny, sour-looking nun occasionally glared down at him along her elegant nose.

And then there was the angel, who drifted into and out of his consciousness like a vision. But she was real. She touched his forehead or his cheeks with tender hands and coaxed him to swallow the food she spooned into his mouth, even when he feared it would only come back up again. When the angel fed him, the food stayed down, perhaps because she did not rush him as the others did, but sat patiently waiting until he opened his mouth for the next spoonful.

Her face was a perfect oval, her hair was so pale it was almost silver. She wore it in twin braids tied with green ribbons to match her deep green wool gown. Her eyes were a soft gray-green, shadowed by some undefined sorrow. She was small and shapely and her voice was like heavenly music. Unfortunately, he could not understand what she said.

She tried to make him understand and he struggled to remember the words she spoke, but his head ached so badly that he could make no sense of her language. It ought to be easy for him. He was fluent in several languages and had the ear to learn new ones quickly.

How did he know that?

As time passed and the pain in his head eased, fragments of memory drifted into and out of his thoughts. Glimpses of scenes bedeviled him . . . a skinny young man throwing a punch at him and missing . . . blinking lights . . . numbers . . . the green leaves of springtime slapping against his face . . . falling . . . falling . . . Where? When? What had happened to him?

What was his name?

COMING IN JANUARY!
HISTORICAL ROMANCE
HUNTERS OF THE ICE AGE:
YESTERDAY'S DAWN
By Theresa Scott

Named for the massive beast sacred to his people, Mamut has proven his strength and courage time and again. But when it comes to subduing one helpless captive female, he finds himself at a distinct disadvantage. Never has he realized the power of beguiling brown eyes, soft curves and berry-red lips to weaken a man's resolve. He has claimed he will make the stolen woman his slave, but he soon learns he will never enjoy her alluring body unless he can first win her elusive heart.

_51920-8 $4.99 US/$5.99 CAN

A CONTEMPORARY ROMANCE
HIGH VOLTAGE
By Lori Copeland

Laurel Henderson hadn't expected the burden of inheriting her father's farm to fall squarely on her shoulders. And if Sheriff Clay Kerwin can't catch the culprits who are sabotaging her best efforts, her hopes of selling it are dim. Struggling with this new responsibility, Laurel has no time to pursue anything, especially not love. The best she can hope for is an affair with no strings attached. And the virile law officer is the perfect man for the job—until Laurel's scheme backfires. Blind to Clay's feelings and her own, she never dreams their amorous arrangement will lead to the passion she wants to last for a lifetime.

_51923-2 $4.99 US/$5.99 CAN